The Rebellious Sisterhood

Female artists...taking their world by storm!

Artemisia, Adelaide and Josefina plan to break the mold the male-centric art world has placed them in. They each have ambitions and are willing to fight for their rightful place—they know their worth, even if society doesn't.

From their base in Seasalter, Kent, the women use the only tool in their arsenal to have their voices heard: their paintbrushes. On their mission, might these rebellious women also find something they weren't looking for— men to fight for and love them?

Join the sisterhood in the new trilogy by Bronwyn Scott

Read Artemisia's story in
Portrait of a Forbidden Love

And look out for Adelaide's and Josefina's stories

Coming soon!

Author Note

The setting for Artemisia's story is particularly exciting historically and in its relevance in modern-day discussion. London's Royal Academy of Arts was founded in 1768, and two of the founders were women: Mary Moser and Angela Kauffman. However, when Mary Moser, who is referenced several times in Artemisia's story, passes away in the spring of 1819, no move is made to replace her or Angela Kauffman with another female Royal Academician, despite female applicants being available. It is not until over one hundred years later that a female is elected an RA.

The first attempt to crack the resistance was in 1860. Laura Herford was the candidate, and you can read more about other stories on my blog (bronwynswriting. blogspot.com). Her attempt was unsuccessful. Men are on record as blatantly saying they didn't want a "female invasion." Annie Swynnerton does become the first female RA in 1922.

Artemisia is named after Renaissance painter Artemisia Gentileschi, who is well-known for her painting of Holofernes and Judith. I do parallel my Artemisia's story with hers.

This is a story about liberation, not just Artemisia's, which is center stage, but Darius's, too, as he seeks to find his own power.

BRONWYN SCOTT

Portrait of a Forbidden Love

HARLEQUIN®
HISTORICAL™

ISBN-13: 978-1-335-50594-1

Portrait of a Forbidden Love

This edition published by arrangement with Harlequin Books S.A.

For questions and comments about the quality of this book, please contact us at CustomerService@Harlequin.com.

Harlequin Enterprises ULC
22 Adelaide St. West, 40th Floor
Toronto, Ontario M5H 4E3, Canada
www.Harlequin.com

Printed in U.S.A.

Recycling programs
for this product may
not exist in your area.

Bronwyn Scott is a communications instructor at Pierce College and the proud mother of three wonderful children—one boy and two girls. When she's not teaching or writing, she enjoys playing the piano, traveling—especially to Florence, Italy—and studying history and foreign languages. Readers can stay in touch via Facebook at Facebook.com/bronwynwrites, or on her blog, bronwynswriting.blogspot.com. She loves to hear from readers.

Books by Bronwyn Scott

Harlequin Historical

Scandal at the Midsummer Ball
"The Debutante's Awakening"
Scandal at the Christmas Ball
"Dancing with the Duke's Heir"

The Rebellious Sisterhood

Portrait of a Forbidden Love

The Cornish Dukes

The Secrets of Lord Lynford
The Passions of Lord Trevethow
The Temptations of Lord Tintagel
The Confessions of the Duke of Newlyn

Allied at the Altar

A Marriage Deal with the Viscount
One Night with the Major
Tempted by His Secret Cinderella
Captivated by Her Convenient Husband

Visit the Author Profile page
at Harlequin.com for more titles.

For HRC and anyone who has ever struggled to break free from their limitations. And for my two girls, may you always believe in yourselves and your dreams.

Chapter One

Somerset House, London—December 1819

There was no more dangerous creature than a man when cornered by a woman, unless it was a group of them, all held at bay by a single female armed only with what was her due and unafraid to ask for it. Artemisia Stansfield stood before the assembly at the Royal Academy of the Arts, believing without reservation that she'd earned recognition as an academician. Unfortunately, she was the only one in the room who shared that opinion, a conclusion that was becoming more evident by the minute.

Benjamin West spoke from the presidential throne, his mouth a grim line set beneath the long straight line of his nose. 'Miss Stansfield, you are probably wondering why the assembly has summoned you?'

'If the summons is not to grant me status as a Royal Academician, then, yes, I do wonder.' Artemisia held the man's gaze, her own steady and firm. She would not allow them to mince words with her, as disappoint-

ing as those words might be. A knot of worry tied itself in her stomach—worry that she had misjudged the
purpose for the invitation to the assembly's December
meeting. She had not thought it would turn out this way.

Was it only this morning she'd awakened jubilant,
convinced that today would be the day she achieved
her dream: earning the honour of signing RA after her
name on her works, being allowed to instruct young
artists as a visiting professor and to direct the development of art in England? She fought the urge to smooth
the skirts of her forest-green ensemble, chosen carefully for confidence. She would not let them see her
fidget as if West's question made her doubt her right to
stand here. She did not doubt. She would never doubt.

'I am afraid we will disappoint you then, my dear
Miss Stansfield.' Was that *pity* in President West's gaze?
Benevolent *patronising* in his tone? How dare he con-
descend to her! Artemisia's temper began to smoulder
as the words came. 'The Academy has rejected your
nomination.'

She let that sink in. *Really* sink in. It meant her name
had been put forward and it meant that not one person
had offered a signature in support. Not a single man sitting here had moved to endorse her, men who had pretended to be her colleagues, men whom she'd thought
had been her friends for years. Men whom she'd thought
respected her. Her gaze swept the room, a defiant stare
that spared no one in its scolding wake. A few of them
had the decency to shift in their seats, others were not
brave enough to meet her eyes. Damn them.

Only Darius Rutherford, the Viscount St Helier, art
critic to the *ton*, met her gaze with an obsidian stare

of his own. Her temper ratcheted another degree to a slow burn. St Helier was not a member of the Academy, but where he led others followed. One word from him and an artist could be launched from anonymity into fame, or quite the opposite. She'd rather he not be here to witness her defeat. He might do her more damage than any of the others put together.

It was no longer a case of 'damn them' but of 'damn *him*', with his dark eyes and darker hair that fell perfectly imperfect over one arching brow and that long, strong nose that ended just above a firm mouth. His was a visage that was confident in its sense of superiority. How many times had she wanted to wipe that confidence off his face as he passed judgement at an exhibition, making and breaking careers with his words? She'd often wondered if those long, elegant hands of his had ever even held a paintbrush? Now the scrutiny of all that superiority was turned in her direction, assessing and waiting.

Waiting for what? A response? An outburst? For her to beg or to wither under the weight of the Academy's judgement? Would he like that? Would he like to see her brought to her knees? He'd made no secret of his dislike for her in years past. She was not the sort of woman he approved of. In evidence of that, he'd never spent more than a handful of minutes in her presence, making it patently clear he preferred to rub elbows with a more traditional crowd. Whatever his dislike of her, though, he had yet to take that dislike out on her art. He didn't effuse praise over her work—How could he? He didn't understand it because he didn't understand her—but neither did he condemn it. He ignored it. Perhaps today would be a turning point there and not for the better.

She let the enormity of the Academy's refusal swamp her. Was their rejection just the beginning of the end? Would this signal the conclusion of her artistic career? What would people say about her? It suddenly seemed paramount that she make a response to Benjamin West's verdict, that she not walk away. If she did, she'd be walking away from far more than just an appointment. It was also of great import that her response be even-toned, that it not be the rebuttal of a disappointed shrew.

It took an enormous amount of self-control to get the words out in cool, objective, professional fashion. 'President West, I would like to remind the assembly of my credentials. I am already a Royal Associate of the Academy. I've been showing work at the Summer Exhibition since I was sixteen. I have even managed to take several prizes.' Even over some of these other artists in the room. Just last year her portrait of Lady Basingstoke and her famed thoroughbred, Warbourne, had taken the top prize in the category, although she refrained from mentioning that at the moment. She didn't want to risk wounding the manly pride in the room. 'I am also an active, working painter under the age of seventy-five, one of the definitive requirements for consideration, I believe.'

The last cast a broad, seemingly inclusive net, a net she'd not thought to question until this moment. She'd been raised by an artistic father who'd not baulked at teaching both his daughters to paint. She'd grown up in an Academy that had two females as founding members at the time. She'd studied with one of them, Royal Academician Mary Moser, always believing there would be a place for her when the time came. Now, the time had come. Artemisia was twenty-eight and proven in her field. Where was that place? Was it not in this room with her colleagues?

'A successful candidate for membership at this level must do more than merely satisfy requirements, as I am sure you understand.' West's gaze slid to the left to elicit support from the Academy's long-time secretary, Henry Howard. In the silence, Artemisia felt what was to have been her triumph, her moment, slip away. How had it come to this?

She'd been so sure of her reception, so sure of the logic of the Academy accepting her nomination. She was still sure of it, why weren't they? Didn't they see that the timing was right, that she was the ideal candidate to fill Mary Moser's vacancy in so many ways? 'I do more than meet the requirements, sir,' Artemisia contested boldly. If they'd expected her to accept their decision meekly, they were wrong. She would not let this go without a fight. 'I studied with Mary Moser, I am the daughter of Sir Lesley Stansfield, a respected artist in his own right. Who better to carry the torch of Mary's legacy than a former pupil and a woman who understands what it is to be a female artist in a male-dominated field?'

Her tenacity had not won her any points with West or with others in the room. There were a few coughs of disbelief at her bold display of argument. From his seat, St Helier, with his dark eyes, met her gaze with a frank look of consideration, but his words were for the room at large. 'I was unaware we'd become a debating society.' Nervous chuckles followed from men uncertain how to take the comment. Was the scold for them or for her?

Artemisia refused to be intimidated, whatever St Helier's intentions were. Something moved in his dark eyes. Had he been intending to help her? Warn her that she went too far? Or was he like so many other men she knew who treated women as invisible objects not entitled to their opinions? Her gaze returned to West. 'Then tell me, what qualifications did I lack? In what way did my portfolio not satisfy?' He could not answer because there was no answer. She had satisfied in all ways except in meeting one unwritten requirement: she was not male. Some time between 1768 with the founding of the Academy and now, that had begun to matter.

'We feel your art needs time to mature,' West said with a clearing of his throat. 'We would like to see more painting from you, something unique, something we haven't seen before. We are tabling the consideration of your membership until the meeting in March. We are giving you a probationary period to prove yourself.'

'Probation? What has these last twelve years been then if not probation? Isn't that the function of the associates' pool?' Artemisia interrupted. 'To create a collection of artists from which future academicians can be drawn? I, sirs, have already served my *probation*. My father—'

'Your father is the only reason we are even having this discussion, Miss Stansfield,' West cut in swiftly. Whatever benefit he'd been willing to give her in the form of pity or condescension was gone now. She'd pushed him too far and he had his own face to save in front of his peers. 'It was your father who put your name forward in the nominating book. It is out of respect for him that we have invited you here today to have this discussion at all.' He made it sound as if the council was granting her a great and tolerant boon in allowing her to stand before them, which they might be. Not even the two female founding members, Angelica Kauffman and Mary Moser, had been allowed to attend meetings on account of their sex. They were represented only by two portraits hung on the wall. Artemisia had not thought of it as exclusionary before. She did now. 'You know, Miss Stansfield, your invitation is not usual protocol for a candidate who has been refused.'

No, it wasn't usual protocol, but she did see what it was protocol for. Her temper went to full boil. She was no longer interested in comporting herself calmly. She was being made an example of in a very public way so that no other woman would try for such lofty status. They would make her request into a scandal while other male candidates were simply notified privately that their membership was not successful. There was no public shaming of them. Some might even try again later for membership.

She glared at West. 'What do you think you will see in March that I have not shown you in twelve years?' The standards of her probation were vague, which no doubt suited the council quite well, but suited her not at all. It was a moving target. Why was she surprised by this turn of events? A man had betrayed her trust before. Why wouldn't others? Why had she thought it would be different? She swept the council with a final challenging stare. 'I do hope whatever you think to see

in March isn't a penis, because I don't think I can grow
one by then. Good day, gentlemen.'

What an unnatural woman she was! From his seat
near the President's throne, Darius watched the exchange with something akin to appalled amazement,
unable to look away like a bystander caught in the
throes of horrified wonder as a disaster played out before their eyes. She reminded him of her namesake, the
Renaissance painter, Artemisia Gentileschi, an uncon-
ventional firebrand of a woman if ever there was one.
There wasn't a meek, repentant, subordinate bone in
Miss Stansfield's body even when such characteristics
would serve her in good stead. Not that such characteristics would have served her today. They would only
have made West's job of dismissing her easier.

There'd been nothing easy about Artemisia Stansfield. Darius had never heard a woman speak like that
publicly in his entire life. He'd never seen a woman
look like that either—at least not one that wasn't a
whore or an actress. The 'look' was something inde-
finable in itself. It wasn't her dress—that was impeccable and above reproach with its high lace collar and
tight, lace-trimmed cuffs peeking out from beneath
the green jacket of her ensemble. But unlike so many
women in London, Artemisia Stansfield was more than
her clothes. No, 'the look' was all that dark hair piled
in unruly curls on her head, that direct, piercing grey
gaze that showed no modesty, no deference even in
defeat, and that mouth which gave no quarter. Darius
would not have wanted to have been West for all the
salt in the sea.

The uproar that met Miss Stansfield's departure was immediate the moment the door shut behind her. He was not the only one who couldn't believe such shocking behaviour. 'It's why we don't want women in the Academy to start with,' Sir Aldred Gray said beside him with staunch authority as if he himself didn't keep a mistress in Piccadilly. There were other comments that ran in a similar vein. They were not kind, but they were also not untrue. The Academy was dominated by males and now with the two female members gone, this was the moment to solidify that maleness behind the message that these higher echelons of the Academy were for males only. Did Miss Stansfield already guess that? Surely she could not be surprised by such a decision. The Academy wasn't the only institution to be restrictive on female membership. In fact, he couldn't think of one that wasn't. Miss Stansfield was an associate, she should content herself with that, *applaud* herself for achieving that much.

And yet, something whispered in the back of his mind—would *he* be content with that? Would he settle for being told what he could or could not achieve no matter the level of his talents? He had settled once. He'd always regretted it. It was the only time he'd ever been told no and likely the only time he ever would be.

It was different for him. As a man and the son of a peer, he need not be constrained by the limitations of others. By definition, the world was his—legally, socially. It was something he had been raised to accept as his natural due. It simply was how the world worked. He'd not questioned it.

Why would you? his conscience whispered. *By the*

*nature of your birth, you came out on the winning side
of life.*

Perhaps if he hadn't, he might be flashing defiant
stares and daring the powers that be to overturn the
natural order of things. It was an interesting thought,
but there was no time to ponder it. The words, 'I think
St Helier should go' jerked him out of his musings.

'Go where?' Darius glanced around the chamber.
What was Aldred Gray up to? He didn't trust the man
as far as he could throw him, as the expression went.

'To check up on Miss Stansfield's work after the
Christmas holidays,' someone nearby supplied the conversation he'd missed.

'We must handle this very carefully.' Aldred Gray,
egotistical spider that he was, was enjoying the attention as all eyes fixed on him. 'No matter how good her
work is, we must be prepared to declare it, or her, unacceptable in March.'

Ah, so the probation *was* meant to be a smokescreen. Darius had thought as much. It was an ingenious smokescreen, one that appeared to offer her a
chance and in doing so, one that would not offend Sir
Lesley Stansfield. The Academy would not want to
risk quarrelling with him, a leading artist and professor
within their ranks. 'Why me? I'm not a member, merely
a critic.' He was an invited guest to these meetings, a
non-voting member of the discussions.

'For precisely that reason.' West took up the idea.
'You will appear entirely objective.' Darius didn't care
for that word 'appear'. He was not in the business of lies
and misleading, nor was his opinion in the business of
being bought. He was an art critic, he didn't take sides.

'I *will* be entirely objective,' Darius asserted. He had his own reputation as an art critic to think of as well.

'It shouldn't be too hard to find incriminating evidence against her character, after all,' Gray said with a nod and a certain knowing gleam in his eye. 'A woman like that, a woman of her age, has no doubt had her affairs.' Gray waved a hand dismissively. 'Of course, she's entitled to them privately, I suppose, but we can't have such behaviour, such lacking in morality, among our academicians. It's hardly the standard we want to set.' The chamber nodded as one, as if they'd all been choirboys, which Darius knew first-hand they weren't.

'If you can't find any illicit behaviour on her part, you can always seduce her yourself,' another near Gray chuckled. 'She said the word penis. Sooner or later she'll show her true colours.'

'That's entrapment,' Darius replied drily, staring the man down. He had no desire to follow up with Miss Stansfield. He was aware of her and the place she occupied in the art world—the talented daughter of a talented artist—but he did not know her well. She was hardly the type of woman the son of an earl would seek out socially. She was far older than the debutantes that peopled his dance card and his mother's expectations. She had no title, no lineage, no age-old fortune. She merely made paintings for those who did.

She was a woman of little note to a man like himself, yet as odd as she struck him, as much as she went against the standard of what a woman ought to be, he didn't want to spend his winter playing her probation officer or, worse yet, deceiving her. From the look on her face this afternoon, she'd had enough of deception.

Whatever she knew of the world or expected from it—and surely at her age she wasn't entirely naive—she'd been genuinely surprised by the rejection today. She'd honestly thought she'd be admitted and that gave his usually rather conservative conscience pause. *Was* she being unjustly denied a place?

He prided himself on being a man of honesty and directness. Deception of any sort cut against that code. It was on the tip of his tongue to say he wasn't their man, but his refusal wouldn't stop the ploy from going through. They would simply appoint another to go in his place, someone who wouldn't supply true objectivity, someone who did not have her interests at heart, someone like Sir Aldred Gray. He found he didn't like the idea of someone deliberately seducing the proud Miss Stansfield for the purpose of using it against her.

'All right, I'll do it,' he found himself agreeing. How hard could it be? He'd planned on spending the winter in town looking after some political and business interests anyway. It would be simple enough to drop by her studio once or twice and see how things were progressing. If his report was too objective for the council's sake come March, that would be their problem. Until, then, however, it looked as though Miss Artemisia Stansfield was his.

Chapter Two

The audacity of them to offer *her*, a professional, active, award-winning painter, probation! As if four months would change anything. The idea rankled on several levels. Artemisia was still seething over the insult by the time she arrived home, her emotions as stormy as the weather. She didn't dare tamp down on her anger yet, though, for fear of what might lie beneath it—tears, grief, despair. She still had to navigate homecoming, still had to face the staff, still had to climb the stairs to her room. Only there would she entertain the notion of setting aside her anger, and then just for a self-indulgent moment or two, after which she would put the mantle of anger on again. Anger was sustaining. It had got her through before when another man had betrayed her.

'Miss, welcome home,' Anstruther greeted her, an expectation of impending good news inflected in his voice. The butler's usually stoic expression held a hopeful enquiry in his eyes. She had none to give him.

'Is my father home?' Her tone was clipped and impersonal as she handed him her gloves and shed her outerwear.

'No, miss. He's gone out to his clubs.' Anstruther was too well-trained to overlook the subtext of her message. There would be no celebration tonight. The flicker of hopefulness in his gaze had been replaced instantly by the professional detachment of his calling. Silently, she thanked him for that. She could not have borne up under his sympathy.

She was glad, too, that her father was out. Perhaps he'd already known and strategically decamped. He'd done his part. He'd served as her nominator. He'd made it clear the rest was up to her, that she must stand on her own feet for reasons that weren't entirely charitable. Sir Lesley Stansfield had a strong streak of self-preservation in him. Still, she'd agreed. She'd wanted her own laurels to rest on, not his, and in that she had failed.

'There you are! At last! I thought you'd never come home.' Her sister Adelaide's excited exclamation drew Artemisia's gaze up the long staircase as Addy sailed down the steps, all exuberance and confidence in her sister's success. 'How did it go? Shall I call for cham—?'

Artemisia hated to disappoint her. 'No champagne, Addy.' She halted her sister's progress with a look and a shake of her head. She could feel Anstruther retreating behind her to give them privacy.

The smile on her sister's face faded. 'No! Never say they denied you?'

'They did.' Artemisia mounted the steps, suddenly weary. She found a small smile for her sister before stalling Anstruther's retreat. 'I'll need my trunk from the attic, please.'

'Where are you going? What's happened?' Addy fell into step, following her to her room where her sister took up her usual post in the middle of Artemisia's bed, skirts tucked about her. 'You'd best tell me everything.' There was comfort in those words and in Addy's presence. Here in the sanctity of her own room, with Addy beside her, she could set aside her armour and let the hurt show. Addy had always been her biggest supporter, her most loyal advocate, a champion who believed she could do no wrong. It was exactly what she needed now.

'I am so sorry, Arta.' Addy squeezed her hand when she finished. 'Did they give a reason? I can't imagine what it would be. Your work is exquisite.'

'It wasn't my work.' Artemisia rose from the bed and began to pace, strength and conviction returning to her. 'It's because I'm not like them.'

Addy's ginger brows knit in puzzlement. 'You're a painter, an artist, a professional. You *are* just like them. How can they say that? You've had more commissions this year than most of them.' Her sweet sister truly didn't understand. 'Surely one of them would have spoken for you.' She could see her sister running the list of names of their close acquaintants, friends of their father, behind her thoughtful green gaze.

'Not like that, Addy,' Artemisia said softly. 'I lack one fundamental quality they all share. I lack a penis.'

Addy covered her mouth in shock. 'Oh! Arta! Don't be vulgar.'

'Honesty is never vulgar.' Artemisia held firm on that. 'Despite the superficial offer of a four-month probation, they don't want women in the Academy. It was made very clear to me today. Their answer will be the same in March.'

Addy was silent for a long while, processing the revelation. Did her sister believe her? As large as the revelation had been to her, it would be even larger to Addy, who was younger and more sheltered from the world than she. Perhaps it was too large of a truth, too heinous, for Addy to allow. It would mean allowing for a certain duplicity in their so-called friends and that would be hard for Addy to accept. At last, Addy spoke. 'Then you'll have to prove them wrong.'

A knock on the door heralded the arrival of Artemisia's trunk, a large, leather-covered pine affair that took two footmen to carry from the attic. 'Just set it by the window,' Artemisia instructed, feeling Addy's eyes on her full of questions.

'I'm going to Aunt Martha's farmhouse in Seasalter,' she announced once they were alone again. Their great-aunt had left it to the girls after her passing. 'I can paint and recoup.' It had occurred to Artemisia on the ride home that she had no choice about the probation. If she didn't show up in four months with something to show the Academy, they would say she had simply refused consideration for membership. The onus of her failure would be laid fully on her shoulders. If she did show up with new art, then the onus would be on them and who knew what could change in that time. She stifled a wry chuckle at her own expense. It was true, apparently: hope did indeed spring eternal.

'Now?' Addy looked disappointed. 'What about the

holidays? Christmas is in two weeks. We'll miss all the parties.'

'*I* will miss all the parties,' Artemisia corrected.

Addy shook her head. 'We. Don't think I'll let you go traipsing off to Kent for months on end without me. We're sisters and this is my fight, too. If the Academy refused you, they'll refuse me in a few years. This is for *us*.'

'You could come after the holidays,' Artemisia offered, knowing how much Addy enjoyed the festivities. Her sister was a far more social creature than she was. 'It will give me time to fix the place up, make it habitable. We haven't been down in years.' In truth, she wasn't sure what she'd find in Seasalter. She only knew she had to go somewhere and that was the only place available that was truly hers, where she could paint in private.

'It will be a real adventure then.' Addy smiled, a spark of inspiration leaping in her eyes. 'I know, we should have a name. Men do it all the time. The brotherhood of this, the brotherhood of that. What would we be? A sisterhood, in our case literally.' She thought for a moment. 'I know, we could be the Seasalter Sisterhood, united in a common cause.' She wrinkled her nose. 'No, that's too tame. You're not a tame woman. We need something more…defiant. Rebellious. That's it! We'll be The Rebellious Sisterhood.'

Artemisia went to her and wrapped her sister in a hug. 'Are you sure you want to do this? To give up your holiday? I don't know what I did to deserve a sister like you. The Rebellious Sisterhood it is.'

* * *

As much as Artemisia would have liked to have left immediately for Kent, the reality was that 'immediately' meant three days later. There had to be time to pack clothes, time to gather art supplies and household goods against the anticipated paucity of the farmhouse, time to send a rider ahead to warn of their coming. With luck, the farmhouse wouldn't be entirely uninhabitable upon their arrival.

Or not. Artemisia dropped the carriage curtain. After a long day of rainy, rough travel, she was ready for a decent hot meal and a warm bed, but the dark façade of the farmhouse, starkly outlined against the grey sky, did not reassure her of getting either unless she provided them herself. She reached across the carriage and gently shook Addy awake. 'We're there.' She offered her sister a smile.

The carriage rolled to a halt and Artemisia jumped down, not waiting for help. With the exception of a cook-cum-housekeeper they would hire from the village, they'd be on their own. She'd best get used to it. The comforts of London were far behind them now and unnecessary, she reminded herself. Living in a farmhouse hardly necessitated the staff and services required for running a town house. She pulled up the hood of her cloak against the rain and surveyed the house, a red-bricked structure built in the classic T style, with a single-storeyed kitchen extension attached on the left of the two-storey structure. A wisp of chimney smoke drifted against the dusky sky and Artemisia smiled. Maybe they had some luck after all.

Where there was smoke, there was a fire, and where there was a fire, there was warmth and perhaps tea.

The front door opened and a stout woman in a white cap and apron beckoned them in welcome. 'I thought I heard horses. Come in, come in, you'll be soaked through in no time standing about like that.'

Inside, the small entrance hall was warm as Artemisia and Addy shed their cloaks. Addy cast her an *I told you so* smile. 'See, everything is ready, Arta.' To the woman, Addy explained, 'Artemisia always expects the worst. She was certain the farmhouse would be damp, no fires, no beds, no hot food.'

'We've done better than that. Get settled in the parlour and I'll bring you tea and ginger biscuits.' The woman exchanged a friendly conspiratorial look with Addy and bustled off before Artemisia realised she hadn't asked her name.

'You've made another conquest.' Artemisia pulled a chair before the fire. Addy was always charming. People were drawn to her sister's open manner and enthusiasm for everything. Not so her. People found her off-putting. Perhaps it was her height—she was as tall as many men. More likely, though, it was her own manner that put people off—a directness laced with cynicism. Beyond Addy, Artemisia trusted no one, confided in no one, a product of an early brush with heartbreak and betrayal. To date, life had proven that decision correct.

The housekeeper bustled in with a tea tray, followed by a pretty blonde girl whose cap couldn't quite hide her abundance of errant curls any better than her clean, respectable apron could hide her abundance of feminine curves. And she was *trying* to hide them, Artemisia thought. Desperately, and failing miserably. Artemisia had instant empathy for the pretty girl. Men were capable of doing terrible things to pristine beauty.

The housekeeper set the tray down on a low table before the fire and Artemisia saw to the business of introductions. 'I'm Miss Stansfield and this is my sister, Addy.' The girl hung back, respectfully behind the older woman, attempting to blend in, but failing in that as well. A girl like her would never survive service in a big house.

'I'm Mrs Harris,' the housekeeper said, as brisk and no-nonsense in her tone as she was in her movements. 'I'll come up during the day and look after the house. There will be breakfast and lunch served and I'll leave supper for you on the stove.' The woman allowed herself a break from the business of introductions as she added, 'I served your great-aunt before she passed. It will be a pleasure to have someone at the house again. I was thrilled to get the news Martha's nieces were coming. She loved to talk about you and the summers you spent here.'

Martha. Their great-aunt and Mrs Harris had been friends. 'I took the liberty of hiring some girls in the village to help get things ready. They'd be eager to work if you wanted to hire.' She gestured for the pretty maid to step forward. 'This is Elianora, she's my niece. My brother owns the bakery in town. She does the baking for me here. It's good to have a second pair of hands, good to not be alone, if you take my meaning.'

Artemisia offered a curt nod in Elianora's direction. 'Thank you for the biscuits, they are delicious.' Ginger biscuits aside, she understood Mrs Harris's meaning. It referred to the likelihood that illicit activity might be got up to in the desolation of the Kent countryside, particularly in empty or mostly empty farmhouses where only a housekeeper worked. The marshy coast was known for its smuggling industry as much as it was known for its oysters. A woman alone might be an easy target.

'I think the two of you will be more than enough staff for the house.' Artemisia was quick to squelch the idea of extra help. The last thing she wanted was a house crawling with maids and footmen. 'We want to live simply and privately while we're here.' She was here to paint, but the housekeeper looked crestfallen.

'Well, it was just a suggestion.' Mrs Harris was all brisk business once more, moving to straighten a pillow on the sofa to cover her disappointment.

Artemisia was aware of Addy's gentle touch at her knee, counselling restraint as her sister softened her inadvertent blow. 'Let's see how things go and how much work we actually require, Mrs Harris. We can revisit the subject after we've settled in.'

That seemed to appease the housekeeper. 'Very good, then. I'll see that your baggage is delivered to your rooms and then I'll be off for the night. There's stew and bread set aside for supper in the kitchen.'

'Times are hard, Arta,' Addy said softly after Mrs Harris left them. 'People will be glad of the work and the holidays are coming. Perhaps we might have a small party here, welcome ourselves to the neighbourhood so to speak. After all, one can never have too many friends.'

She smiled kindly at Addy. Her sister saw strangers as potential friends while she saw them as potential enemies. 'You're right. I hadn't thought of that. I was thinking only of my own privacy. You're too good, Addy.' She paused and sipped the hot tea, swallowing slowly to let its warmth seep through her. 'Still, if we take anyone on, I don't want people gossiping and speculating about what happens up here.' It would only take one wagging tongue, one unkind speculation to somehow reach London, and the Academy would paint her a loose woman. Admittedly, it was unlikely the people of Seasalter had London connections, but one could never be too careful.

They drank their tea in silence, listening to the sounds of trunks being hauled upstairs, the grunt and huff of labouring men punctuated by an occasional instruction from Mrs Harris. 'There's still time to change your mind,' Artemisia offered as the sounds of moving in ceased. Her father's carriage crew would stay the night in Seasalter and return to London in the morning. Addy could go with them.

Addy shook her head, her words coming around a mouthful of ginger biscuits. 'Are you joking? With biscuits like these to look forward to? There's not a chance I'm leaving.'

Artemisia set down her teacup. 'I think everyone's done. Shall we take a tour and see what we're up against?'

There were three rooms on the bottom floor, excluding the extension housing the kitchen: the parlour, a dining room, and long glassed-in rectangular space at the back that ran the length of the house. Great-Aunt Martha had used it as a conservatory of sorts for her plants.

The space was empty now. Artemisia thought it would do well for an art studio. The windows would capture the precious winter light in late morning and afternoon. Upstairs, multiple bedchambers awaited, lining both sides of the hall. Their trunks had been delivered to two of the chambers facing the front of the house with its view of the estuary. Beds were already turned down.

Artemisia stared out the window, seeing the wintery landscape with an artist's eye: blacks, greys, heathers, slate, wheat, copper, sienna, silver, salt. A strong, masculine palette. In the spring and summer the marsh would be full of birds: godwits, oystercatchers, plovers. Today the estuary was deserted with the exception of a flock of Brent geese. It would send a bold message. Women seldom painted in such austere shades. But the icy purples and blues that might be used for a mountainscape simply did not suit the mud of a winter estuary.

'You're busy, already painting in your mind,' Addy said from the doorway.

'Yes, I suppose I am.' Artemisia didn't turn from the window, not wanting to lose the images and ideas it inspired. Her fingers itched for a brush to paint, a pencil to sketch. She would unpack her equipment tonight and be ready to start tomorrow. Excitement thrummed through her as she planned. She would sketch the geese, the brown weeds, the sienna mud, the silver-grey waters of the marsh. She would paint them all from a palette of isolation. There was a metaphor there for her own isolation from the community she longed to be part of. Yes. She would paint the estuary. To the untutored onlooker, it would be a bold collection of nature, but to those who knew better, it would be a protest.

Chapter Three

January 1820

In hindsight, Darius realised he should have protested more vociferously when his father had invited him to the town house for dinner. He'd wanted a quiet supper his last night in town. While dining with his parents in the insulated elegance of Bourne House met that requirement, it did so at a price.

'Have you met any nice girls yet? I thought there were several in town for the holidays this year.' His mother was making him pay for the privilege of her French chef rather early in the meal. Usually, she waited until the cheese was served. He'd barely got through the fish—a flaky sea bass spritzed with a zesty lemon juice served on his mother's Wedgwood creamware. Delicious as it was, Darius wasn't convinced it was worth the maternal inquisition.

Darius drew a deep breath and set aside his fork. Calm was what was required here. The more reasonable he was, the better it would go. 'Not at present, no. But I expect the Season to provide more interesting choices.' As the heir to Bourne, he had only three mandatory tasks in life: care for the earldom, marry and produce a brace of capable sons. On his last birthday, he'd agreed with his mother that it was time to look to the latter two tasks on that list. He'd be thirty-five this autumn. It was time and it was his responsibility. Darius always did his duty.

And so did his mother. She fortified herself with a sip of wine. 'To be sure, this year's crop appears to be extraordinary. It's no wonder so many fine young girls were in town pre-emptively over the holidays, looking to steal a march on the others.' It was the second time she'd mentioned the holidays. Darius was wary. She must have someone in mind.

'Old Worth had his sons' families with him for Christmas. His grandson, Preston, is impressive. He's due for a government post, I think.' She waved a long, delicate hand in his father's direction. 'Bourne would know those particulars,' she said, indicating there was another set of particulars to know and she knew them. 'His granddaughter, May, is a dark-haired, sharp-witted beauty. She's bound to be a diamond this Season.' There it was, the point she wanted to make.

'I am sure Miss Worth is delightful,' he acceded neutrally. Thoughts of another dark-haired, sharp-witted woman invaded his mind juxtaposing the fiery Artemisia Stansfield against the image of the no doubt smooth-haired, porcelain featured May Worth. When his mother had said they'd begin looking in earnest in the new year, he'd thought she'd meant this spring when the Season started, not the moment the calendar turned.

The new year was only two weeks old. 'Unfortunately, I am expected out of town. I am leaving tomorrow.' He offered the news to stall any further incursions on his mother's part.

His father looked up in interest. 'Where to? I've heard nothing of this.'

'Seasalter.' It was an unplanned journey, courtesy of the inconvenient Miss Stansfield. Carrying out his commission for the Academy was becoming far more difficult than he'd anticipated. When he'd agreed to the suggestion it was in part on the assumption that Artemisia Stansfield would paint in London. He'd been wrong on that most important account. When he'd shown up at the Stansfield town house the butler had curtly informed him Miss Stansfield had decamped for Kent, all the while looking down his rather long nose at him as if he were personally at fault for the reasons she'd left.

'Seasalter? In January?' His father made a look of noble distaste, something sly moving in his dark eyes. 'Whatever for? The oysters aren't even in season.'

'It's for the Academy,' Darius answered vaguely, feeling protective of the commission while his mother was in full matchmaking mode. His father's gaze lingered on him for a moment and Darius had the suspicion he'd not escape unscathed. His father was a respected collector of art, the Bourne collection one of the finest in England. His father knew what happened in the art world.

After that, the conversation devolved into general discussion roaming from Parliament to spring work on the estates, to new exhibitions in town, to the upcoming Season. All the while, the tension that permeated the meal never truly ebbed despite the congenial conversation. That was the Rutherford way, Darius had discovered growing up. Everything must be serene and perfect on the surface. Upon meeting the Rutherfords, no one would guess the disappointments that lurked underneath: the multiple miscarriages that had driven a wedge between the Earl and the Countess years ago, that the Countess had once been a talented flautist, despite being the daughter of an earl herself, and laid that talent aside to make an advantageous marriage, or that a quarrel between the Earl and his sixteen-year-old son had nearly torn the family apart. That quarrel was the last time his mother had shown any real fire. These days her energies were bent unconditionally to the task of seeing him wed, her last maternal duty. She'd failed to present the earldom with the necessary pair of young males. She could not fail in seeing the heir wed. In that, Darius's responsibility and hers were intertwined. They could not do their duties separate of one another. He would not fail her. She deserved the best from her one surviving son.

His mother rose, still a handsome, gracious woman at fifty-five who knew her duty at the table even when dining *en famille*. 'I'll leave you two to your port.'

The decanter was brought, drinks poured and Darius waited for his father to take the lead. His father would not appreciate any conversational distractions when he had something on his mind. 'Artemisia Stansfield is in Seasalter,' his father said at last. 'Is your trip for the Academy attached to the trouble with her?' He was only moderately surprised his father knew despite the Academy not bruiting the business about.

'Yes.' Darius had learned the truth was the only path forward with his father. His father learned the truth sooner or later about everything. Best to have it out in the open from the start. 'The Academy would like me to check on her progress so they are prepared for her return in March. I only learned yesterday she'd left town.'

His father cocked a brow and took a long drink. 'She's an interesting woman. Too interesting, if you know what I mean.' Darius did know what he meant. Hadn't those been his thoughts as well? 'Perhaps you can get out of it?' his father proposed. 'I'm sure when the Academy appointed you to the task, they thought she'd be here in town, surrounded by people. Seasalter can be lonely in the winter.' His father gave him a strong look. 'A dishonourable woman and an honourable man are a dangerous combination.'

'I don't think Miss Stansfield is looking for a husband,' Darius replied evenly. It wouldn't do to take offence at his father's insinuation. 'I am going in a professional capacity and I doubt Miss Stansfield will be pleased to see me,' he assured his father. She would be no more pleased to see him than he would be pleased to be there. It was a distasteful business all around. The sooner he dealt with it, the sooner he'd be out of it.

'Just so, be careful. You're an earl's heir, a definite step above her usual, I am sure.' His father tossed back the rest of his drink, signalling the end of the conversation. He rose, confident his message had been delivered. 'Let's go join your mother.' Not because it was the usual etiquette, but because his mother was a constant reminder of those who were counting on him to do the right thing. Perhaps getting out of town for a few days would be a welcome breath of fresh air after all.

The coach stopped in the innyard of the Crown, the only real inn Seasalter boasted, and Darius prepared for the discomfort of the road to be replaced with the discomfort of an out-of-the-way inn not used to regular hospitality. With luck, he wouldn't be here long. He checked his pocket watch. Half past three. He could refresh himself and make the Stansfield residence by teatime. After all, misery loved company. He was under no illusions that Miss Stansfield would be pleased to see him.

His footman opened the door, setting down the steps. Darius stepped down into the mud of the innyard, his boots squelching, misty rain dusting the capes of his greatcoat, and took a deep breath of sharp, briny, Kent air. It was certainly fresher than London, he'd give it that, a small consolation. 'Bring my trunk in,' he instructed. 'I'll let the innkeeper know I'm here.'

Inside was no better than outside, merely darker. Muddy boots had left tracks on the plank floor and no effort had been made to sweep, perhaps because it was a losing battle. A few men lounged by the fire, drinking ale, and there was the smell of hot food being prepared for the supper meal. That was encouraging. He wouldn't starve, not that he intended to be here long enough for such a thing to be of concern. The innkeeper gave him the key and a sly look when he asked directions to the Stansfields'. Apparently Artemisia had made an impression on the community already. No doubt they found a single woman living alone quite the novelty.

Darius found himself wondering as he climbed the stairs to his room if she had enlightened the population about her opinions on the male anatomy. He had an errant image of her, that magnificent mass of dark curly hair wild and loose about her shoulders, storming the public room and spouting her arguments against gender inequality. Some day, she'd learn it was a losing proposition. There was little tolerance in the world for people who thought differently. They either conformed or were stamped out. As a lord's son, he'd learned that lesson early.

Darius fitted the key into the lock and surveyed the room. Objectively, it would do. It was surprisingly clean and of decent size. There was a bed, a washstand, a fireplace, a small table for writing or for dinners when the taproom proved too rowdy. He availed himself of the washstand, scrubbing his face and hands, but was hard put as to what other improvements he ought to make to his appearance. This was an informal place, a village by the merest definition of the word. To look too fine would be to attract further attention.

The farmhouse occupied by Miss Stansfield was just up the road, a half mile or less. The innkeeper assumed he'd walk as, no doubt, most people did in this village no matter the weather. He peered out the window. It was still raining. It hardly made sense to change clothes just to get them dirty when his own clothes had only seen the inside of his carriage. He shook the droplets off his greatcoat and put it back on as his trunk arrived.

'I'll return for supper.' His man would know what

that meant—a bath and hot food should be at the ready, along with a full-bodied red wine if it could be found. Darius pulled his collar up high and headed out into the misty elements.

He found the farmhouse easily enough a little farther up Faversham Road and, in truth, the chance to stretch his legs had improved his mood despite the rain. Smoke curled invitingly from the chimney and a lamp shone through a lace-curtained window, an affirmation that someone was home, that his walk had not been in vain. For the first time in a while, he was starting to feel lucky. He wasn't looking forward to calling on Miss Stansfield, but if he could see her and her artwork today, he could be on the road home tomorrow. He need not prolong his stay to the benefit of them both. The less he saw of Artemisia Stansfield, the less opportunity he'd have to report anything unsavoury.

Darius knocked on the door and it was answered by a round-shaped woman in a crisp apron. 'I'm here to see Miss Stansfield,' Darius offered with appropriate deference. In his experience, it always paid to be courteous to housekeepers.

The housekeeper gave him a swift appraisal, deciding he passed her muster. 'Right this way, Miss Stansfield is in the parlour.' It was no great distance to the parlour. The farmhouse was neat but compact compared to the airy town houses of Mayfair.

'Miss Stansfield,' the housekeeper said with suitable seriousness, perhaps a sign of the impression he'd made on her, 'there's a gentleman here to see you.' She moved out of the narrow doorway so he could step through.

From the green sofa a pleasant-looking young woman with auburn hair looked up from a sketch pad, friendly green eyes mirrored his own surprise. Had he come to the wrong place? Had he misunderstood the directions from the innkeeper?

'Thank you, Mrs Harris. Might you bring some tea? It's a wet afternoon out.' She set aside the pad and rose as the housekeeper hurried off. 'A visitor is always welcome, sir, but I don't believe we've met.'

Darius made a little bow, masking his own surprise. 'No, I don't believe we have. I am looking for Miss Stansfield.'

She gave a light laugh. 'You've found her. I *am* Miss Stansfield. Well, one of them. No doubt you're looking for my sister, Artemisia?' The way she said the last, Darius had the impression she was used to being passed over for her sister. It would be easy to do. She had her sister's confidence, but not her sister's edgy boldness, nor her sister's aplomb. She did have an endearing openness all her own, however. She stuck out her hand in the silence that followed. 'I am Miss Adelaide Stansfield.'

Darius took her hand and shook it. 'I'm Mr Rutherford, I've come from London.' He opted to leave off his title. He was the art critic here, not the Viscount.

'Oh, have you come to purchase a painting? Artemisia will be disappointed to have missed you.'

'She's not here?' Darius enquired, wondering if that was a stroke of luck or misfortune, followed quickly by wondering where she might be. It was raining out and there was nowhere to go unless she'd gone into Whitstable or Faversham.

Adelaide Stansfield shook her head. 'No, she's out sketching today in the estuary. Please, sit down and at least have some tea for your troubles. I'm not sure when she'll be back. She said not to expect her until supper.' There was no question of staying that long, but he had to stay for tea. It would be rude not to. His stomach rumbled as the tea tray came in, reminding him that it would be practical, too. He hadn't eaten since breakfast.

They sat near the fire, the warmth welcome after the damp walk. His eye went to the painting above the mantel—a lone goose on the marsh done in striking blacks and greys against subtle browns and deceptively dark greens for the marsh reeds. In the corner were the initials A.S. He nodded towards the painting. 'Is that one your sister's?' It occurred to him that Artemisia's absence might be a piece of luck after all. He could see her work without having to overcome whatever resistance Artemisia would put up. Now, her work was unguarded except for this more pleasant Stansfield who offered him tea and delicious little lemon seed cakes.

'Yes, do you like it? I'm not sure if it's for sale. It's the first one she's done in a new collection.'

'Does she have others?' His gaze swept the little parlour for other work.

'Yes, in the workroom. They're not up.' Adelaide Stansfield rose. 'Would you like to see them?' She was so earnest he felt a twinge of guilt about misleading her, yet wasn't this better for all involved? There would be no arguments, no unpleasant scenes.

The workroom at the back of the house had been transformed into an artist's haven. He took it in with a practiced eye; a drop cloth covered the floor, speckled with paint splatters, canvases stood propped against a wall, an easel showed a work in progress. In the mornings the light would be fantastic. He stopped and surveyed the sketches on the table. Artemisia had been busy since departing London. 'Might I have some time to study the paintings?' he asked.

'Of course, I'll leave the lamp.' Adelaide Stansfield excused herself, giving him privacy. He held the light up to each canvas, not all of them complete yet. Still, the amount of work she'd done was impressive. She'd have quite the collection to show the Academy in March. They wouldn't like it. Surely she knew that. And she'd done it anyway. The palette she'd chosen was stark and masculine. The Academy would take issue with that. Women should paint flowers and still life. Even Mary Moser had had enough sense to realise that. Women painted in pastels, in bright blues or pinks, not in grey and taupe. No, the Academy wouldn't like it at all, not her palette, not her style, not her subject matter—geese, birds, marshes, weathered boats. She'd depicted a landscape battered by nature. It drew the eye, most certainly, but it did not please the eye, not like Constable's landscapes of southern England with their soft colours and light.

There were quiet steps behind him. Adelaide Stansfield had returned. 'What do you think, Mr Rutherford?' she solicited, her tone clearly indicating she expected him to be pleased with what he saw. He hated to disappoint her.

'I shall have to consider them. They are not what I expected and I'm not sure they shall suit. Perhaps I'll send word from the inn if I decide on any.'

Some of her pleasantness faded. 'I assure you this is exquisite art. You must consider the artist's use of light and receding planes. The simplicity of the work is deceptive, sir,' Adelaide Stansfield argued in spirited defence.

'Miss Stansfield, you do your sister a great credit. But have you considered that you are biased?' He made a bow, 'I do appreciate your time. Thank you for the tea.' He took his leave then before Miss Stansfield could further her case.

The walk back to the inn in the near dark provided an opportunity for reflection. The artwork he'd seen today had stunned him. What did Artemisia Stansfield think to prove? She'd been given licence to promote herself by painting anything she liked, anything that showed her talent to the Academy, and she'd chosen to defy convention on every front. Did she guess the probation was a sham? Did she guess that nothing would change the Academy's mind? If not, why would she tweak their noses and throw away what she perceived as her chance? If so, what did she seek to prove with this swansong of sorts?

Upstairs in his chamber, Darius shed his coat and boots and settled to a warm meal of jugged hare and vegetables accompanied by a more than adequate red wine and fresh bread. He was halfway through the bottle when the answer came to him. Artemisia Stansfield was staging an invasion, one last glorious attack on the bastion of male uniformity. Did she think she stood a chance? That her invasion could succeed? It wouldn't. She ought to save her strength for battles she could win.

Darius set aside his napkin, the tub beside the fire steaming and ready for him. He stripped out of his clothes and sank into the blessed waters, eyes closed. Someone ought to tell her. It would be a painful lesson in the short term, one she would be reluctant to hear, but a necessary one that would save her pain in the long run. Why should she spend her life railing against a system that would never let her in? Why have a life of futile striving and desperation?

Darius leaned his head back against the rim of the tub, letting the heat and the wine do their work. He'd once been enlightened about the limits of his own talents at the impressionable age of sixteen. He would never be anything but a dauber, a hobbyist. Anyone who'd told him otherwise was merely pandering to a lord's son's vanity in an attempt to curry favour. His father had been relieved when he'd set down his brush and focused on his studies. It had hurt, certainly. But in hindsight it was probably for the best. He was thirty-four now and he hadn't touched a brush in almost two decades. Still, he'd found a way to be involved in art as a patron and a critic—both were roles much more suitable for his station. Where Viscount St Helier led, others followed. What more could he want?

Chapter Four

Artemisia scrunched her brow, trying to follow her sister's story as she stripped out of her oilskin slicker and muddy boots. The day had been wet and long as she sketched rain at the estuary. She'd wanted to study the slant of the rain and its sheeting. The outing had been a success in that regard, less so in others. She'd spent the day under a canopy, drawing and trying to keep her paper dry. Now, her sister was talking of a visitor who'd come to buy her artwork.

'He came all the way from London and then decided he didn't like any of it?' Artemisia summarised with some incredulity. It was a long way to come and then not purchase anything, not that she had anything for sale—another reason this story of Addy's didn't make sense. It was also a long way to come not knowing if there was any work to buy in the first place.

'That's what he said.' Addy shook off the oilskin and hung it up on a peg in the hall.

'What was his name? Did he leave a card?' Artemisia worked off her boots. She'd worn trousers today instead of skirts for the wet estuary.

'Mr Rutherford.'

Artemisia's hand paused on her boot. 'Rutherford? *Darius* Rutherford? He was here?' He'd not introduced himself as Viscount St Helier, but as Darius Rutherford, which meant he'd come as the art critic. Rutherford had been here and she had not.

'He didn't offer a first name. He was tall, dark-haired, dark-eyed,' Addy described. 'Do you know him?'

'Know him? Yes, he's an art critic. He was at the assembly meeting in December.' What was he doing in Seasalter? It obviously wasn't coincidence. He'd known she was here, he'd come to the farmhouse expressly to seek her out. A suspicion formed in her mind. Had he come to check on her? To bring a report back to the Academy? Artemisia tensed. 'Did you show him the paintings?' Addy flinched at her tone and she instantly regretted it.

'Yes, did I do wrong? I thought he was here to purchase something,' Addy apologised.

Artemisia shook her head and hugged her sister. 'No, you did fine, you couldn't have known. I'm not mad at you, I'm mad at him.' How dare he come haring over to Kent to spy on her, to mislead her sister into showing him the new collection, and how dare the Academy put him up to it? She had until March and it was only two weeks into January. It was unconscionable. She grabbed her recently divested oilskin and shrugged into it. The Academy had enough leverage as it was, they hardly needed to resort to spying on her. It merely added insult to injury that they'd now taken to invading her sanctuary.

'Where are you going?' Addy cried. 'You just got back, dinner is waiting.'

'To the Crown, to give Darius Rutherford a piece of my mind.' Probably more than one piece, more like five or six. He'd duped her sister and encroached on her studio. He would not get away with either of those crimes.

'What the hell do you think you're doing, spying on me?' The sharp words and slamming door penetrated the relaxed fog of Darius's brain. He sloshed upright in the tub, sending water over the edge as his eyes flashed open. Doom approached in the guise of the long-legged Artemisia Stansfield advancing towards the tub in all her temperamental glory *and* trousers, a full bucket of water in her hands. He didn't think for a moment the water was *warm*.

'Put that down!' The words were out of Darius's mouth as the only defence he was able to launch, caught at his most vulnerable. The words came too late, they couldn't stop her. Artemisia upended the bucket, sluicing ice-cold water over his head.

'Damn! Do you want to kill me?' he yelped, his delightful hot bath completely ruined and his teeth chattering from the sudden shock.

'At least you saw me coming. That's more advantage than you gave my sister.' She pointed a long, slim finger at him. 'You gained entrance through misrepresentation. No one misleads my sister and no one goes into my studio without *my* permission.' She was a stormy sight, eyes flaring, hair loose. Not all that different than in his imaginings.

Even muddy and bedraggled, she was a force to be reckoned with. He was unprepared and he shouldn't have been. He should have known she'd come, that she wouldn't allow his stealthy invasion without retaliation. He certainly hadn't thought she'd come tonight, though. This was the second time he'd underestimated her. He would have words for whoever had not secured his door, but that couldn't change anything now. Darius held up the white towel in a gesture of truce. 'Let me get out of the tub so we can discuss this.'

'You can stay in the tub, for all I care.' She crossed her arms over her chest and fixed him with her grey stare.

'Perhaps I'd *like* to get out.' The water was cold and he recognised a dare when he heard it. Did she think he was such a prude that he'd rather lurk in a tub of cold water than emerge in front of her?

She shrugged. 'Suit yourself.' Her gaze did not waver, making it clear she wasn't going to turn away. If he wanted to get out of the tub, he'd have to do it without the benefit of modesty.

'Fine.' Darius pushed up from the water and stepped out of the tub, making no hurry to dry himself. Let her look if she wanted. He wasn't ashamed and she wouldn't be the first woman to see him in his altogether. He was naked and made no effort to hide it. If she could call his bluff, he could certainly call hers. She had issued the dare and he had answered with one of his own. Perhaps she felt she could *not* look away without admitting her challenge had been a hot-headed bluff, a confession that she hadn't really thought he'd do it, let alone stand there in the buff, taking his own leisurely time towelling off.

He was aware of her eyes on him, aware too that she'd have seen naked men before—artists often did. How did he compare? he wondered. He was conscious of her gaze moving objectively over his shoulders, to the curve of his buttocks as he bent to towel his legs. Her gaze would see him objectively, artistically, all muscle and smooth skin. That was her armour, of course, her protection in the game of dares they currently played. It allowed her to boldly advance. He found he wanted more than that from her. He wanted a subjective reaction, something that said she saw him as a man, not an object.

He straightened and felt her eyes rivet on the core of him, proof that her appraisal wasn't entirely objective. His body stirred from semi-arousal to something more obvious. He had the reaction he wanted, but at a cost to himself. Darius wrapped the towel about his hips. The game was over. A draw. He met her gaze with a challenge of his own. Had she seen anything she liked?

'You're a well-made man, from an artist's perspective, that is,' she answered, unabashed by the bold question in his gaze. She took a seat by the fire and crossed one trousered leg over a knee.

'And from a woman's?' Darius took the other chair, pulling his discarded shirt over his head.

'I'm sure you already know the answer to that.' Artemisia didn't bother to dignify the remark with a response. 'What I'd like answered is what you are doing in Seasalter?'

'I'm sure *you* already know.' He tossed her words back, waiting to see her plan of attack now that her anger had waned—at least he hoped it had. He took a surreptitious look about the room in search of any remaining buckets of water. He didn't care for another dousing.

Subtlety and patience were not weapons in Artemisia Stansfield's arsenal. She went right for the kill. 'I think you've been sent to spy on me so that when I return in March the Academy can move their bar once more and declare my art not suitable for membership.' The last was said with just a hint of an upward inflection. She *wanted* to be wrong. She wanted him to denounce her theory, to suggest that she was seeing conspiracies where there were none. He couldn't do it.

'You're not entirely wrong,' Darius offered after a thoughtful pause. 'I am here to check on you, as you suspect. As to what the Academy will do with that information, I can't say.'

'Can't say or won't say?' Artemisia corrected.

'Miss Stansfield, I understand you are disappointed,' Darius said, hoping to soothe her.

Artemisia snapped at him for his efforts. 'Disappointed? I am *beyond* disappointed. I am in absolute disbelief that a group of men are so intimidated by a single female's talent that they would deny her membership for no reason other than her gender. But I am *furious* over the lengths to which they'd go to obscure that truth. They've set up a probation, knowing full well they never intend to honour it. I could paint the damn *Mona Lisa* and it wouldn't be good enough for them. Whatever standard I meet they will make another.'

She gave him a hard stare. 'So, don't sit there and patronise me when you are part of the problem simply by being here, by acting as their tool.' Darius stiffened at the affront. Men had been called out for less. How inconvenient that Artemisia Stansfield was very much a woman, trousers or not.

'Have you considered you do yourself no favours? I saw the artwork—it will not appeal to them. You are tweaking their noses and cutting off your own in the process.'

'Shall I paint flowers, then? I promise you they won't like them either,' Artemisia retorted.

'Since there are no flowers, I can only report on what I saw,' he reminded her. Someone needed to counsel her to caution.

She gave a humph. 'Cut and run, is that it? Did you really think you could avoid seeing me? That you could dash into the farmhouse, sneak a peek at the artwork and call that a report?' She rose and began to pace, her temper visibly riding her hard. 'Do you know how it made me feel today when I heard you'd been there, in my studio? I felt violated, as if someone had looked into my soul, into the depths of me against my will.'

He gave her a sharp look. 'Against her will' was a far stronger phrasing than merely 'without my permission'. This was the rhetoric of rape. What did Artemisia Stansfield know about that which caused her to align it with his visit today? He had no sympathy for men who raped and, in its strictest sense, it happened far more often than he liked to admit. 'I am sorry you see it that way.'

'Apologies are cheap and easy after you already have

what you wanted.' Artemisia was not fazed. 'Far easier to apologise than to ask for permission,' she said sharply.

'Are you never not the cynic?' Darius retorted. 'Not everything is a conspiracy, Miss Stansfield.'

'Are you sure about that? Try seeing the world from my point of view for a few days and let me know your answer then.'

Darius blew out a weary breath. This was going nowhere and he desperately wanted to go to bed. The day had been long and full of disappointments. 'What do you want, Miss Stansfield? If it's to vent your anger and give me a piece of your mind, you've done that. If it's something more, I haven't any idea what it is. If you could tell me, perhaps I might be better able to provide it.' Appeasement wasn't always the best conflict management strategy, but it would get him what he wanted. She would leave, he could go to bed and in the morning *he* could leave and get back to his life.

'I want you to give me a fair report.'

'I will. I saw the paintings today.'

'Did *you* like them?' Artemisia probed, leaning against the small mantel like a gentleman in the drawing room, an entirely manly posture. One of many that she had—the way she'd crossed her leg over one knee, her tendency to shake hands. Another survival technique she'd perhaps adopted to assimilate into the male world of art, part of the armour he was coming to recognise.

'My personal opinion is not relevant.' He watched the fire pick out the amber highlights in her hair, flickers of flames among coals. It was a losing battle. No one would ever mistake her for a man.

She arched a slim brow in challenge. 'Since when is the opinion of an art critic not relevant? Isn't your job all about opinions?'

'Objective opinions, opinions based on the founding principles of good art. Not opinions grounded in nothing but subjective emotion. Everybody has one of those.' He was having one right now, in fact, one that concluded Artemisia Stansfield was an unconventionally attractive woman, even in trousers.

If she'd thought trousers made her appear less feminine, she was mistaken. Those trousers were accentuating her long legs and compactly rounded backside in ways a ballgown never would, while the mannish shirt she wore billowed gently over the high full curves of her breasts, fooling no one as to her gender.

But that slender body of hers wasn't the sole attraction. There were other attractions: the slim column of her throat, matched by the proud patrician length of her nose, the curve of her cheekbones which had the potential to lend her both the look of angel or Fury depending on her mood, and those alert grey eyes. A man looking for an ornament on his arm could do no better. But that man would miss the truth of her.

She was all fire, that was her chief attraction. Men were drawn to flames, to the danger fire posed. Some to quench it, some to revel in the thrill of fighting it. Others to be consumed by it. Still others to tame it. What a feat that would be, Darius mused, to tame the fire that was Artemisia Stansfield. Taming might start with telling her the truth while she still had time to correct her course of self-destruction.

'The Academy won't like the paintings. Objectively, they don't fit the English tradition. But you already know that.'

'Why show them something they've already seen?' Artemisia gave another of her shrugs. He didn't believe she was as indifferent as she let on. 'They wanted something different, something fresh.'

'Not really, we both know that. You'll make it too easy on them to dismiss you.' Her stubbornness would be her undoing if she wasn't careful, and she wasn't.

'I don't want to be a copy of Constable or Gainsborough.' She paused. 'My work is better than that. There's a subtlety to it that transcends the instant satisfaction of pretty colours.'

Darius recognised the remark for what it was, a direct shot across the bow of the Academy's flagship—Constable with his hues and hazy light that lent his paintings a near-fairy-tale atmosphere. 'I don't think such an argument will help your cause,' he cautioned.

She shook her head. 'Nor will your hasty judgement. I don't think twenty minutes with my collection will render a fair assessment, especially since it is not even half-done.' She nodded towards his trunk in the corner of the room, still strapped and unpacked, or was that already re-packed? 'You were leaving tomorrow, thinking your job done.' It was a blatant accusation on par with her bold critique of Constable. 'Thought you'd seen enough?'

'I thought *you'd* prefer it that way,' Darius offered carefully. He'd been sent to see the art, but he'd also been sent to see her, something he'd been trying to avoid. He was an art critic, he was not an arbiter of morals. The idea that he was supposed to pass judgement on her lifestyle sat poorly with him no matter how unnatural she might be. She was certainly unlike the women he knew, but that did not give him the right to destroy her. It struck at his standard of fair play.

'I'd prefer you'd not come at all,' she answered honestly. 'But since you have, it's best to carry out your task right.' She was challenging him again and his own tired temper began to stir. How dare she suggest he wasn't giving her fair consideration? She had no idea that he was trying to avoid letting her hang herself with her own noose. Had she no idea what men like Aldred Gray suggested behind her back? The longer Darius stayed, the more he'd see and the more opportunity she'd have to be the author of her own demise.

'Are you asking me to stay in Seasalter and monitor your work? Forgive me if it seems an odd request since it's the very thing you came down here to condemn me for.'

'I condemned you for invading my privacy and misleading my sister, for *not* asking permission,' she corrected. 'You may monitor my work on my terms.'

'Which are?' Darius drawled.

Her eyes glittered dangerously in the firelight.

'You wait until the end of February to make a report when my portfolio is done.'

The end of February! That was six weeks away. The minx was holding him hostage by giving him what he'd wanted: access to her art. Why would she do that? He'd been about to protest and thought better of it. Perhaps she *wanted* him to disagree. Perhaps she thought she could turn this visit against him and argue he'd not given her fair consideration if he left early. Perhaps she wanted the satisfaction of having driven him off, never mind he'd been about to go before she'd shown up. Now, leaving wouldn't be of his own accord, but something she could take credit for.

He would not be manipulated. 'Fine, I'll stay until the end of February.' She might regret this later even if she felt victorious now. As for himself, he was regretting it already. Six weeks in Seasalter in the middle of winter had a certain death knell to it that pealed as loud as a winter of matchmaking in London, although he was sure Artemisia Stansfield would make Seasalter interesting.

Chapter Five

It had been an interesting argument with an intriguing outcome. Even now, tucked up in the window seat of her room, ready for bed, Artemisia wasn't sure who'd won. Had she? She'd got her conditions. There would be no premature report, no fear of having her probation terminated early. She'd trapped him here. She'd seen how unsatisfactory the thought of staying six weeks in Seasalter was to him. Six weeks of inn living would seem like purgatory to a man used to the finer luxuries of life.

However, he did get to remain *and* she'd have to endure his company. Did that mean he'd won? Surely not. She'd seen the look on his face. He hadn't wanted to stay, although he'd get to make a very thorough report. It wasn't clear to her exactly why he'd wanted to rush back to London other than the obvious: Seasalter lacked a certain charm when it came to entertainments. Was that all it was?

Artemisia flipped open her sketch pad, lines and form coming to her absently as her mind continued to run over the evening. Perhaps no one had won. Perhaps they'd both lost in their stubbornness. He was forced to stay and she was forced to endure his company by a snare of their own obstinate makings. She looked down at the drawing—the shape forming on the page was of a man emerging from the bath, a very familiar man. It was no wonder that her hand had chosen to sketch that which was imprinted on her mind: Darius Rutherford naked. Despite her claims to artistic objectivity, her body's reaction, all warmth and liquid heat at the sight of him, had been something else entirely. Her eye might have seen him as an artist's subject, but her body had responded to him unmistakably as a woman responds to a man, proof that she'd not been in nearly as much control as she'd liked to have been.

If her reaction, if her loss of control, had been a revelation to her tonight she had only herself to blame. Her reckless behaviour had invited such consequences. When one charges into another's private rooms, anything could happen. She knew this first-hand. Isn't that how it had happened with Hunter McCullough, although he'd been the one doing the charging into her private quarters. What had started as harmless kisses without witnesses had escalated into something far more dangerous and damaging. One would think she knew better these days. Apparently not. Darius Rutherford was more handsome than McCullough and far more adept.

She sketched more slowly now, thoughtful with her lines and shading as she recalled the image of him in detail. It had been no hardship to let her gaze roam the broad muscles of his shoulders, the sculpted curve of his smooth buttocks, the length and sinew of his legs, long and strong to support his height, but it was the core of him that had captured her attention, riveted her gaze and turned her insides to liquid.

She'd never seen a man with a chiselled midsection that looked as if it could have been made from marble and just as strong. It was a good thing she hadn't attempted punching it. The exquisite musculature of him drew the eye southwards to the iliac crest of his hip and the pelvic girdle that housed the manliest part of him. Even in a state of semi-arousal there'd been a strength to him in that place, to the weighty sway of his testicles, low and heavy behind his phallus, entities of strength in their own right, reminding the viewer they were no mere dossal ornamentation.

She stopped and studied her work. What would the Academy think of that? If she painted him, their beloved critic? *A Lord's Bath*, she'd call it. A naughty smile teased her lips. She would make a subtle satire of it, a palette of fleshy pinks and peachy oranges against the backdrop of the fireplace. She could do a good imitation of Constable with those colours. Perhaps she would, if it amused her. It wouldn't amuse him, but he'd be hard-pressed to find technical fault with it. What a rather awkward position he'd be in. It would serve him right. Didn't he know that was the risk of angering an artist? The artist might put you in their painting. She thought of Gentileschi's *Judith and Holofernes*. It had been no accident Judith had worn Gentileschi's face and the doomed Holofernes had been the face of her attacker, a man allowed to walk free from his crime, just as McCullough had walked free from his. But never again. Never again would a man get the better of her, not even one as handsome as Darius Rutherford. She would make sure of it. She was wiser now.

Artemisia yawned, the day spent out of doors catching up with her at last. She needed her sleep. She would be up early. There was more sketching to be done and she didn't intend to be easy to find when Rutherford showed up to do his monitoring. She'd only asked him to stay until February—she'd said nothing about making herself available.

She wasn't available when he called the next afternoon at the farmhouse, or the afternoon after that. Two missed visits was enough to convince him her absence wasn't a coincidence, not when it was coupled by a scowling Mrs Harris at the door who was all too pleased to inform him neither Miss Stansfield was receiving. 'Miss Artemisia has gone sketching.' She wiped her hands decisively on her apron as if she were wiping her hands of him, making it clear that he wouldn't be getting even a crumb of the kitchen's lemon cakes in the near future. The feminine population of the farmhouse had closed ranks against him decisively.

He couldn't blame them. He might have handled things differently if he'd imagined he'd be staying in Seasalter for six weeks and dependent on their hospitality. He needed to apologise to Adelaide for allowing her to believe his business was different than what it was and it was a point of pride to charm himself back into the good graces of the housekeeper. But both of those tasks would have to wait.

The larger issue at hand was what to do about Artemisia. It was clear that he could call for the next six weeks in a row and she wouldn't be at home. She was deliberately thwarting him in carrying out the duty she'd charged him with. How could he observe her work if she wasn't there to be observed?

Darius reached the end of the muddy drive. He could either turn right and head back to the Crown for another unproductive afternoon in the taproom or he could go in search of her. His legs, and perhaps the other parts of him that found something akin to enjoyment in sparring with her, liked the latter idea better. Artemisia challenged him. She'd poked at his assumptions about the world and its fairness, stirred old desires, ones he'd thought were long buried, and then, just when he thought he'd glimpsed a piece of her, she had retreated, once more shrouded in mystery, a mystery he very much wanted to solve. He wasn't one for idleness of any sort—mental or physical. Between the journey here and the subsequent afternoons, he'd been too idle for his body's tastes. Spending time with Artemisia satisfied both needs.

He turned left up the shore road, wondering where to look first. There wasn't much to do in Seasalter except catch oysters. He had to think like an artist. Would she seek out views? He scanned the flat horizon. There were no cliffs in Seasalter. Expanses, then. There was the marsh and the estuary that looked across the Swale to Sheppey. A lone curlew cried overhead, settling his decision. The estuary it would be. She would have water, mudflats and winter wildlife to choose from for sketching.

* * *

He found her down on the beach, snugged into a sheltered space set back from the muddy shore. She sat cross-legged on an old plaid blanket, dressed once more in trousers and boots, her wild hair tamed into a single thick, tight braid hanging over one shoulder, sketch book in her lap, her gaze and thoughts absorbed by whatever was on the paper. She looked…peaceful, restful, two words he wasn't used to ascribing to Artemisia Stansfield.

There was none of the storm about her today, none of the rage. He hesitated to intrude and risk bringing them back. Darius allowed himself the indulgence of studying her a moment longer. This image of Artemisia Stansfield was just as beguiling in its tranquillity as the dark-haired fury who threw cold bathwater on a naked man, or the virago who challenged an entire assembly with the flash of her grey eyes. This image of the sketcher at work tempted him. His fingers twitched at his side out of old reflex for a pencil, wanting to capture the moment. For the second time in two days, he wanted to draw again. No, that was yet another temptation she offered and must also be resisted. His drawing days were in the past. He'd made that decision decades ago.

He took his imaginings in hand and strode forward into her line of sight, hands thrust deep into the pockets of his greatcoat. 'You've found a good spot,' he called out.

'And *you've* found *me*.' Artemisia set down her pencil with a sigh that was half-irritation, half-resignation. 'I suppose discovery was inevitable.'

'May I join you?' Darius took a spot on the sand,

careful not to infringe on her blanket. It was unexpect-
edly temperate in this little place of hers. The wind off
the water missed them and one could almost forget they
were on a beach in January. 'You're a hard person to
find. But I am always up for a challenge.'

He leaned back on his hands and crossed his legs at
the ankles, his pose as casual as his words. There was
no need to be antagonistic, she would hear the reprimand and the rule without being goaded. She would not
be allowed to elude him. He would hold her accountable
to their arrangement. 'What are we sketching today?'

'Birds.' The answer was succinct. For a moment he
was taken aback by the abruptness. Then she reached
into a covered basket beside her and drew out a bread
crust. She broke it into crumbs and scattered it several
feet from her on the sand. 'They'll come close if we're
quiet.' Her voice was pitched low, a throaty, exotic murmur. He nodded in understanding. An artist often liked
to work in silence, to be alone with their thoughts.

Darius reached into a deep pocket and brought out
his journal. He seldom went anywhere without it. He
flipped to a blank page and settled in. From the looks of
the empty beach, they could be here awhile. He made a
habit of journaling, something he'd begun doing at Oxford to keep track of professors' lectures and to keep his
hands busy sans paintbrush. Afterwards, it had trans-
ferred into a record of his days, who he met, what he
did, thoughts about life. Some entries were more philo-
sophical than others. Today, however, he didn't want to
write. He wanted to draw. Before his mind could gainsay his hand, the pencil was moving of its own accord.

'A curlew, look.' Her voice broke into the silence,

quiet and slow, and then, a little later, 'A godwit.' When the bread was gone, she reached for more. The afternoon became punctuated by three words here, two words there, scattered out like her bread, drawing him in as surely as the crumbs drew the birds.

At last, she laid aside her sketch pad and stretched her back. 'I think that's enough for today. Would you care for something to eat?' She reached into the basket once more for the rest of the bread and a large, carefully wrapped wedge of cheese. 'Mrs Harris always packs enough for two.'

Darius gave a wry chuckle and shut his book. 'She might not have done so if she thought you'd be sharing with me. She made her opinion of me quite clear when I showed up at your door these last two days. Not that I didn't deserve it. I fear I've got off on the wrong foot at the farmhouse.'

'Mrs Harris is quite protective.' Artemisia sliced into the bread and the cheese and handed him a chunk of both. 'She also doesn't like to admit when her own judgement is wrong and you had her charmed from the start.' She nodded towards his book 'What do you write in there?'

His hand moved protectively to touch the worn leather cover. 'Just notes, observations that are of no account to anyone but me.'

Artemisia lifted her dark brows in a teasing arch. 'Private thoughts are interesting to everyone just because they're private.'

'I assure you mine aren't.' Darius tucked the book into his pocket in case she thought to make a grab for it.

She would laugh if she saw his efforts today. He wasn't even sure he wanted to look at them. He'd probably tear the page out tonight and burn it. He cocked his head towards a bird at the edge of the marsh standing on one spindly leg, a long, slender beak pecking in the mud. 'What kind of bird is that?'

'An avocet.' She reached for her sketch pad in measured movements, careful not to startle their visitor. 'I've waited all day for one of those.'

Darius waited for her to finish sketching, seeing the bird through her eyes; its black beak, its black-and-white plumage, would make an ideal addition to her stark palette of winter greys and browns.

'Very impressive, Miss Stansfield, you know your birds,' he said once the bird had flown away and she'd gone back to eating her bread and cheese.

'Painters have to be a little of everything: historian, scientist, anatomist, philosopher, social observer, ornithologist, otherwise their paintings will never be original, just flat copies of what others have already done.' She shifted on the blanket, untucking her long legs. 'Birdwatching is no hardship for me. Some people might think it's boring to sit on a beach all day waiting for a bird, but I like it. It's a practice in patience and perseverance, which I desperately need, and it reminds me of my great-aunt.' She favoured him with a rare, genuine smile that lasted only a moment.

'My sister and I spent our summers at the farmhouse. She would bring us out here and teach us all the names of the birds.' The farmhouse she'd inherited. He was starting to see why she'd fled here. This farmhouse in the middle of nowhere wasn't nowhere to her. It was a sanctuary, a place where she could refill her well of creativity and find her centre while Mrs Harris stood guard at the door. In the moment, he envied her that—a place to take shelter from the world. But that envy was short-lived, cut down by the knowledge that Artemisia Stansfield *needed* refuge, that the world was not the same oyster for her as it was for him. When one version of himself hadn't worked out, he'd been allowed to reinvent himself. But she would be relegated to anonymity.

Artemisia rose and began to pack the empty basket with her sketchbook and pencils. He grabbed one end of the blanket and helped her shake it out before she tucked it away in the basket, too. 'Let me carry that,' he offered.

'Thank you, but it's not necessary. I carried it down here, I can carry it back.'

'I am sure you can, but for the sake of my pride, I'd like to carry it.' He flashed her a grin. 'I don't want anyone thinking I'm sloughing off my duty as a gentleman.'

She handed over the basket with a saucy smile. 'All right, then, for the sake of your fragile male ego, you can carry it.' She was probably only half-joking. She knew precisely the lengths men would go to protect that fragile ego.

They walked in silence back to the farmhouse. Unlike many women of his acquaintance, Artemisia Stansfield didn't feel the need to make idle chatter. She was comfortable with herself just as she was. He liked to think the silence was a sign that she was also comfortable with him, but it was too soon to make any assumption there. He'd been unlucky regarding assumptions and Artemisia. She was, no doubt, resigned to tolerate him, yet he did not think it was an entirely unpleasant resignation. They'd spent a companionable afternoon together, they'd eaten together and she'd told him about the farmhouse. Surely that signalled at least modest liking.

At the farmhouse drive, she took the basket from him. 'I am sketching the oystermen tomorrow at the beach.'

'I'll take that as an invitation and as a humble endorsement of my company.' He gave her a half-smile.

'Don't read too much into it. What cannot be avoided must be endured,' she replied, but there was no rancour in it. He took that very small victory with him as he left, but it didn't quell the growing emptiness the further he got from the farmhouse. He pictured Artemisia going inside, setting the basket down in a warm kitchen filled with dinner smells, imagined her telling Adelaide about the birds. She might mention his presence in minute passing, affording him perhaps four brief and nondescript words in the recollection of her afternoon.

Darius Rutherford was there.

Not St Helier. Not the title, but the man. Of course. Artemisia Stansfield would never be intimidated by a title nor would she conflate a man with his title as too many did, as his mother did, calling her husband Bourne, even within the intimacy of the family dining room.

He smiled a little to himself. What else might she tell her sister? Would he feature further in her recounting? If he was lucky, he might get three more words later when she discussed her plans for tomorrow.

Rutherford is coming.

He laughed out loud. She would say it just like that, too, as if he were a bothersome schoolboy tagging along. But she hadn't minded his company, not entirely. They'd got along well at the estuary today sitting in, if not an exactly companionable silence, certainly not an uncomfortable one.

The Crown would seem lonely tonight. He knew no one else here and, like most small towns, Seasalter's inhabitants weren't keen on getting to know strangers, especially well-dressed ones from London. He liked to think that explained his nascent obsession with Artemisia Stansfield. She was the one person he knew here, the only person he had any connection with, tenuous as it might be. It was perfectly understandable to gravitate towards her, to fix his attentions on her. In the absence of other acquaintances and other work, where else would he fix them?

Chapter Six

He was still 'gravitating' a week later. His days or-
bited around her. He rose in the mornings, responded to
correspondence sitting next to the window in the taproom as he ate his breakfast. Stretched his legs with a
mid-morning walk around what passed for 'town', and
then it was time to seek out Artemisia, time to watch
her sketch, time to sit quietly and contemplate her over
the pages of his journal, his own pencil scribbling or
drawing away in efforts he'd not yet had the courage
to go back and assess.

'You will never be nothing but a dauber.'

Eight words that had changed the trajectory of his
life, assuming that heirs ever had choices about their
trajectories. At the time, though, he'd thought he had
a choice. Those words had meant everything, defined
everything. It was the only time he'd ever felt limited.

Artemisia looked up from her pad, her gaze con-
templative. They were back at the beach, watching for
winter birds. He took advantage of the moment to initi-
ate conversation. She spoke little when she worked and

he found her words to be like golden grains, treasured for their scarcity. 'When will you paint?' As much as he was enjoying the outings this week, it had occurred to him that perhaps these outings were another of her strategies to keep him out of her studio, but she couldn't sketch for ever.

Her sharp grey eyes dropped to the journal in his hand. 'There's a reason I don't press you about your book. An artist's work is very private. The studio, be it a journal or an actual space, has an intimacy matched only by the bedroom.'

His blood began to rouse at the potent image drawn by her words. Had she done it on purpose? It was the most telling statement she'd made all week, even more revealing than her story of the farmhouse. It had occurred to him, of course, that she was no stranger to passion in all of its guises. She was not an eighteen-year-old debutante, but a woman in her late twenties, the daughter of an artist who ran an eclectic household without a motherly figure at the helm.

Her own temperament and views suggested that she held society's foibles in contempt. There was plenty of ground on which to speculate and speculate he had. It was, admittedly, one of the more decadent things his mind had wondered about during this week of silent study. What type of man would such a woman take as a lover? How often? He didn't want to know the answers. He'd have to report them to the Academy if he had knowledge of them. The Academy would pillory her for passions indulged.

'You want to watch me paint, Mr Rutherford.' It was a quiet accusation. She might as well have said, 'You want to see me naked.' To her it was likely the same thing. He recalled her earlier reference to the studio as a bedchamber, an intimate space.

'Well?' He rose to the argument. 'You've seen me naked in my bath.' Surely, this confident woman was not intimidated by him watching her paint. Her talent was already proven, even if it was not accepted by the Academy at the higher levels.

'You had nothing to lose, it's hardly the same.'

She really believed that. He gave a short chuckle. 'My dignity? My pride? Those are no small things.

'What does it cost you if I watch you paint? You've already said you think it hardly matters what you come back with in March. Perhaps you, too, have nothing to lose.'

She did *not* believe that. She put her pencil away and closed her sketch pad, signalling the end of the session. 'I have everything to lose and you hold all the power. Your words *will* matter, far more than mine. A man's testimony always carries more weight than a woman's.' Her stare was piercing, forcing unspoken truths to surface. They both knew it was true. How many times was a woman believed in a court of law over a man? How many maids didn't dare lay a complaint against the molesting lord of the manor in fear of their jobs? Never and none. His thoughts stalled on the last. It wasn't just men, then, that she referenced in her shrewd comment, but men with status, a subtle reference to the power of his title and perhaps to something more.

'If there is any sway to be had,' Artemisia said with deadly quiet, 'it rests with you, Mr Rutherford.' There it was again: the tellingly formal *Mr Rutherford*. Proof that, for her, nothing had changed in their week. There was no intimacy in her address and something in him rebelled against it. He didn't want to believe they were the same people they'd been five days ago. Perhaps because he wasn't the same. Something in him was beginning to wake up, to hunger for things he'd not allowed himself in years. He wanted to paint again, wanted to defy the conventions that said he shouldn't, that such dabbling was beneath him.

Rebellion whispered softly at his ear, *If you shook off those shackles, what else might you shake off?* An intriguing thought. Perhaps that was the real power of Artemisia's influence and he wanted more of it, wanted to see where it led.

'Darius, please. We do not need to be enemies, Artemisia.' He tried out her name. Would she correct him?

'At least not in Seasalter?' There was no correction, but she was wary of the offer, perhaps already concluding he should not have made it. 'What about London? I can't imagine this fragile truce has a chance of lasting once we return to town.' Fragile on so many levels, not just the Academy. He was heir to the Earl of Bourne. He could not imagine presenting her to his parents. To be seen with her would raise eyebrows and speculation. He would survive it. Men were expected to have mistresses. She would not, even if the speculations were untrue.

'London is complicated. It need not be that way here,' Darius said simply. He couldn't win the argument and he wouldn't give her lies. He rose and offered her a hand up from the hard-packed sand but she refused it, rising on her own to stand toe to toe with him. Dear heavens, what had he said now to irritate her?

'Is that a proposition? If so, I won't sleep with you for a decent review.' She tossed her plait over her shoulder. 'I am not for sale.'

Darius had not thought she was. Her accusation inflamed him. 'It was nothing more than an offer of friendship for the duration.' Darius's own temper began to slip its leash. This was the damnedest waltz, one step forward, two steps back. Just when he thought they were making progress, she put up another wall, each one higher than the last.

'Am I really such a monster?' He could see the dark flecks in her grey eyes, could almost see the thoughts that flitted behind them, could almost catch them. Almost. Nothing about her was easily caught.

'You are worse. You are the monster's tool.'

He did not like the sound of that and it broke the last of his restraint. He'd taken enough of her insinuations this week, but he would not stand for slander of his personal honour. 'Be careful with your words, Artemisia. I am my own man and I do not need to bribe women into my bed,' he growled the caution. 'You know nothing about me.'

'I know you are here, sent by men who would destroy me. That seems sufficient enough to make the case.' Artemisia knew nothing of caution. His warning had not been heeded.

His dam of restraint broke. 'I am here because those men would indeed destroy you, *if* given the chance. *I* came so they might not have that chance.' He was suffering six long weeks in Seasalter for that decision. He need not suffer her accusations as well.

She rolled her eyes. 'So now you're my saviour? Every woman needs a protector, is that it? You want to be my knight in shining armour? I assure you, I am no damsel in distress.' She made to turn from him. 'I can handle myself.'

'By shouting "penis" to a room full of men?' No one turned their back on him and it was time someone took this brash young woman in tow with some hard truths. Darius reached out a hand and gripped her wrist, unprepared for the electric frisson of awareness that jolted up his arm at this first contact, skin-to-skin, a reminder that there were more feelings at play here than anger and pride. 'Listen to me, Artemisia, I was in that room after you left. I heard what they said and it's all you can guess and more. In March, maybe you get accepted, maybe you don't. If you're accepted, it should be on your own merits, not because of who your father is. If not, it shouldn't be because they're holding you to an unfair standard that they would not hold themselves to.

'You are making it too easy on them. There were plenty of men in that room willing to come and make sure you were found unsuitable, but they asked me, because an art critic is supposed to be objective. I am willing to be your fighting chance, but you have to let me in, you have to stop thinking of me as the enemy.' The ardour of his argument surprised him.

He almost had her. Something had got her attention. He could see her thinking through his words, weighing them against the truths she knew. He pressed his case.

'I can offer you objectivity, a fair hearing. Perhaps I am the only one who can or will.'

'You want me to believe you're on my side?'

'I am not on anyone's side. I'm objective, remember.'

'Nice try.' She shook her head. 'That's not possible. Everyone's on a side and, in the end, you will be, too.'

'Not me,' he assured her, loosening his grip on her wrist. He was close. He had to make her see *he* was in her best interest. She would not get a better chance. When had he started to care so much what happened to one rebellious artist? 'You're not the only one who can't be bought.' She was softening. He couldn't lose her now; the reasons were myriad and confusing if he focused on them for too long. Not all of them were about access to her art. Some of them, frankly, were about access to her. He'd not been intrigued by a woman this intensely for a long while. It was an unseemly attraction and a dangerous one. Developing an attachment to her would jeopardise the objectivity he promised her. If that attachment were discovered, it could be used against him if he rendered a favourable opinion of her art.

He ought to walk away, he ought not to stoke the sparks that leapt between them. But he didn't want her to go, not back to the farmhouse where she'd be alone with her thoughts, where she'd convince herself that he was the enemy once again. Alongside that, though, was another reason that had emerged steadily over a week of watching her, of noting her habits and words. He *wanted* to talk to her, talk without quarrelling, without debating. What more might he discover about her? She was full of fascinating ideas and perspectives. Where did they come from? What fuelled Artemisia Stansfield?

How did he make her stay? He thought fast. 'Come have dinner with me at the Crown. Let me show you who I am. I've earned your tolerance, now let me earn your trust. I am not the monster you think and the wine will be a more than adequate compensation if I'm wrong.' He offered a wry smile.

She cocked her head and made him wait for an answer. He jotted another mental note. Everything was done on her terms, even answering invitations she didn't issue. 'All right, *Darius*,' she said at last. 'One dinner and you'd better be right about the wine.'

Chapter Seven

He wanted to be her fighting chance. The words played through her mind as they sat for dinner at the Crown, not in the crowded main room as she'd anticipated, but in a private parlour.

'Here we might talk,' he offered, his voice low at her ear as he held her chair inside the cosy room. A fire crackled in the grate, the heavy oak door shutting out the din of the taproom, emphasising their privacy. 'It would be too noisy out there. I'd have to ask you to repeat every other word. Wine?' He moved to the oak sideboard where a bottle waited and poured two glasses.

His manners were smooth, effortless extensions of himself. Even in sand-speckled clothes, there was no mistaking him for other than what he was: a peer's son, a man raised to navigate society with the subtle inflection of a single word, a single look designed to create a desired impression. Today, the impression had been one of possibility. On the beach, he'd almost made it seem as though she had a choice, that she could make the Academy accept her, that she had a choice in allow-

ing him into her studio, or that she had a choice about
dinner tonight. Technically, she supposed she did, but
refusal was costly and served no purpose except to be
the tool of her own defeat.

Rutherford handed her a glass of deep ruby wine
and took his own seat across from her at the small,
square table. It was oak like the sideboard and lacked
a tablecloth. Instead of white linen, it sported a generation of scars and burns. It was not an elegant table,
but Rutherford sat at it as if it were polished mahogany,
transforming the humble furniture with his own innate refinement. 'Cheers.' Rutherford clinked his glass
against hers and they drank.

The wine went down as smoothly as his manners.
She had to wonder, was he navigating her as he would
a ballroom? Easily? Effortlessly? No matter how sin-
cere the offer of friendship sounded there was no denying it was convenient for him. It gained him all he
wanted. Why was he so adamant that she listen to him?
Was it truly for her own good as he argued, or for his?
They both knew he couldn't go back to London empty-
handed.

'Well? What do you think?' he asked as she swallowed.

'It *is* good.' Artemisia gave her assessment. 'A
French burgundy. Probably smuggled.' She added the
last offhand and was gratified when Rutherford choked
on his swallow. 'Well?' She cocked an eyebrow at him.
'Where did you think the proprietor of an out-of-the-
way inn of meagre means would get such a fine vin-
tage?' Rutherford no doubt drank smuggled brandy at

his London clubs, but he'd likely not been so close to the supply chain before.

'Touché.' He grinned, taking the ribbing good-naturedly, and took another swallow as the innkeeper's two gangly sons entered with dinner on heavy trays and set out the dishes. The savoury scent of a roast and potatoes filled the room and Artemisia's stomach grumbled, a reminder that she'd forgone the usual late lunch on the beach when they'd quarrelled.

The boys left and Rutherford carved the meat, offering her the first slice and topping off her glass. He was giving new definition to the concept of being wined and dined. When the firelight played across his face, accentuating the firm, straight line of his nose and the strong angle of his jaw, it was hard to remember this was a show for her benefit, an attempt to persuade her that she could trust him. Despite her past experiences with such persuasion, she'd *like* to trust him. She chewed her roast slowly, thoughtfully, as she mulled the idea over.

This week hadn't been unpleasant. He'd been good company, respectful of her need to work in silence. He'd not intruded on her privacy with words or useless small talk. And he was easy on the eyes. There were far less attractive companions one could have. Tonight, he was giving her a taste of what friendship would be like with him: quiet evenings, good wine, pleasant banter and the same freedom he'd given her all week to speak her mind, to be herself. It was a dangerous mixture, a tempting cup to drink from, and she was not unwilling to stir that cup a bit, but with a caution born of experience that said men betrayed. But before that, how far would he go to win her trust? How much of himself was he willing to reveal in order for her to do the same?

'So, *Darius*...' the taste of his name was still new on her tongue '...why does an earl's son spend his time as an art critic?'

He laughed and set down his fork. 'Why not? I have the time to spend precisely because I *am* an earl's son. What else shall I devote my enormous amount of discretionary time to? Mistresses, gambling, dangerous carriage races? I have time on my hands. Why not do something meaningful with it?'

'But why art specifically?' Artemisia pressed, unwilling to be lured away from her question by debate on the virtues and vices of a gentleman.

'The Bourne family has always been supporters of art. Throughout the generations the Earls have collected art, paintings particularly. I grew up surrounded by the grand galleries at my father's various houses.' The answer was too polished, too quickly given. He'd been asked that before. He'd been ready for her.

Artemisia was familiar with the Bourne catalogues. They possessed one of the finest private collections of paintings done by the English school in the country. It was a patriotic point of pride with the current Earl. 'A critic is not the same as a collector, though. You could have just continued the work of collecting, supporting artists through patronage.'

Darius furrowed his brow and fixed her with his dark eyes. 'There's not such a great difference between a critic and a collector—both are trendsetters in their own ways, both lend value to an artist's work.' He'd been ready for that, too. She wasn't doing a very good job of getting under his skin. He was too well-armoured.

'Or not.' She was quick to respond. 'When a critic suggests someone's work is inferior you ruin their career. Do you ever consider that when making your opinion public? A critic's opinion is far more widespread than an individual's single like or dislike. Others are inclined to adopt a critic's stance as their own. A critic's words spread like a contagion.'

'Contagion? First you make me a monster, now you make me a disease.' Darius chuckled and then sobered. 'If I am anything, I hope I am honest, even when it hurts, even when it's hard. Catering to an artist's ego helps no one in the long run. I would not want to give anyone false hope about their talents.'

'That's a very cold nobility.' Artemisia sipped her wine. 'An artist puts their heart and soul into a work, regardless of its quality. To have that work brutally, objectively destroyed with words is like ripping out that heart.'

'Is that what I did to you with my remarks about your new collection?' he parried. 'I doubt it. Any artist who seeks a career needs a thick skin. It's part of being an artist, part of being in the public eye.' He rose and moved to the sideboard once more where a mince pie waited for dessert. 'We are not so different in our backgrounds, I think. I grew up surrounded by art. You did as well. It is no surprise we ended up where we are today. What is it like growing up with a famous father?' He served her a slice of pie and resumed his seat.

'Probably the same as it is growing up an heir to an earldom. Pressure to be successful, pressure to put forward a certain image.' She took a bite of pie and gave him a cool smile to let him know she was on to him, to his smooth manoeuvring of the conversation away from himself and over to her. 'I thought tonight was about getting to know you?'

'And you have.' His smile spread slowly across his face, warming something deep at her core, further proof just how dangerous Darius Rutherford could be. 'You've been watching my every move since we arrived. Getting to know someone is about more than words.' He leaned across the table, capturing her gaze with his, his dark eyes steady and intense, his voice low and intimate. She concluded he had not exaggerated. He probably didn't need to bribe women into his bed, not when he possessed a look like that, a look that made one the centre of his attentions and shrank the room to only the space between them. Even forearmed, Artemisia's own breath caught.

He reached for her hands, gripping them in his. 'I see you've decided you *can* trust me in your studio. Now, you just have to decide to let me in and accept my opinions whatever they might be.'

There it was again, this illusion that she had a choice. She fought the urge to look away. She'd never been read quite so thoroughly before, or so correctly. 'We cannot be friends.' It would be a slippery slope to disaster. If friendship with him was this intoxicating, how much more so would other intimacies be? It was not hard to imagine those intimacies here in the firelit privacy of the dining parlour with his eyes on her, his hands wrapped about hers, strong, capable and long fingered, the firelight glinting off the sapphire ring on his right.

These were a lover's hands, sure and confident. Despite the wine, her throat was suddenly dry. She should not have gone down that particular rabbit hole. She did not want to think of him as a lover, her lover, those hands on her skin, that mouth at her ear whispering impossible nonsense.

'Why can't we be friends? Because we might disagree? Friends are allowed to disagree. It would be boring, otherwise.' He sat back in his chair, arms crossed over a chest that she knew was well defined beneath his coats and shirt. 'Or is it something more? Is it that this friendship has not been offered on your terms? Is that what makes you uncomfortable? No one is permitted to take you by surprise? Artemisia Stansfield must always define the rules of engagement?' That hit too close to home. She'd not defined the rules with Hunter McCullough and she'd paid for that.

'Perhaps I don't believe there *are* any more surprises.' Although he'd surprised her plenty tonight. He saw too much of her. She didn't dare risk him seeing any more. That was the problem in getting others to expose themselves—one often had to expose oneself in return. She wasn't comfortable with that. Artemisia stood up and gathered the plates. That he could see through her made him even more dangerous. 'A woman needs her protections, Darius. She can't just let anyone in.' Not into her bed, her studio, her thoughts, her soul. There was a reason her circle of friends was small. She'd learned that through difficult choices, but, once learned, she was not keen on making those mistakes again with a man who was handsome and well mannered.

She could not let herself forget for a moment that he was a critic, he was a man and he'd been sent by those who wanted her to fail, three very potent strikes against him. Yet she'd nearly forgotten those tonight for a short while. Even now, remembering his sins, she was still tempted to overlook them, all for that smile, those eyes, those hands, those words of assurance that what happened in Seasalter, would stay in Seasalter, but too many men did not keep their word.

She set the dishes down on the sideboard. She needed to get out of here while some semblance of good judgement remained to her. 'Thank you for supper, it was enlightening. I must go. I don't want Addy to worry.' In her haste, she was clumsy, her senses focused inward. She'd not heard him leave the table. She turned from the sideboard straight into the hardness of his chest.

'Stay, just a while longer.' His hands were at her waist, steadying her, his eyes hot on hers, dark mirrors reflecting his intentions, the only warning she had before his mouth claimed hers.

His kiss was warm, his mouth firm, confident. He knew what he was about with a caress of mouths, a slow, lingering exploration of lips, of tongues. He tasted like dinner's wine, dry tannins mixed with buttery oak, complex and intriguing, hinting at depths that would please a more sophisticated palate should one wish to explore. And she did wish it, another reminder that she was not as in charge of her responses around him as she'd like to be. The lapse was easily reasoned away, a moment's exploration would hurt no one. She let her own tongue trail over his lips, trace the lines of his teeth. This was kissing at its slow and exhilarating best, the kind of kissing that could easily segue into other exhilarating activities. *Those* she could not afford, not with him, not now.

She gave his lip a final nip, catching it between her teeth as she pulled away, taking refuge in a reprimand. 'Why did you do that?'

His eyes glistened, two black diamonds shining with secrets unrevealed, secrets close enough to the surface to tempt. What did the perfect Darius Rutherford have to hide? 'To prove there are still a few surprises left.' For whom? she wondered. For herself? Or for him? More importantly, why did it matter? Nothing good could come of exploring what those surprises might reveal and they both knew it, which made the temptation all the harder to resist. That kiss had become a veritable tree of knowledge in the garden of their desires, the root of good and evil.

Chapter Eight

Darius Rutherford was positively inscrutable. One would think, after a kiss, there would be some kind of unveiling, the lowering of one's guard. If anything, Darius's guard was more alert. His secrets, which had once tantalised her with near capture, lying on the surface of him, now evaded her entirely. For all the openness he seemed to evince, that same openness only served to shield him more completely. Perhaps it was his version of hiding in plain sight. She knew no more about him now than she had at the start. It hardly seemed fair when she'd let him into her studio to watch her paint.

Artemisia picked up a penknife and sharpened her sketching pencil. She hazarded a look over the top of her easel at Darius, who'd taken up residence on the old sofa across the room and was once again busy with his ever-present journal while it rained outside—a perfectly dreary day to be indoors with her speculations. What *did* he write in there? Her curiosity was starting to get the better of her. She didn't doubt he'd told her the truth, that he wrote down thoughts and observations. But what thoughts? What observations? What did Darius Rutherford think, see, feel? Were they observations about *her*? Surely some of them must be.

Seven days ago, you didn't care. Last week he was nothing but a nuisance following you to the beach, her conscience prompted.

Not all week, though. By Wednesday he'd stopped being annoying and had become a somewhat comfortable appendage who had invited her to dinner and kissed her. It mattered little to her *when* he'd become an accepted fixture in her routine. It mattered more as to *why*. What had changed? She'd gone from wanting to know nothing about him to wanting to know everything. What was in that leather journal of his? What secrets lurked behind the guarded gates of those dark eyes? Why did she care? A week ago, she'd have said Darius Rutherford could keep his secrets. This week, she wanted to know them. It would be better not to. Knowing his secrets was akin to naming a stray dog. Both were a step closer to an attachment she didn't need. That didn't seem to stop the wanting of it, though.

She set aside the knife and went back to outlining on the canvas, but even work couldn't quite distract her. That kiss had taken her over temptation's edge, just far enough to want to know more about a man who kissed not like sin but like sincerity. It was the sincerity that was hard to resist. Rakes were easy enough to ignore, she had no interest there. But Darius Rutherford was not a rake. Society defined him by titles: art critic, gentleman, heir to an earldom, a viscount. But he spoke of fairness and objectivity, showing himself to be a man who was not limited by those titles.

She did not know many of such men. Even her father was defined by his title. The 'Sir' in front of Lesley Stansfield's name meant everything to him—at times she thought it meant more than his own daughters. It signified his level of accomplishment, the quality of his expertise, his standing in society. But where Darius was more than the sum of his titles, her father was not. Therein lay the intrigue. What sort of man lived beyond social constraint? These musings were proof she should not have kissed him. It had opened a Pandora's box and all nature of curiosity from the esoteric to the sensual had flown out, not to be put back in.

Artemisia finished the outlining, satisfied with its initial lines. It was one of the oystermen and she had great hopes for it; it was different than birds and wildlife. Now, it was time to do something about that journal. She carefully put her tools away and approached the sofa, slowly, cautiously. They'd been wary of each other this week, careful not to tease, not to stir the pot of temptation knowing what waited there. 'Is that old thing comfortable enough?' She tried for a comfortable conversational tone. They were both adults, neither of them untried by passion and lovers. One kiss should not have them on edge like adolescents.

Darius looked up from the journal. 'Absolutely. Sometimes old sofas are the best sofas, especially on rainy days.' He gave her a smile that roused the butterflies in her stomach. 'Come, sit.' He patted the spot next to him and she did, knowing full well they were playing with fire now, the tacit agreement to keep their physical distance when together had been just as tacitly set aside. Had they learned their lesson?

'Are you done for the day? Did the outlining go well?' He was always so conscientious not to interrupt when she worked.

'Well enough. I'll know for sure once I start to paint.' She settled on the sofa cushion, legs and skirts tucked around her in a casual pose. 'And your writing? How was your journaling this morning?' They knew too much of one another's routine. Such knowledge made a mockery of the distance they'd tried to impose. Distance wasn't only about space, it seemed.

He gave his customary shrug regarding his journal. 'Fine.'

'Fine? Is that all?' she queried, temptation whispering loud now, too loud. 'Perhaps I should be the judge of that.' She made a lightning-quick grab for the open journal in his lap, snapping it up before he could stop her.

'Artemisia,' he warned, 'give that back.'

For the space of a heartbeat she almost did, so firm was his request. 'Fair is fair. You saw my paintings.'

'Your paintings were meant to be public, meant to be seen.' His eyes glinted dangerously. She wondered what he'd do if she dared him to come and get it. Old sofas and rainy days were made for such dares.

'But they were still a secret,' she countered. 'They were not meant to be seen *yet*, like a bride on her wedding day. A piece of your soul for a piece of mine, Darius. You must pay the forfeit,' she teased, glancing down at the pages prepared to see words. She saw drawings instead. She recognised the beach, the godwit, a boat from the oystermen. She stared at them, letting her thoughts settle before she looked up. It made sense now, how he knew when to stay quiet, how he seemed to respect the process. He wasn't merely an art critic. She felt his eyes on her, still and waiting. She looked up.

'I've misjudged you.' Her earlier assumption shamed her. 'I was wrong,' she confessed. 'I was thinking you were one of those critics who'd never held a paintbrush. But you're an artist, too.' She handed the journal back to him. 'Why didn't you say anything?'

'Because it's not relevant. It's not who I am any more.' He rose from the sofa and tucked his book into the pocket of his coat where it hung from a peg.

'Any more?' She picked up on that one word. 'Does that mean at one time you were?' She asked the last quietly, holding her breath in anticipation of the answer. These were the unlooked-for depths she'd dipped her foot in last night.

'Yes.' Darius didn't shy away from the truth now that the subject was broached. 'I enjoyed painting in my youth, but I haven't any notable talent.'

She thought there might be some room for disagreement on that point. 'Those are good. You use perspective well.'

'One needs more than technical expertise.' He was uncomfortable with the subject. He didn't come back to the sofa, but paced the length of the glassed wall. 'Technical expertise can be bought with the best of instructors. It cannot, however, make one an artist.'

No, that was true. One needed some other intangibles for that: passions, experiences, a raw look at life for instance. She had that in spades; a mother dead before she was ten, an infant sister to raise, a father who'd travelled his daughters all over the Continent while he struggled to make a life for them. Those were experiences an earl's heir was unlikely to have, but Artemisia held her tongue. There were more important things to discuss. 'When did you stop?'

'I put away my paints when I went to Oxford.' It was offered tersely, but there was history behind Darius's sparse words. It prompted more questions. Why? What had happened to cause him to give it up?

'Not everyone has to be hung on the line at the Academy to be an artist. If it brings you joy, you should do it.' She couldn't imagine giving up painting. Even if she never sold another painting, she would still paint. She *had* to. It was in her blood.

He gave a rueful smile. 'I'm not you, Artemisia. I have other things that require my attention.'

'Attention and joy are not the same thing,' Artemisia pressed, her curiosity surging with the rain against the window. What brought him joy?

'No, they are not.' It wasn't an answer. He wasn't ready to share.

'Thank you for letting me see them,' Artemisia offered. Drawings, writings—those were personal things not shared lightly.

He chuckled. 'I didn't think there was any "letting" about it.'

She shrugged and gave him a teasing smile. 'I suppose you could have taken the journal back by force if you'd been so inclined.'

'Maybe I should have,' He was teasing now, too, the stiffness of unplanned revelations and the reminder of a kiss fading just when they needed the reminder the most. This way lay danger, a delicious, delectable danger.

'But then I would never have known you painted. You never would have told me, otherwise.' Something potent was simmering between them again, hot and searing and undeniable. The question was whether or not it was resistible or inevitable. She was aware of everything in those moments: the persistent drum of rain on the glass, each breath she took, the heat of his gaze.

If they acted now, they wouldn't be able to excuse it as the product of wine and firelight. This would be an admittance of attraction. She ought to fight it, it was too dangerous to indulge, but something in his eyes was irresistible.

There was a suggestion of genuine human need in the hoarseness of his voice when he spoke. 'Artemisia, do you ever get tired of being alone?'

His raw need threatened to undo her. She wanted to reach for him, to wrap him in her arms. Instead, she whispered, 'Yes.' Yes to all of it: to secrets she had to hide, to wants and needs denied, to dreams deferred, to always being her father's perfect girl—the heir to his greatness—to disappointments she bore behind a brash façade that said she didn't care a fig for the world's rejections even when those rejections cut her to the quick and stripped another piece from her soul until alone was all she could be.

'Me, too.' His gaze was melting her. He reached for her because she hadn't reached for him. She froze.

'Darius, we cannot risk it again.' What she really meant was that she couldn't risk it. The power balance between them would shift dramatically. That shift would not work in her favour and when he betrayed her, as he surely would, this decision would ruin her, yet it beckoned.

He wanted to be her champion, to give her the objectivity her art needed. He wasn't Hunter McCullough, who felt he was trading up with her. Darius Rutherford was a viscount. She was beneath him. Perhaps that was reason enough if not to trust him, then to indulge. There it was, that ridiculous logic that seemed to resurrect itself when Darius was around, proof that she wasn't as in control as she'd like to be when it came to him.

'Please, Artemisia, don't make me beg, don't deny yourself, don't deny us.' Darius's words were a plaintive growl. 'Just for a moment out of time, I don't want to be alone and neither do you.' He read her mind, her body so completely, and she knew when a battle was lost.

She gave herself up to his mouth, to the press of his body on hers. She lost herself in the moan that worked its way up his throat as he, too, gave over to the moment. Her hips dragged against his, her hands in the glossy wave of his hair and at his back, digging into the fabric of his clothing, feeling the muscle and flex of him, the need for release riding them both hard.

His mouth moved to her neck, to the vee of skin exposed by her blouse. His hand, that glorious, elegant hand that had taken up so much of her speculation last night, kneaded a breast, a thumb running over a nipple beneath the linen until it puckered and strained for more. Heat pooled low at her core, a sigh escaping her. As if drawn by that heat, his mouth moved to kiss her belly through her clothes, his body slid down the length of her until he straddled her thighs, his hands running up her legs, pushing back skirts, her skin bared at last. It was something akin to relief to feel his hands warm on her flesh, confident and caressing as he spread her, exposed her most deliciously.

Her core was weeping when his mouth took her. Had she ever needed anything as much as she needed this right now? She gave herself over to his tongue, each stroke, each lick. Each decadent flick of its tip over the tight, hidden nub of her sent her closer to pleasure's paroxysm. But not quite. He was very careful to make sure she waited, that she not claim that pleasure too soon. Neither did she intend to wait too long. She raised her hips against him, urging him on, the need for completion racing through her, raw and wild and untamed, and he answered, his own back heaving in the borrowed pleasure of her pleasure, until at last she broke in a wave of sighs, each one deeper, more shuddering than the last as they peaked, and then softening as they ebbed, taking pleasure's sharp edge with them, a little bit at a time, like the tide going out.

It was good while it lasted. Artemisia sighed against Darius's shoulder. They laid length to length on the sofa, holding on to the pleasure and all it brought as long as they could. There was freedom in the pleasure, freedom to float, to forget, freedom to relinquish burdens and fears. What did Darius relinquish? What did he forget? Had he forgotten, like her, that for all his arguments to the contrary, they were on opposite sides? When would he remember?

His arm moved around her, keeping her tight against him. She shut her eyes, letting herself imagine that this moment out of time could stretch on. That this hand-

some, strong, insightful man was her lover in truth—
would he be her shield if she asked? What would it be
like to have such an ally?

It was a fairy tale, of course. She'd never asked a man
for such protection and none had ever offered. Even if
they had, she wouldn't have believed them. Everyone
wanted something. No one did anything without cause.
For the first time since she was eighteen and still dewy-
eyed about the world, she wished it could be different,
that men could be trusted, that women could be treated
as their equals. No, not that all men could be trusted.
Just one man would suffice. *Her* man. Whoever he was,
if *he* was trustworthy, that would be enough.

'Have you reordered the world to your satisfaction?' Darius's voice was a drowsy drawl at her ear.
He smelled of clean linen and bergamot, all citrus and
spice.

'Not quite.' She breathed deeply. 'You remind me
of the south of Italy.'

His chuckle rumbled deep in his chest, beneath her
ear. 'I'm sure the weather is better. Have you been?' His
hand ran up and down her arm, an idle caress.

'Yes. My father took us when I was ten, right after
my mother died. We rented a villa outside Naples and
played on the beach every day while he painted.' And
drank and hunted for oblivion, but she left the last part
off. She understood now that he'd been grieving. He'd
lost his wife, his newborn son, and inherited sole care
of two daughters just as he was on the cusp of his fame.

'It must have been a difficult time,' Darius em-
pathised.

'Yes, but good came out of it. My father started to

take a real interest in me. He began cultivating my talents. He taught me to paint that summer.' It had been a very formative summer in other ways. A ten-year-old was a smart, impressionable creature. 'I think that was the summer I grew up.' Although she hadn't known it at the time, it had been the first step towards self-sufficiency and a step away from trusting others. Even those you loved had the power to fail you; her mother had died and her father had seen to his own grief first.

It had been up to her to see to Addy, who'd been not much more than a toddler, and it had been up to her to carry the torch of her father's artistic legacy. 'I had to be perfect. I had to be all things to all the people I cared about in my little world.' She sighed softly against him, marvelling that he'd done it again. 'How do you do that, Darius? How do you make me tell you things I don't tell another soul?' She never talked about Italy, or her mother, or that her father was only the first man to fail her.

'Because you like me, Artemisia,' he murmured. 'You just don't want to admit it.'

No, she didn't want to admit it. If she did, she'd soon be admitting other things from which no good could come. Now it was his turn to reciprocate in kind. He'd had his pound of flesh and she'd have hers. She levered up on one elbow. 'Now, will you tell me something, Darius, something from your childhood?'

Chapter Nine

Darius shifted uncomfortably. She was making him pay for his curiosity earlier and quite possibly this was the price for his pleasure as well. The balance of power was ever foremost on Artemisia's mind. It spoke volumes of what her experiences growing up had extracted from her. Artemisia must always have a level playing pitch and in one fell swoop of a question, she achieved that levelling, although that was likely by chance. She couldn't possibly guess how much the question discomfited him.

'Does an heir ever truly have a childhood?' He offered a question in answer to her own. 'I think I was twelve when I realised, though, what it truly meant to be the Earl,' Darius said after a pause, selecting his story carefully. 'There'd been fever in the village that winter and several had died. My father took me to the funerals. He didn't miss a single one. Each death grieved him. Another tenant lost, another friend gone. I watched him comfort the families. I watched him tell the widows who had no man to work the fields not to worry about their tithe this year. I watched him take a moment with the children and leave baskets my mother had packed.'

'Your father sounds like a good man.' Was she equating his father with hers? A man who had seen to his own grief over caring for his daughters with a man who shared his grief with his community and his support? Was she concluding his father was a saint? It was all part of the perfect surface the house of Bourne curated so well and it was a myth. Something in him stirred, compelled to disabuse her.

'My father tries to be a good man. He does not always succeed. Without my father, the village would have failed. I learned two lessons that day. First, a lesson in compassion, but secondly, and perhaps more importantly, I saw how deep my responsibility ran for others. The people of Bourne must always be my first priority, just as they have been for my father.' A priority that came before his son, his wife. He served Bourne and they must, too.

'Then we are indeed true opposites.' Artemisia said quietly. 'While I was learning self-sufficiency, you learned the import of caring for others. I wonder who learned the better lesson?'

'The word "better" assumes many things, Artemisia.' He wasn't convinced either lesson was essentially 'good'. 'Both come with prices.' Darius gave a long exhalation. Serving Bourne meant subjugating oneself, one's preferences, one's passions. 'But those are not thoughts for today. Today, we are just Artemisia and Darius. A moment out of time, remember?'

'And tomorrow? Who shall we be then?' In looking ahead, Darius sensed, she was already retreating, already playing with the idea of regretting their choice today. Reality was encroaching on her pleasure and he wanted her back. He wanted the Artemisia who let passion purl up the length of her throat, who arched into that passion with all she was.

She stretched and sat up, taking the last of the interlude with her. She combed her fingers through the tangle her hair had become. She did not look at him as she did so, keeping her back to him. Darius had the distinct impression she might be combing through a tangle of another sort with her long fingers, as if she could comb away what had happened this afternoon. 'This must truly be a moment out of time. I will hold you to that, Darius. This cannot be repeated.'

Darius sat up beside her, unsurprised by her announcement. Artemisia was fortifying her citadel. He would allow it because he understood how much she needed to do it. She would not feel safe with him otherwise. He swung his legs over the side of the sofa and held out his hand, unwilling to relinquish the private peace of the afternoon all at once. There were other ways to be intimate beyond the physical.

'Will you show me the progress you've made with the paintings? There's nothing I'd like better than to see your work through your eyes.' He offered her a warm smile. 'It would be the perfect ending to a perfect day.' It would be dark soon and he would go. But not yet. As long as there was art to discuss, they could be alone together for a little while longer.

She took his hand and led him to the far side of the room where her paintings awaited. She walked him through the narrative of each. She'd chosen a stark palette and yet there was a warmth in those greys and browns that depicted the marsh in winter. That warmth took him back to the first day he'd found her on the beach and the seclusion of their spot by the rocks where one could forget it was January. Her paintings were stark, but they were not cold, not lifeless. 'The marsh is a refuge, you've made it a place of safety,' Darius mused. Her skill confirmed that painting was more than putting colours to canvas. It was skill in manipulating a brush stroke, intelligence in thinking of the subtle messages being conveyed, making the most of every line.

'The marsh *is* a refuge. Kent is temperate. Birds flock here for the winter.'

It was more than that, although he declined to say so. She'd also made it an allegory. She'd flocked here, this was her sanctuary, the place where she could be safe from winter's winds. He paused at a painting depicting an avocet and godwit side by side. This was a place where all were welcome despite their differences, unlike London where the rule was, uniformity, conformity and adherence, like with like. 'This is exquisitely done,' he complimented. 'Your father would be proud.'

She dismissed the remark. 'Proud? To date, I've failed him. I'm his great legacy and I cannot enter the great ranks of the Academy.' That was telling. Artemisia Stansfield wasn't as self-sufficient in terms of detachment as she pretended. It did matter to her what certain others thought. He'd heard it in her tone earlier when she'd talked of Italy, of raising her little sister while her father mourned. She was acutely aware that Addy relied on her, that in his own, perhaps selfish way, her father relied on her as well.

He didn't think they were as different as she thought. People depended on them both. They asked themselves to be all things to those people counting on them. He rather thought her father asked too much of her and gave too little in return. That had hurt her, shaped her early. Men had betrayed her, starting with the one man who should have been her rock.

It occurred to Darius as he stared at the last painting that it wasn't a singular man who could be blamed for her inherent distrust of men, her fire against them, but a covey of them who'd systematically ruined her faith until she was left with faith in no one but herself. Her earlier references to free will, intimacy and access in all ways: to her body, to the world of men, teased at secrets yet unspoken. What shape had that ruination taken?

Whatever shape, it had not broken her, had not ruined her, as it would have other women. It made her stronger, too strong perhaps so that now she thought to wage an impossible war. An idea began to light within him, a warm, glowing coal of insistence—a singular man hadn't ruined her, but perhaps, a singular man could save her, could repair her faith. He wanted to be that man.

Even as the thought came alive, he knew it to be as impossible as her war against the Academy. To restore her faith, he'd have to reorder the world he knew, turn it on its head and his own assumptions along with it. His father would never forgive him. He would say the house of Bourne was not worth one woman's life.

'Penny for your thoughts,' Artemisia's throaty tones interrupted.

Darius looked away from the painting. 'I'm thinking

it's getting dark and I must go.' He lifted her hand to his lips. 'Until tomorrow.' She did not gainsay him, but something moved in her eyes that made him wonder if he'd put too much stock in the assumption, or perhaps it was only that he was dangerously close to overstaying his welcome.

'Mr Rutherford stayed a long time today,' Addy observed over ham and potatoes that evening. It was just the two of them, Mrs Harris and Darius having both left. Darius had offered to walk the housekeeper home, cementing himself in her good graces. 'I thought he might stay for dinner.' Addy offered the last as a quiet accusation of how long he'd been at the farmhouse, apparently too long in her sister's opinion.

'We had a lot to discuss. I've started outlining on the canvases for the last set of paintings.' Thank goodness he hadn't stayed for dinner. She wasn't sure she would have been capable of keeping a guilty look off her face. It was hard enough now to offer plausible explanations for Darius's prolonged presence today.

'I can't imagine what you have to discuss. He's here nearly every day. Pass the potatoes, please.' Addy served herself another helping before she launched her next salvo. 'He sees more of you than I do and you don't even like him.' Artemisia was aware of her sister's hazel stare. 'That's still true, right? That you don't like him?'

Artemisia cut her ham into tiny cubes. She wouldn't lie to her sister, but she knew Addy would disapprove of this afternoon's interlude. 'It's a little more complicated than that. He should not be defined by his task. He's in a difficult position.'

'*You're* in a difficult position,' Addy pointed out. 'More so than him. He's supposed to report back to the Academy about you, but who reports about him? Who holds him accountable for his words? He can go back and say anything he likes.'

'All the more reason to play nicely with Darius, don't you think?' Artemisia argued. 'I can't imagine what rudeness with him might gain us.'

'Darius? Is that what you call him now? How nice are you playing with him, Arta?' Addy set her fork aside, evincing genuine concern. 'Have you forgotten that he came in here on a lie and wormed his way into your studio?'

'No, of course not, but that's not the whole of him.' It was easy to forget, though, when he told her stories of his childhood, when he talked of growing up or when he'd allowed her a glimpse in his journal. There'd been a vulnerability to him then, a humanness that made one forget he was an art critic, that he could influence her future with a word.

'I think you do forget. He's very handsome and he does seem taken with you. It would be easy to fall for him. Perhaps that's why I am worried, Arta. I don't want to see you hurt again.'

'That was a long time ago. No one has hurt me since. I'm quite capable when it comes to managing men,' she reminded Addy with a reassuring smile. She'd not been managing Darius today, though. Today hadn't been about manipulating or negotiating for relational power. It could be though, she supposed, seeing the afternoon in another light. Would he keep his word that whatever they were to each other, whatever they did together, would stay here? What if he told the Academy about what they'd done on the sofa today? It would paint her as a woman of loose morals. She could make it uncomfortable for him if he did, but in the end, she would be the one who lost. She liked to think that was all unnecessary speculation. He seemed to be a man of his word. She was counting on that. But should she be?

'Perhaps I should be the one worrying about you?' Artemisia teased, wanting to move the conversation away from her own situation. 'I hear Bennett Galbraith is quite taken with you.' She nodded to the vase at the end of the table. 'Are these from him? One wonders where someone finds flowers in Seasalter in January.' Addy blushed, but Artemisia could see the notion of Galbraith's attentions pleased her. 'What do we know of Mr Galbraith?'

It was a successful diversion and they spent the rest of dinner probing the depths of Addy's suitor, of which Artemisia didn't think there was much. Bennett Galbraith seemed an insincere dandy, but perhaps it was too soon to tell, or to worry. They would be in Seasalter until the end of February and when they left, Bennett Galbraith would cease to matter. Darius Rutherford, however, would continue to matter. He would follow her to London. In hindsight, she knew she'd behaved imprudently today. She *was* allowing Darius to get too close. She said goodnight to Addy and went into the sitting room. She would send a note to Darius, asking him not to come tomorrow, to give her a little distance.

She drew out a sheet of paper, a large part of her already missing him tomorrow. Perhaps she was more vulnerable than she realised. She had been alone a long time, *careful* for a long time in her determination not to repeat the debacle with Hunter McCullough.

She'd been eighteen, impressionable and arrogant, thinking she was worldly enough to understand men. Hunter had been twenty-six, a good-looking, sweet-talking Irish painter, her father's latest protégé at the time. She'd fallen for every line, every look, never guessing he wasn't above using her to secure her father's coat-tails for himself. He meant to marry her, but for all the wrong reasons. It wouldn't be the last time she encountered a man who had such designs on her person.

The page before her was still blank. How did she explain all that to Darius? How did she explain why she needed distance? That no matter what he said, she couldn't allow herself to believe him because the risk was too great, to her regret. She took up her pen. She would begin with an apology, she would take responsibility for her actions. He would understand that.

Chapter Ten

It was not a good morning for the mail. Artemisia's note had been on top of his correspondence when Darius had gone down for breakfast. It was not the way he'd wanted to begin the day. Artemisia was retreating, much as he'd suspected. He reread the opening of her note. She felt her self-sufficiency was under attack. Darius saw that much in the first line. It was carefully coded in an apology that was meant to remove any sense of burden from him for what had passed between them in the studio. She didn't want to see him this afternoon or the next. He could come around and view the progress on the paintings while she was out on the third day. He was welcome to send her a note if he had questions about her work. This part was also clear. She meant not to see him again for the duration and that was unacceptable.

He crumpled the letter in his hand. Damn right he had questions. Not about the paintings, but about her sudden burst of misgivings. She was regretting their afternoon lapse. Which only meant one thing: she

doubted him. The trust he thought he'd won was a façade. The realisation was awkward and disappointing,
especially given his own reflections on the afternoon.
He'd felt a connection that was electric and genuine,
not just in their sport, but in their conversation. For
him, there'd been no thought of using those intimacies
against her. It stung doubly that she thought he would.

The afternoon had left him hungry for more. More
conversation and, yes, more pleasure. Why should they
not indulge? They were both adults with no fairy-tale
expectations. Surely, that was enough to ensure the
balance of power between them remained even? There
were only four weeks left to them before they returned
to London. Why not enjoy this newfound and short-
lived passion between them? Last night, he'd been hard-
pressed to imagine anything else; four glorious weeks
with Artemisia, a woman who embraced her passions
as fully as she embraced her opinions and challenged
his own.

What an about-face his thoughts had done from a
month ago when he'd sat at the assembly meeting, finding Artemisia outspoken and odd, to translating that
unconventionality into the source of his intrigue with
her. Those very same attributes drew him and ulti-
mately it was those attributes that were reshaping how
he viewed not just her, but her art, and other women.

Darius poured himself another cup of coffee and
took a long swallow, as sobering as the realisation itself. *Was* it possible she was right? That women were
deliberately kept in their place not for their own good,
as Darius had been raised to believe, but for *his* own
good, the good of collective man? For a man who prided

himself on keeping a code of honesty, that supposition seemed decidedly dishonest.

He thought of his mother, who had given up her flute to marry his father. Had she been pushed to it by her parents? Had the choice been hers? He'd always assumed it had been. That was how it had been presented to him through the years. Perhaps it hadn't been any more her choice than it had been his choice to give up painting. Why had he not thought of it before? Because she was a woman? A wife to a titled man? That being a mother to an heir was the greatest achievement she should strive for? He knew what Artemisia would make of that. He knew what his father would make of it. The question was, what should *he* make of it? That would require a complex answer.

Darius reached for the next letter in the pile and his hand stilled—this one was from the Academy. He could guess its contents: a polite note to enquire about his progress. Harmless in and of itself. Perhaps less so, considering the thoughts running through his mind at present. They'd not sent him here to have his head turned, or to start a revolution. Is that what was happening? Had his head been turned? Would he be having these same thoughts if he wasn't smitten with her?

Darius wrapped his hands around his mug, letting its warmth focus his thoughts. Had Artemisia done it on purpose? Did she distrust his motives yesterday afternoon because her own were suspect? It certainly put a different cast on things—those invitations to the beach to watch her sketch issued just reluctantly enough to be believable; her penchant for arguing with him, which gave her licence and a stage from which to share her radical thoughts. He gave a self-deprecating chuckle. If so, he'd been played by a master. He'd been so focused on winning her over he'd not been aware of her ideas taking root in his own mind.

Then there'd been yesterday afternoon, the coup de grâce. She'd reeled him in with a collection of intimate moments physically and emotionally. By the time he'd asked to see the art and she'd agreed, he'd thought it had been a sign of mutual trust, a pact between them. He'd spent a heady hour, his arms wrapped about her, breathing in the soft winter-spiced scent of her, as she'd shown him the works in progress, discussing each thoroughly as they went, each one a rebellion in its own right, each one brilliant. He'd given her the perfect stage and a willing audience with whom to make her argument once more: that the Academy was deliberately denying her on grounds of gender.

She'd made the argument so compellingly that he was sitting here with his coffee, poised to write his report, while the question ran through his head: What if she was right? He'd promised the Academy only that he'd be objective. Was that wrong? Perhaps he was panicking too early. Objectivity by definition meant he was required to look at both sides. There was nothing wrong with considering her perspective.

Darius felt a bit better after that. He slit open the letter from the Academy. It was as expected up until the last lines. Those gave him pause.

'In closing, the Academy knows it can rely on you to see our standards upheld. The word of a critic of your stature is beyond value, something one does not give lightly or without due consideration.'

Adoration or extortion? Perhaps Artemisia was getting to him, after all. A week ago, he would have thought nothing of it beyond a bit of flattery. Everyone wanted a good review from Darius Rutherford, some were even happy to get a bad one. Any notice from him was still publicity. He had more exhibition invitations than he had time to attend. Now, though, with Artemisia's theories pounding in his head, he saw the sinister context of the words. Did the Academy mean to blackmail him into compliance?

Darius fingered the note, rereading. They meant to turn their backs on him if he endorsed her. They'd denounce him and discredit his opinions. They would discredit her in the process as well. That wasn't any different than the current plan. Either way, Artemisia lost. But the former would be far messier than what they preferred. They wanted him to do the dirty work for them. If he didn't endorse her work, no one would expect them to override his opinion. They were simply following the suit of an expert with a good opinion. Should he not offer that opinion, he would go down with her. Or at least they would try to take him down. It would be a nasty fight. He might survive it, but not unscathed. It would require hard choices, hard sacrifices.

Darius put his head in his hands. This was supposed to have been an easy task aside from the inconvenience of it. It was not supposed to cause him a moral quandary, to force him to question the order of the world, *his* world. Should he retreat the field, his honour intact in exchange for publicly decrying Artemisia Stansfield? That was merely the personal quandary. It had become so much more than it should have been. It wasn't supposed to cause him to dream old dreams, to pick up a sketch pad or to question the order of things. Men protected women, children, all those who were beneath him, and in return the protected kept their place, like the tenants in his father's village. Everyone understood and accepted their place in the scheme of life. Until now. Until Artemisia.

He was not prepared for what happened when a woman exceeded her place. It would have been no hardship to carry out his task if her work had been poor. But it wasn't. It was different and rebellious, and pointed, but it was good. If a man had produced this work, he might be hailed as a pioneer, taking the English school in a new direction. But a woman? And those who endorsed her? He would be risking his very reputation.

On *her*, a woman who might have manipulated him into this very dilemma. Was she worth it? Had she been coaxing him into taking that risk? He hoped not. He did not like thinking of yesterday's magic, of the sweet taste of her, her soft moans as he put his mouth to her, as part of a play, something designed to unman him.

Perhaps she is counting on that, his conscience whispered in wicked punishment. *Your own ego can't admit it wasn't pleasure for pleasure's sake.*

But he'd seen her face, felt her body's response. Those had not been lies. His heart knew what his mind denied, but how to prove it?

He sifted through the pile of letters, finding Artemisia's note. A smile coming to him. *This* was the proof. She would not have warned him away if it had simply been a manoeuvre. Her reaction had caused her to withdraw, to reconsider the nature of her association with him. Her concerns over that association were clearly implied. She feared he would use any intimacy between them against her. A woman who'd wanted those intimacies, who'd wanted them as tools for directing his responses, would not have pulled away when the fire was hot.

He folded the note and put it away, some of his anxiety easing. This made for an interesting dynamic. Whether Artemisia liked it or not, they were now in this together. Only he had no idea how to resolve it in a way that protected both her and his honour. He knew only that he would not betray her for the sake of his reputation.

His conscience couldn't resist getting in one more jab: *perhaps that was what she'd been hoping for all along.*

His father would be displeased. His admonitions had not gained purchase with his son. Darius pushed a hand through his hair. There was nothing like having one's world upended and then questioning the legitimacy of that reality.

Darius stayed away for three days, but it did not provide him with distance or clarity. He hoped Artemisia was doing better, that the space she'd asked for was giving her peace of mind. Not so for him. For him, there was no space, no separation and too much reflection. She was in his thoughts everywhere he went: the beach, the little harbour while he watched the fishermen repairing their boats, even the tavern wasn't safe from her. There was no privacy in the private parlour for him, only memories of the dinner they'd shared and the kiss that had followed. There was certainly no privacy in his room. Its most noted feature now was the place where she'd doused him with cold water in the bath.

In the time he'd been here, Artemisia had imprinted herself on his space, his mind and his body. She dominated his routine. His days had been built around her. In this unlooked-for interim of absence, his days were shattered. With the spare time on his hands he couldn't stop thinking about her, about the direction of his life, about what he'd given up to get to this point, about what was expected of him back in London. And how it might all come undone in a single decision.

He wandered Seasalter with an uncanny ability to find himself watching the farmhouse at a distance and to linger imagining what was going on inside; Artemisia would be in her studio, in her smock, her hair in a plait, curls straying despite her best efforts, her brow forming its little furrow as she assessed her work. Then, he'd imagine Mrs Harris catching him and coming outside to scold him, undoing his hard work to get back into her good graces.

That usually got his feet in motion and his thoughts refocused on the situation at hand and brought them full circle to the same conclusion he'd arrived at on day one: he couldn't resolve this without her. Any solution he arrived at involved her compliance, more specifically, her cooperation, the two things Artemisia Stansfield was least likely to give. He'd have better luck asking her for the moon. He pushed a hand through his hair, damp from the perpetual winter mist of Seasalter. He *had* to see her, had to confront her and hope she'd be truthful. He was tempted to storm the farmhouse and demand answers. Artemisia would never respond favourably to such a tactic. It would give her reason to withdraw further.

He could not go to her with demands. Neither could he go empty-handed. He needed a peace offering, something to convince her of his integrity. There was one thing that might suffice: an honest opinion. Darius turned from the farmhouse drive and retraced his steps back to the inn. He would write his report as proof of his intentions and hope it would be enough to persuade her. He'd pack a bottle of the red she liked as well. Perhaps wine would persuade her if words would not.

Chapter Eleven

'Come walk with me.' The words brought Artemisia's eyes up from the easel. Darius stood there as if conjured by her very thoughts. Painting had been difficult today. She'd not been able to concentrate without thoughts of him interrupting. Painting the estuary only served to call up memories of their days sitting on the beach, of watching him unaware, the little gesture he made to sweep that imperfect fall of dark hair to the side out of his eyes. She'd heard his voice in her head all day and now that voice and the man it belonged to stood in front of her.

He was dressed in his greatcoat and boots, misty droplets glistening in his hair. He looked elemental and raw, less like London. 'You can't paint much longer. The light is nearly gone for that,' he coaxed, looking entirely too attractive. A three-day interim had not dampened his appeal. Neither had a three-day absence settled her thoughts about him. It had only made her crave his company, his presence. She'd *missed* him. It was the last reaction she would have thought to have.

Artemisia made her decision. 'Yes, help me wash the brushes out.'

Cleaning up didn't take long and they were on their way, the wind fresh in her face after a day indoors. He hadn't even been with her and he'd known what she needed. They walked down the road in silence, neither one saying a thing; perhaps he, like her, was simply letting the other happen to them all over again. She was refreshing her memory of him, of his long stride, of the way he shoved his hands into the pockets of his greatcoat, how the breeze played with his hair.

They reached a vee in the road and veered towards the beach on the estuary. Sand stuck to their wet boots and she smelled the familiar brine of the marsh. 'What brought on this visit?' she asked at last. 'I thought my note was clear.'

'Very clear, but I needed to see you.' There was raw honesty in his voice and a heat in his gaze that prompted her next careful question.

'For what reason?' The rawness in her own voice mirrored his, a tentativeness, unsure of what path his answer might take and how she might respond. 'Have you come for work or pleasure, Darius?' There was only one acceptable answer, only one they could have. He did not choose it.

'Both.' His voice was quiet beneath the wind and it sent a trill of wicked want down her spine. 'I have to talk with you and I need you to be honest with me.' He made a gesture with his hand, drawing her gaze towards the sheltered area where she liked to sketch. A small campsite had been set up, a blanket laid out, a basket at its centre and a firepit at the ready waiting to be lit.

'This sounds serious.' Artemisia slanted him a considering glance, trying to read him, but he was inscrutable as always.

'It is.' He knelt beside the fire, retrieving a flint from his coat pocket and striking a match. He fixed her with his dark stare as she settled on the blanket. 'This is very difficult to ask and, the more I thought about how to ask it, I realised there was simply no good way to put it.'

She smiled encouragingly. 'It's rather refreshing to see you off tilt. Well? Give it your best shot.'

He balanced on the balls of his feet, stoking the fire with a spare stick, gathering his words as he held her gaze. 'Artemisia, have you been seducing me to your side? I need to know. If you have, just say so. You are in an untenable situation with the Academy. I wouldn't blame you, but I do need to know.' The fire crackled between them, sending sparks into the dusk.

She stared back, letting the long silence speak for her while she chose her words. 'I already told you I wouldn't sleep with you for a good review.' But if not for the business of that review hanging between them, she might have been tempted. She wouldn't sleep with him for a review, but for herself, for satisfying the curiosity that burned between them, she might consider it. If only the playing pitch between them wasn't already so uneven.

He knew it, too. She could see dark acknowledgement flicker in his eyes. That kiss at the inn, that afternoon on the couch, all evidence that something existed between them, something they had only partially resisted and even now was tugging them towards some inevitable conclusion. Or was she being played? Was all of this part of a deeper game? The old cynicism reared its head. 'Do you think my words are a lie? That my resistance is a coy strategy?'

'I don't want to think that.' Darius's voice was quiet across the fire. 'I want to think that our rainy afternoon was a moment out of time for both of us where agendas were suspended. I want to think that such moments might happen again.'

Artemisia fought the urge to soften at the words. She wanted that, too. If the three days apart had shown her anything, it was that she desired him, that there was pleasure to be had with him, a connection that, if explored, might be more than physical. But the risk was too great to merely explore a curiosity.

'Perhaps I should be asking you the same,' she replied. 'Why do you suppose I wanted some time apart? Those same questions haunt me as well. Perhaps *you* are seducing *me*, hoping to report to the Academy that I am too immoral for them. You could ruin me in more ways than one, Darius. Whereas I can do nothing for you.'

He chuckled and poked the fire with a stick, watching the wood catch. 'You still think I am the one with all the power. You're wrong. There *is* something you can do for me, that we can do together.'

There was a ruefulness in his gaze when he set the stick aside. She did soften at that. Something more was on his mind. 'While we have been wondering if we can trust one another, something has happened. What is it, Darius?' It must be terrible indeed to drive him to such considerations.

He came around the campfire and took up a spot on the blanket. 'I've had a letter from Aldred Gray at the

Academy. You should read it.' He reached for the basket and pulled out a bottle. 'It will go better with wine.'

Artemisia took the letter and settled against a rock. The letter was nothing short of a covert confession regarding her suspicions: that the Academy had never planned to approve her work or her membership. It wasn't surprising, but it still hurt. More surprising was the closing salute.

She took the wine glass from Darius and sipped thoughtfully. 'They want to blackmail you. They must not be sure of your compliance if they think such measures are necessary.' She took another swallow, getting her thoughts around the reasons for that. 'They must think I'm a femme fatale, an irresistible Circe, that I'll lure you to my bed and infect you with my ideas of feminine equality.' The letter all but called her a whore. 'What will you do?'

'What will *we* do?' he corrected. 'There's something else you should read.' He reached into the basket and pulled out a sheaf of papers. 'This is my report on the progress I saw here.'

'Is this what you've spent the last three days doing?' Artemisia took the considerable collection of pages, feeling a little quiver of anxiety move through her. 'Passing your verdict?' Would it be favourable? More importantly, would it be truthful? If he found her work lacking, would that be the truth or would it be his way of saying he had no choice, that no matter what he thought, he would cater to the Academy's whim?

'Just read. I'll roast us some dinner.' Darius busied himself stabbing two thick sausages on to sticks and holding them over the fire. Despite her curiosity about the report, Artemisia found it hard to look away. The firelight and fading dusk did beautiful things to him, limning the planes of his face, flickering over the blue-black highlights of his hair, outlining the contours of his body.

He caught her staring. 'Read, Artemisia. Please,' he scolded. 'It's important and the light is fading.'

She did read, glancing up every so often to reconcile the man at the fire with the man who'd written these words. 'You liked the collection?'

'You sound surprised.' Darius took a sausage from the fire and passed it to her. 'I have bread to go with it. Just give me a moment.'

'I am surprised.' Artemisia twirled the stick in her hand, sniffing appreciatively at the smell of cooked sausage. 'When you first saw them, you told me everything that was wrong with the paintings.'

'I told you what the Academy would see,' he corrected. 'They will still see that, but that's not what's there. The paintings are brilliant. To someone who understands them and their painter even more deeply, they exceed brilliance.'

She was glad of the darkness so he couldn't see her blush, couldn't see how the words pleased her. 'But you can't print this.' She put the pages back in the basket for safekeeping.

'Why not? It's the truth.'

'They will ruin you for it.' Artemisia bit into her sausage, letting the hot juices dribble over her tongue.

'Yes, they will try.' She felt Darius's gaze on her mouth, watching her eat.

'You don't think they'll succeed?' She reached for

her wine. Despite the conversation, this was turning out to be a delicious picnic.

'I'm not sure what I know right now. That's why I wanted to see you. I wanted you to know what they'd done, not just to you, but to me. I thought...' Darius paused and refilled her glass '...together we might find a way to thwart them.'

Artemisia sighed. What interesting bedfellows adversity made. Given her state of mind when it came to Darius Rutherford, she needed all of her wits about her because he suddenly needed her, or, at least, he thought he did. 'You are looking to save yourself.' Weren't all men? Something in her deflated a little. She'd wanted him to be different. This was where he proved he wasn't and she would remind herself she wasn't disappointed, that she'd had no expectations.

'You don't need me to save you, Darius. The power to do that has always been within your grasp.' Because he was a man, a man with a title and influence, a man to whom people would listen even if he was stark, raving mad. 'The answer is easy.'

Something sparked in his eyes. 'I will not give my name to a lie.'

Ah, she saw it now, in a brilliant flash the way lightning reveals a landscape in the dark of a storm, the dilemma that plagued the honourable Darius Rutherford. He felt duty-bound to tell the truth, even when it could save neither of them. Perhaps he did need her to save him after all, not from the Academy, but from himself.

'I was always going to burn, Darius,' she said with quiet acceptance. 'You needn't burn with me.' All he really needed from her was her permission: permission to separate from her, permission to say whatever was needed in his review to assure he fell into step with the Academy. Only she would know that for a moment he had contemplated doing otherwise.

The fire crackled between them, a shower of sparks lighting the night. Overhead, the first stars were birthing in the sky, in the marsh a rambler gave its night cry. Artemisia stretched out on the blanket, her head propped on an elbow as she nibbled the rest of her sausage and bread. 'I trust that was the business end of your reasons for seeking me out. Now, we can move on to the pleasure, starting with how you learned to cook like this?'

'We haven't decided anything, Artemisia.' Darius's gaze was intent.

'What is there to decide?' Artemisia gave him a half-smile. 'You can't possibly submit the review you've written.'

'I can't avoid submitting something, if that's what you're suggesting.' He answered her half-smile with one of his own, full of wryness and rue. 'You were right. I have to pick a side.'

Artemisia laughed. 'You can't pick mine, Darius. It will ruin you and you know it.' So much for being her fighting chance, her champion. It had been a nice thought while it lasted. At least he was honest about it. She set aside her empty stick and folded her hands behind her head, looking up at the sky. 'What will you say about me? Perhaps you will say I am overly simplistic, that the paintings show no depth of mastery with light and colour.' She chuckled. 'Maybe I will help you write it—it could be an entertaining exercise being the author of my own demise.'

She felt the nearness of him, the heat of him, as he rolled to his side, his body closer now, his words an earnest whisper. 'Stop. Go back. Why wouldn't I pick you? Why do you assume I wouldn't choose your side?'

She turned her head to watch his face in the firelight. So this was what an idealist looked like: handsome, strong, his belief in doing the right thing chiselled in every plane of his visage from jawline to brow. It wasn't naivety or a blindness to the reality of the world. Darius Rutherford knew what the world was like and he chose to be a champion for right regardless.

'Because it will be the undoing of you, Darius,' she reminded him. 'Save yourself for a fight you can win. We both know I was never going to be victorious.' She rolled to face him, reaching a hand up to smooth back that errant swoop of hair that fell across his face. 'Thank you for the thought, though. I've never had a champion before. It was nice.'

'Was? *Am.* I *am* your champion, Artemisia. The work you've done here is outstanding. I've seen nothing like it. You should be recognised.' His hand closed over hers. 'Why are you so willing to give up? The woman I saw in the assembly hall wouldn't have given up.'

'I am not used to having others involved. You needn't sacrifice yourself for me. I'm used to being alone.' She'd been alone the day she'd faced the assembly. She was alone when she painted. No one but she decided what she painted, how she painted. She didn't even paint with her father's other pupils, hadn't for ten years. Art was a solitary pursuit—to make it otherwise was to pollute it with agendas and compromises. 'Up until now, I couldn't really hurt anyone but myself.'

She wanted to keep it that way, but it was hard to remind herself of that with Darius Rutherford's long length stretched out before a campfire on the beach, tempting her with all nature of persuasion to rethink her association with loneliness. To have an ally who understood her, who saw her passion, who saw her, who didn't want to change her, was a heady temptation indeed. She felt like the sticks on the fire; one moment strong and whole, the next, ash, overcome by the flame.

There'd been men before who sought to be her patron among other things, men who thought to raise her up in their image, polish the diamond in the rough, never understanding this particular diamond liked her hard edges. She had, on occasion, given one or two of them her body when the loneliness became unbearable, but she'd never given them her soul, her heart. They wouldn't have known what to do with it.

How could Darius be any different despite his protestations? How could he fulfil the promises he made with his words, his eyes, his body when he was so highly placed in the hierarchy of men? What did he stand to gain? 'Darius, why do you care what happens to me?' The fire popped as if to emphasise that this was indeed the burning question. What could matter so much that he would take such a risk? She wasn't sure she wanted to know. But it was too late, the question had already been asked and his answer was swift.

Chapter Twelve

The words were breathtaking and offered without hesitation. 'Because you, Artemisia, are the most incredible woman I've ever met. You are beautiful and bold, courageous and talented. Such things should not be crushed by the world, not if I can help it.' And he thought he *could* help it. But she couldn't. In that moment, she couldn't help her body, couldn't help the wanting of him. At long last she was going to stop resisting, she was going to give in.

He reached for her, his hand was in her hair at the base of her neck, his body gathering her close, his words low at her ear as if they were the fine words of a lover. 'What good is my voice if I cannot use it to fight for right? What good is it if I am only giving voice to others' vision? Doing what others want?' He kissed the inside of her neck beneath her ear and a trill of want shot through her, wild and wicked. She wanted to possess this man, wanted to drink from the intoxicating cup of his goodness, his rightness, his honesty. Just one night, with no artifice. Had she ever been able to say that about a lover?

Darius's mouth kissed the racing pulse at the base of her throat. 'You've brought me alive. I'd forgotten I was dead until I met you.'

Yes, she breathed against him. That exactly. With him, a tiny part of her was slowly allowing itself to wake again, to stretch its limbs. It had been dormant so long she'd almost forgotten it—that piece of her that didn't need to fight, to rebel, to defend, only to be, to trust, to live simply in the moment. She wrapped her arms around him, answering his closeness with hers, hips, mouths, bodies pressed together, knowing he needed from her in equal measure that which he gave. In this moment, in this place under the stars, beside a crackling, snapping fire, she was content to give it. Solace, in its finest form.

This was communion in its most intimate form. Darius breathed her in, drinking from her lips, his body rising against the curves of her, feeling her tremble with the same desire that shook him in waves of need and awareness, of him, of her, of who they might be together—something as dangerous as it was powerful. The unknown beckoned and Artemisia was the gateway to it, to earth-shattering passion, to dreams he'd long since stifled in exchange for the mantle of responsibility. Her hand moved between them, seeking and finding the hardness of him. She moved over it, tracing his length through his breeches. He let out a hard breath, part-arousal, part-pain, as his body strained for the freedom of release. Her nimble fingers responded, unbut-

toning his fall and seeking him with an intrepid hand
that closed over him, firm and confident, yet needing
to hold him as much as he needed to be held, touched,
roused to the full extent.

He groaned against her, his own hands working the
frogs of her jacket open, cursing the buttons of the linen
blouse under his breath until his mouth, his hands, had
access to the warm, bare skin of her breast. She was
firm and full in his hands, her nipples puckering and
taut as his mouth closed over them, sucking, teasing,
his tongue licking and laving each in turn. She was not
shy. She moaned her delight in honest gasps, her hand
tight about him in return, stroking his length in mirror
of his own machinations.

He moved against her, hips to hips, his hand seeking
the hem of her skirts, rucking them up as she arched
into him, letting out a breathy laugh of pleasure as
he shoved his trousers down past his hips, wanting to
match her bareness with his own. He felt the coolness
of the evening on his buttocks, the heat of the fire's
flame. He felt her tremble against him. 'Are you cold?'

'No.' Her hand found him again. 'You?' Her voice
was low, throaty, seductive rasp.

'No. If I tremble it is with desire.' He sought her
mouth with his, giving proof to words. He could not
recall a raw wanting of this magnitude, of wanting to
lose himself in her. His body wanted to go fast, wanted
to push with all speed to that point of release, the thing
it sought blindly. But his mind wanted to savour this,
wanted to build slowly towards that release.

She wrapped her arms about him, holding him
against her, her thighs parting, offering the hardness

of him a resting place between her legs. He was welcome here. She moved again, her intimate curls damp against his phallus, a petition for ingress. 'Don't wait on my account, Darius,' she breathed the heady invitation against his neck.

He needed no further encouragement. He braced himself on arms taut with his weight, corded muscles straining beneath his shirt, and entered her. She was his estuary, his refuge, and he buried himself deep in the wet heat of her, feeling her legs lock about his hips, her hands grip his shoulders, his back, as her body took up the rhythm of retreat and surge with him, their cries joining with the sounds of the night. He thrust hard, his own body tightening as climax approached. Not yet, not yet, he cautioned. He wanted to wait for her, but soon he would be beyond waiting, soon pleasure would overwhelm him like a wave, pushing him along at its own speed, not his. 'Come on, Artemisia, come with me, now,' he groaned at her ear. 'Look at me, open your eyes, and look at me.' His body was straining hard, slipping its leash at the last.

When he quickly withdrew and release overtook him, she held him tight, a sigh escaping her lips, but her eyes remained shut and he couldn't shake the sense that for as pleasurable as the joining had been, she'd not come with him, not all the way. Yet, when she snuggled against him, there was a weary contentment in her body and in her voice. He would have to settle for that, *this* time. It was enough. Even in its incompleteness, there was a kind of wholeness.

Her hand rested on his chest, drawing idle circles, her voice soft in the night. 'You never did answer my question. How does an heir to an earldom learn to cook outdoors?'

'My father taught me. There was a place we'd camp on the edge of our land. In the autumn, when he was home from London, he'd take me out every year for a tour of the estate on horseback. We were gone three days. Three days of meeting with tenants, seeing the fields, the forest, the river. We'd fish and swim, and hunt.' Darius sighed. Those days seemed a long time ago, boyhood was another lifetime. 'I used to live for those trips and those times when it was just my father and me.'

'They sound wonderful. When did they stop?'

'The summer before I went to university. My father was in London for Parliament and, in the autumn, I left for my first term.' He might have felt adulthood had begun at twelve when his father had started his official instruction in the earldom, but childhood had lingered a few years in the transition. Pulling away in the carriage for Oxford had been a farewell to more than his parents that cold autumn morning. Watching Bourne Hall fade from view had been like watching the last of his childhood fade as well. Part of him had died that day. Part of him had died a few months earlier.

'I was glad to leave, though,' he confessed. 'I think the camping trip would not have been the same that year even if we had gone. My father and I had quarrelled frequently that last winter and spring before I left.' He never talked about that final year at home. He tried to think of it as a beginning, not as an end when he thought of it at all. Even almost two decades later, it was painful to think about.

Artemisia's circles on his chest had slowed to long, thoughtful ovals. 'That must have been difficult. You seem very close to your father from the way you speak about him.'

'My father is a good man, I admire him and, growing up, it was important to me that I had his admiration as well. I think discovering that you disagree with your parents, especially when you admire them, is hard for a young person. You have to choose. Who is right? You? Your parents? If you're right, then your parents are wrong. But how could that be when they've been infallible your whole life?' Darius smiled and looked down at her head resting on his shoulder. 'Have you ever quarrelled with your father?'

'Yes, countless times.' Artemisia laughed with a sigh. 'I'm always right, though.'

'Of course you are.' That didn't surprise him in the least. Artemisia with all her self-sufficiency would never doubt herself, would never choose another's rightness over her own. In that way, they were very different.

'There are so many things I want to ask you,' Darius murmured. 'But we're out of time.' Beyond them, the fire had burned down and their pile of reserve sticks was spent. The wine was gone. It was time to go. Darius eyed the sky, unable to resist the urge to show off. 'Do you want to know what time it is? It's half past eight.' He drew his watch out from a pocket and passed it to her without looking, 'Check it.'

'You'll owe me a forfeit if you're wrong.'

'Then you'll owe me one if I'm right.' Darius buttoned up his clothing.

Artemisia flipped open the timepiece with a saucy

smile and studied the watch face, tipping it this way and that to catch the last of the firelight. She shut the lid and fixed him with a stare. 'Half past eight,' she admitted. 'Very good. You would have made a fine sailor, navigating by the stars.' She handed the watch back to him. 'Shall you claim your forfeit?'

Darius shook his head, tempting as it was, though. 'I shall save it for a more auspicious moment.' He shook out the blanket. 'I hope you are generous in defeat,' he joked.

'Only to those who are humble in victory,' she teased as they picked up the campsite. 'Did you set all this up yourself?'

'No, I had help. I had the two boys at the inn get it all ready. I had my hands full making sure you came out walking with me.' Darius offered her his arm. 'I am glad you came.'

'I am, too.' She leaned her head against his shoulder as they strolled back towards the road. 'Thank you for sharing that review tonight. Thank you for being honest about the Academy and the position they've put you in. I don't know many men who would have been as honest or even consulted me on the details.'

Old doubts stirred in Darius against the evening's pleasure. 'Did you make love to me to thank me?' Did that explain why she'd not been with him at the last? Had he misread her desire? Had this been a courtesy? A favour to him?

Her head came up from his shoulder and he immediately missed the weight of it. He'd grown used to the presence of her, the touch of her in such a short time. 'No, I am not in the habit of taking lovers haphazardly, whatever you may have been told.' Some of her sharpness was returning and Darius regretted his question. He'd meant to protect himself, but he'd insulted her in the attempt.

'I've been told nothing,' he replied quickly in hopes of salvaging the walk. The evening had been too good to end in a fight, too good to give his father's words any purchase.

Perhaps she felt the same. They did not speak again until they reached the farmhouse drive. A lone light burned in the front window. Artemisia's voice was soft when she spoke. 'I made love with you, Darius Rutherford, because you are the most incredible man I know. You are bold and courageous, willing to stand up for what is right, willing to change your own opinion when you feel it no longer serves the truth. Such things should not be crushed by the world, not if I can help it.'

Darius smiled in the darkness. 'It seems I've heard those words before, or close enough.' The first bit had been his, but the last was all hers. It touched him that she saw the man he wished to be. It wasn't who he was, though, not yet. If she knew the truth of him, she'd realise she gave him too much credit.

She reached up and kissed him on the mouth before he could argue the compliment. 'I am sketching in the Oare Marshes tomorrow, weather notwithstanding. There's one last drawing I need. Come with me. Bring lunch and wine.'

How was he supposed to sleep tonight with a kiss on his lips, her invitation on his mind while his body still hummed with the echo of her on his skin, on his tongue? He waited until she was gone from sight. He juggled the basket on his arm and moved the blanket under the other and started the walk back towards the Crown. He didn't mind the walk. It gave him time to mull the evening over. Sweet heavens, she got to him like no other, perhaps because she didn't care he was the heir to an earldom. She wasn't trying to please him. No, certainly not that. Artemisia Stansfield was a woman who pleased herself in life and in passion.

Because she trusts no one to do it for her, came the rejoinder.

Darius laughed aloud in the night. Of course. She'd kept her eyes shut, the gateways to the soul. She wouldn't relinquish that innermost piece of her to anyone. Her body was one thing, her soul was another. Even then, she hadn't given her body to him. There'd been no submission tonight. She wasn't capable of it and, in truth, he didn't want it. He wanted a partner in this dilemma.

He knew people like that, those who held their innermost self in reserve, kept it apart from the swirls of life. They were people who'd been hurt, who'd learned the lesson in hard ways, and he knew she numbered among them. She'd shown him that much that rainy afternoon on the couch, whether she'd meant to or not, and in other ways, like the way she spoke about men and power and her father.

Anger on her behalf began to churn. He would like to call them to account, all of them, anyone who'd hurt her. He wanted to make them pay for hardening the edges of her, for making her unreachable even in moments of abject pleasure. But even that thought mocked him.

That's how the world of men dealt with their problems. It was not what she wanted.

Artemisia didn't want men punished for crimes that could not be erased. She wanted a better world where such crimes didn't happen in the first place. *That* might be beyond even him. It was humbling to recognise that even if he made it the work of his lifetime it might not be enough. It might take two lifetimes, or more.

At the inn, he left the basket downstairs with tomorrow's order and climbed the steps to his own room. It was still early by town standards, barely half past nine, and sleep was beyond him. He turned up the lamp and reached for his journal, his fingers already itching for a pencil before the images of her could fade. He wanted to capture her as she'd been tonight on the beach. This was what she'd brought him to—full circle back to the boy he'd been at sixteen, who'd sketched, who'd painted, who'd imagined a different life for himself, who'd given up those dreams for the sake of his father's.

He was more conflicted than he'd been in a long while these past weeks, but he was also more alive than he had been since the day he'd left Bourne Hall for Oxford and traded in his pencil for politics and history, and all the things an earl's son should know.

He looked down at the sketching, seeing Artemisia as she'd been tonight, as she'd fiercely announced, 'I am always right.'

But she was wrong about him. He wasn't as brave or courageous as she thought. When he'd had a choice between himself and his father, his *family*, he'd chosen peace within his family.

How could you not have? You were a sixteen-year-old boy.

He could still see his mother's face, stricken and pale by the words he and his father had hurled at one another.

'You will never be anything but a dauber. You would risk all this for that, for a middling talent?' his father had shouted—the perpetually level-headed Lord Bourne had actually raised his voice and laid his hands on Darius, as if he could shake sense into him. Perhaps he had. His mother had cried out and he'd capitulated at her distress. The family had recovered, but all three of them still bore the scars from those days—words that could not be taken back, things that could not be unsaid.

He'd not stood up for himself. He'd given up the one thing he thought had mattered more than all the rest. He would always wonder if he'd been weak, if he simply hadn't had it in him to persevere when it had become difficult. Had he given in too soon? Artemisia didn't give in. Artemisia didn't bend, except apparently where his reputation was concerned. That was both admirable and frightening about her. He worried greatly that her stubbornness would be her undoing one way or another unless she would allow him to pave the way for her. He would see this fight through. He needed to for both their sakes. Artemisia would be his redemption just as he would be hers.

Chapter Thirteen

He wanted to redeem her. It was the one thought that had doggedly stayed with her all night and into the morning. She was struck by the oddness of such a choice as she gathered her supplies. One would think other things would be more prominent in her mind regarding last night other than redemption—things like the wickedly sinful passion they'd engaged in, the feel of his hands, his mouth on her body, the knowledge of her own fierce response.

Artemisia tucked a cloth around her sketch pad and pencils in the basket to keep them dry, a little smile twitching on her lips. She could feel evidence of that response today. She was deliciously, ever-so-slightly sore from making love on a beach. It had been a delight for the senses: the smell of brine and campfire mixed with the scent of cooked sausage, the stars overhead, the sounds of night birds, the touch of a man who knew how to please a woman. Even now, in the businesslike brightness of the morning, her body stirred at the echo of his touch. But such thoughts gave him little credit.

Last night hadn't been solely about technical expertise. To say it was reduced it greatly.

She had hungered for him, she'd wanted *him*, not just what his proficiency could do for her physically. That had scared her this morning. It still scared her. That was new territory and, once realised, she'd withdrawn from it at the end. She might have been ready to exchange physical pleasures, but she'd not been ready for emotional pleasure, for admitting the way she felt with him was unique to him alone, that no one else could conjure that reaction. This wasn't about orgasm and that gave her a huge fright.

Orgasm she could deal with. Emotional investment, she wasn't sure. She didn't want to care about Darius Rutherford in that way, but it seemed she had little control as to where her feelings led, especially if those feelings were in any way reciprocated. Heaven help them both if they were. This would be so much simpler if it could have just been physical pleasure.

She looked up at the sound of horses in the drive and smiled at the surprise. Darius had brought the coach today, in the likelihood that it would rain. They would go to the Oare Marshes in style. What a treat it would be to ride somewhere after six weeks of walking everywhere.

Artemisia grabbed her heavy cloak and hurried out of the studio. She could hear him chatting with Mrs Harris in the entry. Mrs Harris was thoroughly smitten with him these days, after their rough start—not that he hadn't worked hard for her appreciation. He brought their housekeeper all sorts of thoughtful little things: some spices he'd ordered from London or a nice roast from the butcher in Faversham. Part of her wished he didn't make such gestures. The last thing Artemisia wanted was more Darius Rutherford supporters in the house. It was easier to not like him when Mrs Harris wasn't singing his praises. At least Addy was still a voice of reason, thank goodness.

'Are you ready?' She looped an arm through his, abruptly interrupting the conversation with Mrs Harris, but not before she noticed he'd brought a bottle of wine for the housekeeper's stores.

Darius grinned, taking the interruption in his stride. 'I am. Mrs Harris was just telling me about the party tonight at Gann's oyster mill. The whole town is invited, it seems.' He arched an eyebrow to suggest that somehow she'd hidden this piece of news from him. 'There will be dancing and good food, I am told.'

'Oh, yes, milord,' Mrs Harris enthused, oblivious to the quelling glance Artemisia shot her direction. 'It's one of the winter highlights in Seasalter. It breaks up the long stretch of nothingness between Christmas and spring. Folks hereabouts look forward to it.' She seemed to recall who she was speaking to. 'Of course, it might not be fancy enough for town folks.'

'I like to think I'm not so high in the instep, Mrs Harris, that I can't enjoy a good party.' Apparently, Darius had made his decision. He favoured Mrs Harris with a dazzling smile. 'We can all go in my coach. I'll have Artemisia back by five from the marshes, it will give you ladies a chance to change and I'll call for you around seven.' If there had been any lingering resistance to Darius on Mrs Harris's part it was entirely dispelled now. She was beaming like a young girl when they left her, already dreaming of her evening out with a lord and his coach.

'You've quite turned her head,' Artemisia commented drily as Darius handed her up into the coach.

'Are you jealous?' Darius teased, taking the seat opposite. 'You were quite abrupt back there, as if you didn't want me to say too much.'

'I didn't want to give us away,' Artemisia confessed. More to the point, she hadn't wanted to give herself away, not sure how she would react seeing Darius this morning. Would she do or say something that might indicate a shift in the nature of their association?

The coach lurched into motion and Darius fixed her with one of his intense stares. 'Why didn't you tell me about the party? Mrs Harris seemed to imply that you and your sister already had plans to go.'

'People will make assumptions, they will talk.' She wasn't ready to explain she and Darius to anyone. She had no idea what it might mean, or if it meant anything at all. Until she did, she wanted it to remain just between them.

'I doubt they will say anything at all except that I came with the household I am here to visit. Just so you know,' he teased, 'it's quite normal to invite your guests to attend outings with you.'

'You're mocking me.' Artemisia suppressed a little grin. 'It's just that I've been relatively private since I've been here and I don't want people speculating.'

'I'll be sure to dance with all the girls, if that's what you're worried about.' Darius winked and settled back against the squabs. 'Now that's settled, tell me about today's sketching session. What are we looking for?'

It was the perfect question to ask. It gave them a comfortable space in which to interact. Discussing her work allowed conversation that skirted last night's interlude without being stilted. They fell into a pleasant rhythm and Artemisia began to relax. Perhaps Darius, too, had decided it was best to leave well enough alone. Last night didn't need to be dissected or analysed or understood if it was meant to be another moment out of time. She could live with that.

The day was overcast and likely to stay that way, but there was brightness behind the clouds and the light was good in the marshes when they arrived. Darius found them a spot out of the wind and went about making a camp for them while she wandered in search of the ducks. She found the pintail on the edge of the marsh, paddling in still waters with others. She retreated to a discreet distance and began to draw.

'I can see why you wanted to sketch him, he's a very handsome duck.' Darius came up quietly behind her, his voice a mere whisper, careful not to startle her or her model. 'His colouring is ideal for your collection.'

She nodded abstractedly, making notes for later reference lest she forget the details: the chocolate head of the duck, the black-tipped wings, the white underbelly, the perfect colours for her palette without any need to improvise. It was more than colouring, though, that drew her to the idea of the pintail. It was what the duck in winter stood for, a symbol of her own retreat, her own refuge, waiting until spring to return. She finished and closed her pad. 'Do you want to walk on the beach?' It wasn't much of a beach, just a strip of land at the edge of the tidal pools, but the view was clear and the length was long enough to stretch one's legs.

He reached for her hand as they walked, their fingers interlocking of their own accord. The ease with which their bodies gravitated towards one another was something of a marvel to her, a marvel she could carefully enjoy with limitations—always with limitations. There was safety in boundaries. She brought his hand up to study it, her fingers stretching the length of his and coming up short. She turned his hand over in hers. 'You've been sketching again. You've got smudges.'

'Guilty.' He smiled, but offered little more explanation. 'I was up late last night and needed to do *something* before I could sleep.'

It was the ideal opening for a naughty rejoinder. Too perfect and Artemisia was too smart to take the bait. She knew he would talk about last night's intimacy if given the chance. She'd rather talk about his sketching, his secrets. 'Why did you stop painting?' She'd seen his sketches, they were more than proficient. He had not given himself enough credit when she'd first mentioned it. Instead, he'd brushed off the compliment, but that was last week. It seemed a lifetime ago. So much had changed between them. There was a new closeness between them now, even if it couldn't last.

'Other things needed my attention. University. The earldom. There simply wasn't any more time. I suppose, in a way, I outgrew it.'

She shook her head and made a dissatisfied frown. 'That's what you said last time. I want the real answer, Darius. Someone who has your talent doesn't simply just stop. I couldn't stop, even if I wanted to.'

'It was a long time ago,' Darius prevaricated. 'It hardly matters. It's not who I am any more or who I will be again.'

'You miss that person. I can hear it in your voice. He needn't be gone. You can start again.' Artemisia stopped at the edge of the water. Their little camp was coming into view. 'I could teach you, help you refine your skill. We could start today.' She gave his hand a tug, already imagining them sitting beside the campfire drawing together.

'No, Artemisia.' His voice was firm and it dampened her spirits as he likely meant it to. 'Those days are gone for me. I don't want them back.' He paused. 'They were troublesome times.'

Because of the painting?

'But you're sketching again,' she argued.

'To pass the time. Nothing more.' His dark eyes were shuttered. She would get nothing further from him. She let the subject drop as they set out their lunch and enjoyed the small fire, but her mind kept working the puzzle. He might not have told her more today, but she knew more today than she had last week. She took out the pieces of him and fitted and refitted them into different configurations throughout lunch, a picture slowly emerging as they ate.

She finished her bread and cocked her head to one side, seeing him through the new lens she'd constructed from all the pieces and parts she knew of him: Darius as a young artist, a young heir, a boy born into one of the most privileged families in England. Not many great artists came from great privilege. The privilege always seemed to get in the way. Responsibility, Darius had said, that had been the root of his rearing and education. Responsibility for others, for the land, to the title, to a father he adored. There would be little room for putting oneself first.

'It's me wanting a penny for your thoughts this time.' Darius gave her a slow smile, catching her lingering perusal.

'They might be worth more than that,' she replied in all seriousness. 'Perhaps I should keep them to myself. You might not thank me for them.' It was enough that she knew, that she'd figured out his reticence to discussing his artistic past.

'Tell me, or you'll be thinking about it, whatever it is, all day, and then I'll be thinking about it, wondering. It will distract us both. Besides, you know what curiosity did to the cat.'

'You won't like it,' she warned once more. He shrugged as if liking was of no consequence. 'Very well, if you insist on knowing. I've been thinking about why you gave up painting. I've had to generate my own answers since you won't tell me,' she reminded him.

'You mean why I stopped.' Darius's tone was sharper now, a definite sign that he did not like the topic despite his curiosity. Perhaps he thought, *wished*, she'd been thinking of something else. Goodness knew there was plenty she might have been concerned with: London, the Academy, whether or not they should make love again. But he had trumped all that. Perhaps that should be a surprise in itself, one she should examine later as proof she was getting in too deep with Darius Rutherford. She was caring about the person, forgetting about the issues.

'No, I mean quite deliberately "give up". Stopping and giving up are two very different things,' Artemisia corrected. To stop was to separate from something, to depart from it intentionally. But to give up was done with resignation, a surrender to overwhelming circumstances. 'You gave up painting for your father.'

There was nothing but the soft sound of lapping water and the occasional squawk of water fowl in the silence that followed and the hard, dark stare of a man whose fortress was under siege.

Damn her. She hadn't even bothered to do him the courtesy of making it a question, of at least the pretence of enquiry. She was that certain she was right. Of course she was. Artemisia Stansfield never suffered doubt. She wore her boldness as her armour, he'd known that from the start. She made no secret of it, whereas so many others wore boldness as a façade— once penetrated, it crumpled, nothing more than an illusion. Not so with her. Artemisia's boldness was real.

'A man likes to keep one or two secrets to himself,' Darius said drily. 'But you seem intent on wanting to strip me bare.'

'I want to *know* you, Darius, not expose you.' She tilted her head to the other side and he braced himself for another barrage of insight. 'It embarrasses you, doesn't it? That you gave up your painting. That's why you don't want to talk about it.'

'Can you blame me? As a fellow artist, I am in your shadow. Your skill overwhelms my meagre talent. You fight for what you want, what you think you deserve, and I gave up at the first hurdle.'

Artemisia stretched her legs out on the blanket, a worrisome sign that she was settling in. She would be relentless. She patted her lap. 'Come lay your head and tell me about it. Tell me your story, Darius.' A siege indeed and a sensual one at that. But he did as asked, recognising that this was a different type of lovemaking. Perhaps by telling his story, she might, at some point, tell him hers. These were real stories, real truths about who they were, the things they hadn't told another soul. If there was to be genuine intimacy between them, genuine trust, perhaps it started here.

'Painting is not a fit enterprise for an earl's heir,' Darius said, looking up into her grey eyes. 'It didn't matter when I was younger. It seemed natural that the son of a great art collector would pursue the arts as a means of educating himself about the family collection. My father hired several art tutors and I continued to paint when I went away to Eton. I had an instructor there who was exceedingly encouraging. He felt I had real promise.' Darius paused. This part was harder to tell. Artemisia's hand stilled in his hair.

'That's good, isn't it?' she coaxed.

'It would be if he'd been telling the truth. Maybe he was. I'll never really know. People tell earls' heirs whatever they want to hear in the hopes of currying favour.' He blew out a breath. 'The instructor in question was removed from his post before I returned from the summer recess. He'd made the mistake, you see, of writing to my father about my talents. I was fifteen, a most pivotal year with university looming. My father and I fought over my art, over the instructor's dismissal, over my future—I wanted to do a grand tour before university, just a short one to study in Italy. We fought constantly until the day I left for Oxford.

'I thought about running away, but I never could bring myself to do it. It would have killed my parents. I was angry with my father, but I didn't want to destroy him, so I gave up my painting. It was the only path to peace.'

'That doesn't make you weak.' Artemisia's voice was soft but firm. 'I think it makes you stronger than any man I know. Sacrificing oneself for another's happiness is a rare form of bravery. But I am sorry for what it cost you.'

He sat up. 'That's just it. Maybe it cost me nothing. Maybe I was no good. I might have risked my family, my future, for something that never existed. I'll never know just as I'll never know if I would have had the tenacity to see it through. Perhaps I'd have crumpled in the face of adversity. I think it's the uncertainty I dislike the most.'

Something moved in her eyes. 'Is that why you're an art critic, so intent on giving everyone the truth?'

The question filled him with a certain relief, a certain satisfaction that she saw him so clearly when others did not. She understood his painting was not a gentleman's pastime, but a calling that went far deeper. 'It is and it's why I want to tell the truth for you, because you should know you are brilliant, Artemisia. Everyone should know.'

The sharp planes of her face softened, her voice a quiet whisper. 'I could kiss you for that, Darius Rutherford.'

'Then perhaps you should. We have a little time left before we have to return for the party.'

Artemisia gave him a slow smile. 'Then let's not waste it.'

Chapter Fourteen

Owen Gann had wasted no space in turning the floor of his oyster fishery into the largest dance hall in Kent. A stage had been built for the musicians at the far end and groaning refreshment tables lined the other while overhead the balcony that housed the managers' offices was decorated in garlands of dried reeds hung with shells and other tidal bits. 'How inventive,' Darius complimented appreciatively as they looked around, getting their bearings in the crush.

They'd got home slightly later than expected from the marshes. Artemisia had rushed to change, but as a consequence the party was well under way when they'd arrived, the fishery already crowded with people excited for a break in their winter routine, Mrs Harris and Adelaide among them. The two had left them at the door to join various groups of their acquaintants. 'We won't see Addy again until it's time to go home,' Artemisia laughed, searching the room. 'There is someone I want you to meet—Owen Gann, our host.'

Artemisia steered him through the room towards the

men gathered at the ale kegs. 'I think you'd like him and he's the only person I really know here.' She nodded her head towards the dance floor where Adelaide was already in a set forming for a country dance. 'My sister is far more social than I am.'

'Why is that?' Darius snatched two mugs of ale off a passing tray and offered her one.

'I like my privacy.' Artemisia took a healthy swallow and frowned as she studied the dance floor. 'I don't like *that* at all.' She was aware of Darius's gaze following her own.

'What is it?' Darius asked.

'It's that fellow she's with. Bennett Galbraith. Something's off about him. He's just too much, everything about him is too intense, too perfect. It's hard to describe. I don't like him, but Addy's smitten so I suppose he must be tolerated for the time being. He's up at the farmhouse all the time. That's one thing I won't mind leaving behind.' She wished she hadn't said it, wished she hadn't given life to the one topic they'd assiduously avoided today: London and March and all the decisions Darius wanted them to make, although she suspected he wasn't looking for her input as much as he was looking for her agreement, that he'd already made his decisions.

She didn't agree with them, which meant to discuss them would only lead to more argument and to more questions. What did he want from her? As an artist? As a lover? On those grounds, the situation between them was confusing and complicated. She didn't want to talk about any of that tonight. She far preferred other, more simplistic grounds: sketching, painting, picnicking on deserted beaches, kisses before early evening campfires, even lovemaking beneath the stars without expectations. Those were things she could commit to, things that could exist in the vacuum of Seasalter. Those grounds were comfortable. She could navigate them with a clear beginning and a clear end and, in between, she could have the company of an incredible man.

Artemisia caught sight of a tall, blond-haired man weaving his way towards them through the crush and gave thanks for perfect timing. 'Here's Owen, now.' There'd be no chance for Darius to bring up difficult subjects.

'Miss Stansfield! What a pleasure to see you here tonight and you've brought a guest.'

'This is Mr Darius Rutherford. He's come to look over some of my paintings.' Artemisia made the necessary introductions, leaving out his title. Owen shook Darius's hand and she watched as the two men sized one another up, Darius's dark eyes meeting the blue-grey gaze of the factory owner. The two men were at once a study of contrasts and similarities; both were tall, muscular men, but Owen's blond Saxon good looks were a rugged foil to the polished Norman darkness of Darius's features. There was no mistaking who was the nobleman and who was the oysterman, even without titles.

'This is an impressive facility,' Darius complimented. 'I would like to come and see it in operation some day.'

'You are welcome any time,' Owen offered graciously. 'We are the largest processor of oysters on the Kent coast. We supply the finest restaurants in London and the markets. We also pickle them here to transport inland.'

'He's being modest,' Artemisia put in. 'He even exports his oysters to the Hapsburg Court.'

Owen Gann shrugged. 'You are too gracious, Miss Stansfield. We are just a humble business. I regret there's not much to see at the moment. Winter is quiet here, but in the spring and summer, we run at full tilt, almost sixteen hours a day when the fishermen are out.'

They talked a few moments longer before someone needed to consult Owen on the state of the kegs. 'He's an interesting fellow,' Darius remarked as Gann took his leave.

'He's a self-made businessman.' Artemisia led the way to the refreshment table. They hadn't eaten since lunch and she was hungry. 'He's grown up here. I knew him when we were children and spent our summers here. I was too young for him to take note of—seven years' difference in age is a lifetime apart when you're children. He was fifteen when I was eight and of course later there were other differences too.' She'd been the daughter of a newly minted knight of the realm, from a family of some substance, while he went out every day to the seabeds with the men to harvest the oysters.

'When the son of an oysterman turns sixteen, they earn the right to farm their father's beds. He started to see the possibilities of what he calls vertical business integration.' Artemisia waved a hand, 'I don't pretend to understand all of it, but it was quite ingenious and his rise has been rather meteoric. He's elevated himself and the town.'

'You admire him.' Darius began to fill a plate from the table.

'Yes. He's turned oyster farming into a personal fortune and given back to his community.' Artemisia slid a sideways glance at the handsome man beside her. Was that jealousy she heard in his tone? 'He's admirable in an objective sense. I don't fancy him, if that's what you want to know. He's married to his work.' She nodded upwards. 'He spends his days in those offices. Some people gossip he has a bed up there and he sleeps here five nights out of seven during the oyster season.'

She pointed to a tiered tray of chilled oysters. 'Get plenty of those for our plate,' she advised. 'I thought you'd like to meet him. He is like you, responsible for the livelihood of others.'

When their plate was full, they refilled their mugs and found a quiet place on a step where they could eat and talk and watch the party going on around them. 'It's not as quiet as the beach.' Darius laughed as she leaned forward repeatedly to hear what he had to say.

'Nor as private.' Artemisia smiled, thinking of how they'd made use of that privacy last night, and this afternoon. Two very different uses for privacy, each one delicious in its own right. She leaned close, her voice low for him alone. 'Thank you for today, for telling me. I know it was difficult.' There would be no more exchanging of deep truths or surprising revelations here among the noisy revels. She suddenly wished they were alone in a firelit dining parlour, in her studio or on a beach. She watched as he took an oyster on a half-shell and slurped it down and reached for another. 'Go easy on those,' she cautioned.

'They're delicious. I hear they're also an aphrodisiac,' Darius whispered wickedly.

Artemisia laughed, allowing herself to enjoy the evening and the company, even as her mind whispered its usual cautions. Darius was entirely too easy to be with when they weren't arguing or carefully dancing around the other. It was something of a comfort to know those arguments would return, would remind her of the realities between them. That this evening, that last night, could not last. They weren't meant to. They were just meant to be enjoyed in the moment.

'I think aphrodisia is a mental concept.' She picked up an oyster, locking eyes with him to demonstrate the point. She smiled, running a tongue over her bottom lip, and then sucked down the oyster. She gave a throaty chuckle at the sight of Darius's gaze turning obsidian at the sight of her. 'See? It's your imagination that makes the oyster sexy.'

'Hmm? Is it? What about your imagination, my dear?' Darius's gaze stayed locked on hers, hot and searing, his eyes a seduction unto themselves. Good lord, she knew too well how that gaze could arouse with just a stare. He took another oyster from the plate, his gaze hot on hers over the shell as he swallowed. 'Remind you of anything, my dear?' His voice was a sensual husk.

Oh, indeed it did, of a rainy afternoon on a couch, of his mouth on her. The too-familiar warmth began to unfurl low in her belly at the remembrance of his mouth, his tongue, how they'd pushed her towards unspeakable pleasure, a pleasure she'd not dared to let herself claim in full last night on the beach. She took another oyster, determined to not be outdone.

'If you put another oyster in your mouth, be warned you are playing with fire,' Darius growled, desire riding him precariously hard at the moment. Dear lord, certain parts of him had become granite in the middle of a country party watching Artemisia Stansfield seduce him with oysters. Not that he was alone in the arousal—this was a rather mutual game of public seduction between them. It was unfair, though, that her arousal was less obviously displayed than his. He didn't dare stand up for a while.

'You've quite the…um…imagination.' Artemisia gave him a wicked, teasing smile, her eyes flicking to the fall of his trousers. He was glad he'd not worn breeches tonight. Trousers were only slightly less tight, but he'd take any relief at the moment.

'My "imagination" wants to step outside and take you hard against the nearest wall.' He leaned in, stealing a kiss, his tongue licking the briny salt of the oyster from her lips. 'You taste like freedom, Artemisia,' he whispered at her throat. Freedom and redemption, possibility and promise. Yet he was aware that so much lay unresolved between them and aware, too, that Artemisia had agreed to nothing—nothing permanent, nothing irrevocable. Neither had he. Nothing was decided that could be binding. He found he was having too much fun tonight to want to force those decisions. They could wait for a more solemn time.

She answered him with a kiss, long and lingering, her tongue taking its turn to taste him and he let her.

This was a country party in the middle of nowhere. No one noticed, no one cared who kissed whom in the shadowy recesses of a fishery floor. No gossip column would make a scandal of this indulgence. He took the kiss from her, deepening it, his hand in the pretty twist of hair at the nape of her neck, guiding her mouth against his. Had any kiss ever been this sweet? Maybe aphrodisiacs *were* purely mental exercises. They'd not made love on the beach at Oare today, although their kisses had left him primed.

He was still primed. His senses had been primed all night from the moment he'd picked her up in the coach, seeing her in the dark blue gown with its subtle indigo pattern of palm fronds and the vee of her bodice showing off the firm curve of her breasts, the simple gold locket at her neck begging a man to kiss that long, slim, elegant column and the pulse at its base. He knew how that pulse could race. He placed his hand over it. It was racing now. For him. Because of him.

'Shall we go outside, Artemisia?'

'Yes,' she breathed against him.

He led her out into the darkness, her hand gripping his tightly as they sought privacy. He steered them around a corner of the building and pulled her against him with a hard kiss, his hands on her buttocks, pressing her close as he lifted her. She moaned into his mouth, her legs wrapping about him, her skirts falling back in the effort to reveal long, slim thighs. He held her tight, balancing her against the wall with one hand as he opened his trousers with the other. 'I did not think it was possible to be this hard,' he breathed the erotic compliment against her neck.

'Nor I. That's very impressive, Mr Rutherford,' she whispered with a throaty chuckle, moving against the long shaft of him with her hips, the scent of her own arousal unmistakable between them. 'Are you going to do anything with that?' Her eyes glittered in the dark, both of them too far gone with the need for immediate gratification to care for much foreplay.

He thrust into her then, hard and sure, setting the pace for a fierce, fast joining that would be intense and explosive when climax came. It would come quickly, already he could feel his own body tightening, gathering in response to hers. Artemisia's breaths came in pants, his own breathing nothing more than ragged inhalations. They were rough with one another, her teeth at his neck, his thrusts taking her hard against the brick of the wall. They would be marked by this, but they couldn't stop. He felt her nails dig through the fabric of his coat in an effort to rake him.

She let out a harsh breath, devouring his mouth with hers. 'I want you naked.'

He could not give her that tonight, not here with the public only feet away beyond that corner. Some day soon, he vowed in the passion-riddled corners of his mind, they would make love in a real bed. But right now, release would have to be enough. He took her once, twice more before release swamped them, her cries muffled against his shoulder, his own groaned against her neck.

Damn it all, though, he couldn't see her eyes. Were they open? He wanted them to be open, he wanted to know her pleasure was complete as it pulsed over them in hot, reckless waves that shook them both. He felt it in the tremble of her legs about him, heard it in the shakiness of her breath. Physics and the wall kept them both upright in pleasure's immediate aftermath. Had lovemaking ever felt like this? Had it ever left him so completely drained and yet so completely fulfilled even after a heady interlude that had begun merely as a flirtation over oyster shells? He'd not expected this.

'You might be the death of me, Artemisia,' he said, his voice still shaky as he laughed. He lowered her down, disengaging her legs gently from his hips. 'Are you all right?' They'd become rough at the end. A part of him that was imbued with a gentleman's ethics felt he should apologise for it—the primal part of him disagreed.

'I'm fine.' Artemisia smiled, affirmation that the roughness had been part of the intoxication. He passed her a handkerchief and turned his back, giving her a moment to put herself together. For him, it was his thoughts that needed putting together. What did this fire between them mean? He knew what she would say, that it meant nothing, but he could not believe that. He could not let that answer stand. It was a convenient means of ignoring that something did indeed lay between them.

'Would you like to walk a bit?' He wasn't ready to surrender their intimacy to a crowd. He'd rather stay in the darkness with her a little longer.

'Yes, I can't imagine going back inside and dancing now.' Artemisia slipped her arm through his.

'Me neither.' They walked in silence, enjoying the quiet lap of water in the distance against the shore. There was peace between them now that the fires of passion had been sated. Darius was loath to break it, but his code as a gentleman demanded it. They'd made love twice and there'd been the implication that there would be another time. In a bed, preferably, but beds came with implications of their own such as premeditation and permanence. He was starting to think Artemisia preferred wilder, more spontaneous encounters. Perhaps she felt she didn't have to be accountable for them.

They stopped at the edge of a sea wall, the oyster fishery behind them, the sounds of the party filtering through the darkness. He had to ask the question and there was no time like the present before things went further, before they *could* go further. Patterns without parameters were dangerous creatures, creating assumptions where none might exist. 'What are we doing, Artemisia?'

'Enjoying one another's company through a bleak winter.' Her answer was straightforward. She knew precisely what he was asking. He appreciated she'd not played coy with a flippant answer.

His heart sank a bit at the response. It was a plausible answer. This they could do. Such an answer fitted their circumstances. It was what they could reasonably give each other. He should not expect more. While he found the answer satisfactory, it was not satisfying. 'We are to be neutral lovers, then, and go our own way at the month's end?' A month with Artemisia, a month of being alive to weigh against all the years of responsibility and duty yet to come. What of her? What did this mean to her?

She gave him a sideways glance full of challenge

as she pushed an errant strand of hair out of her face, blown there by the breeze off the water. 'What else is there, Darius?'

Chapter Fifteen

Artemisia did not let her gaze waver. She wanted there to be no mistake. He needed to understand explicitly that she *was* daring him: daring him to argue the answer with her or to recognise the limitations of his fantasy. Perhaps he would respect the answer if he made it himself instead of listening to her protest. Her answer would be honest, blunt and likely unappreciated. But tonight, he didn't want to settle for the truth behind her honesty. It was there in the set of his jaw, in the tenseness that rippled across his shoulders. He wanted none of her realism.

He would argue against her truths because he wouldn't like them, and she would argue against his, because his were impossible.

What else is there?

It would be better if he'd answer her question. Through his own words, he would be forced to admit the limitations of the unreality he sought, limitations which did not end with his position as an art critic but extended to his family, his title, everything he'd worked for and sacrificed for. One mistake with her would undo all of that, just as one mistake with him would undo her. They would ruin each other if they allowed this interlude to get out of control, if they allowed themselves to think it could be more.

He wrapped his arms about her and drew her to him, her back against the warmth of his chest. 'There is exploration. I have no idea what we can be yet. I'd like to find out. I don't want to stop at neutrality and a date on the calendar unless *I* decide to.' His mouth was low at her ear. 'If we are a one-month wonder, so be it. But what if we are more?' he whispered his temptation. 'Wouldn't it be a shame to throw that away? To never know?' He kissed the back of her neck, sending a warm, slow shiver down her spine, a reminder that she could have a month of such kisses.

She turned in his arms, her voice infused with disbelief. 'It can't be more. What is the use of pretending it could be? What is the use of exploring a useless possibility? This can only be about lovemaking, Darius. It can't be about the Academy.' She cocked her head, seeing his disagreement in his eyes. 'Darius, how do *you* think this ends?'

'I'm working on that,' He smiled, undaunted by her reaction. Then he sobered. 'Unless this is your way of signalling your interest is not as shared as I thought it was?'

'It's not my interest that isn't shared. It's the optimism.' She twined her arms about his neck. 'Darius, there'd be more than one scandal if we associated with one another in London. Your family...'

'My family, and London are miles and miles away.'

He kissed her, a slow, lingering kiss. 'I won't have them intruding on tonight or any other night for the duration of the month. Can we make a pact, Artemisia? Will you give me—give us—the month?'

A month, a year, a lifetime.

His beautiful dark eyes made her reckless. She would give him anything right now with those eyes looking down at her, his arms wrapped about her as if the very strength of him would be enough to keep the world at bay. What might she discover about him in the span of a month? What other secrets might be unearthed? Exploration indeed. But that went both ways, didn't it?

A burst of caution pushed its way forward. To explore him, to explore *them*, she would have to consent to being explored, exposed, too, and for what purpose? Even if she was interested in a 'them', a future was irrelevant. She had to protect herself from hurt. What if her interest did come with a deeper emotion attached to it? There would be heartbreak to navigate. There was more than one reason to be careful here, yet she wanted to throw caution to the wind, let it be carried away on the tide.

'I swear to you, I won't hurt you, Artemisia.' Did he know what he was promising? There were so many ways to hurt a person, before, during, after an affair. The opportunity never really went away. She shouldn't agree to it, but what she ought to do held little sway at the moment. She would be smarter this time, she knew how to protect herself. Perhaps she could afford the luxury of enjoying this man.

'All right then, you have a month.' This was what happened when one agreed to a dinner. It was never just dinner. Then she added, before he could relax in his victory, 'But I am warning you, Darius. I have been down this road before.' Even if he didn't agree, she would hold herself to her own parameters. This would only be about the physical.

'Duly noted.' Darius's mouth quirked in a wry smile as he bent to seal the agreement with a kiss. 'This time, it will be different, vastly different, Artemisia. You'll see.'

That's what they all said, Artemisia refrained from pointing out. In the days that followed, though, she would have been proven wrong. Being with Darius *was* different, noticeably so, in good ways and in bad. He did not seek to dominate her time. He did not assume once they'd committed to a relationship of sorts that he would become her top priority. Nothing changed in that regard.

There were delicious afternoons of lovemaking on the beach, but he never sought to assume such idylls would take place in her home. They would talk, they would sketch. They would share their work. He was open to suggestions about improving his work and they were open with each other about their thoughts and opinions, free to disagree with one another.

Arguing the merits of art was a pleasant way to spend an afternoon between bouts of lovemaking with a well-educated man. She learned he liked the work of the Renaissance painters, while she preferred Vermeer and Brueghel, who had made a point of breaking with the Italian school.

She learned little things about him, too. His favourite colour was green, his favourite food was chocolate cake. He had an enormous sweet tooth. And he was considerate. It was in every gesture he made, large or small, not only to her but to those around him: Mrs Harris, Addy. It was often subtly done. No one would ever mistake him for a pushover.

But for all the perceived openness and increasing closeness, there was the constant nagging reminder that this was a façade, that this gradual accumulation of facts didn't matter. They could change nothing. At the end of the month, all of this would be over, no matter how they felt about one another. But discussion of that inevitability was a taboo subject. Neither did they discuss whatever Darius's plan was that he'd alluded to regarding the Academy. She didn't necessarily want to know. No doubt his agile mind was working on some sort of solution to the twin dilemmas facing them. It would be her job to shoot it down, whatever it was. Soon.

February sped on. She could see the time passing in the accumulation of finished paintings lining the walls of her studio, a beautiful palette of protest and productivity. She saw it in the dwindling pile of sketches she'd so aggressively accumulated in December and January. There were just two left to put to canvas: the pintail duck and one other that was just for her. It would be her own farewell of sorts to this unlooked-for idyll in Seasalter.

Mrs Harris had politely enquired earlier in the day about arrangements for the small staff they'd acquired. When should they expect to close up the house? It had forced Artemisia to give words to those details she tried hard to ignore. Two weeks, she'd told the housekeeper just this morning. Artemisia looked over the easel, studying Darius in his usual place on the worn couch, his gaze intent on something beyond the window, a squirrel perhaps. *Two weeks and one day,* she silently amended.

It was a leap year. There were twenty-nine days in February and she would take them all, to her great surprise. Darius Rutherford had arrived as the enemy. He was not leaving as one, but *he* was leaving and *she* was leaving. Their real lives awaited. This life, this fiction, by necessity had to be left behind.

Artemisia began cleaning her brushes, her work finished for the day. It had become their signal that their day could move into something less formal. She pictured in her mind Darius rising from the couch, crossing the room to her, in three, two…there it was, his kiss at her neck, his arms wrapping around her as she rinsed the brushes. 'This is the best part of the day,' she murmured. It was also the most dangerous. She could lose herself in him and what he offered. She could forget there was a battle she needed to fight in the world beyond Seasalter, that her career hung in the balance of what happened out there.

'I think so, too.' Darius nuzzled her neck. Perhaps he forgot about those things, too. 'Dinner tonight at the Crown? I heard rumours they'd got a new shipment of wine.' He chuckled. 'I've become quite adept at determining which nights the smugglers' boats are in. I try to make myself scarce.'

'If you stay long enough, they might ask you to join

them.' Artemisia laughed and unbuttoned her smock. 'Mrs Harris made you a chocolate cake. Maybe I will engage in some smuggling of my own and bring it with us. We can have it for dessert.'

'Or perhaps for dinner.' He nibbled suggestively at her ear. 'Why not eat dessert first?' Darius whispered. Why not? Life was too short, time was too precious to waste it on proprieties for their own sake.

She turned in his arms and claimed a kiss. 'I'll get the cake.'

'Maybe you *are* cake.' Darius's eyes glinted dangerously dark, desire evident in his gaze. 'I think you and I understand dessert differently,' he drawled. He claimed a kiss this time, one she felt to the depth of her toes. 'Tonight, I will make love to you in a real bed.' Her breath caught and her mouth went dry at the words. 'No more sand, Artemisia, no more wind, no more fumbling with copious amounts of clothing, no more rushing. Just us, tonight, skin-to-skin. You can weigh that against eating dinner in a more linear fashion,' he teased.

The images his words invoked were no joking matter. They lingered through the walk on the beach, through the beef stew and fresh bread dinner at the Crown, the bottle of rich red wine that accompanied it, and through the moist slices of cake purloined from Mrs Harris's kitchen. It was a rather intoxicating and thorough bout of foreplay, leading her for hours. For his part, despite his counsel to eat dessert first, Darius was in no hurry, which was proving maddeningly irritating as her own desire acquired a certain fevered pitch to it.

'More cake?' Darius offered as she took her last bite,

well aware that he was only halfway through his. On purpose? she wondered. 'More wine?'

'No, I'm quite full.' Her suspicions were growing. There was a glint of laughter lurking in Darius's eyes and it occurred to her he'd dragged this dinner out deliberately. Artemisia set aside her napkin and gathered her willpower in the hopes he wouldn't see the lie. 'I am in no hurry. Take your time, enjoy your cake.' There. That should take some starch out of him. 'We have all night.'

And she didn't want to waste a moment of it.

His eyes held hers with great solemnity. 'Yes, we do.' He set aside his cake fork and reached out a hand, raising her from the table. 'Allow me to do the honours.' His voice was a seductive husk that heated her blood even as his touch stoked it to a slow, searing roil. His fingers were at the buttons of her blouse, the undoing of each one a seduction of its own, revealing her bit by bit as the fabric fell away. He would burn her alive at this rate.

His hands skimmed the curve of her breast rising above her chemise. 'Silk—somehow I knew you'd wear silk underthings,' he murmured against her skin, his breath warm as his hands worked the fastenings of her skirt free. She barely felt it slide down her legs. She was more interested in his mouth, his kisses, in the warmth of his hands at her hips as they took the hem of her chemise and pulled it over her head, rendering her bare to his gaze, except for her stockings. She was acutely aware of them against the stark relief of her nudity.

'Leave them for now. I'll take care of them,' Darius instructed in a low growl. 'Sit for me. Here, at the edge of the bed.'

She trembled as she sat, a hot knowing look passing between them. 'Like this?' she breathed, hitching her legs slightly apart.

'Yes, just like that.' There was a hoarseness to his husk now. He was as aroused as she. 'I want to worship all of you.' And worship he did. Her mouth, her throat, her breasts, her belly, the curls between her thighs. Artemisia lay back on the bed and gave herself over to his mouth, his tongue on her skin, her body remembering. Oh, what divine loveliness. She knew this road, knew the pleasure he could bring. But this lingering was so much better than the previous pleasures.

He blew against her curls and a little moan of contentment escaped her. He would put his tongue to her seam and she would writhe... *No*. She gave a mewl of disappointment and struggled up on her elbows. 'Darius', his name a plea.

He grinned from the province of her thighs. 'Not yet. Stockings first as I promised. It's less fun when you anticipate my every move. A good lover isn't entirely predictable.'

Nor would she have predicted the sheer sensuality of having her stockings removed: the slow roll of silk down her legs by warm, confident hands, a trail of kisses left at the sensitive parts of her skin—inner thighs, the backs of her knees, the inside of her ankle— and back up again. This time there was no mistaking how it would end and she was twice as ready for him. She fell back on the bed, wet and wanting, giving herself over entirely to his mouth until pleasure over-whelmed her.

His hands gripped her hips, his head resting on her mons as it took her. Had she ever felt so completely wor-shipped? He'd seduced her with a reverence unparal-leled and her body had gloried in it, held nothing back in return when the pleasure had come. There'd been pleasure in it for him as well. She felt it in the heave of his back where her hand rested.

As the pleasure calmed, he came along beside her, his dark head propped on a hand, his eyes hot. 'I want you to be like that when I come inside you. I want you to lose yourself, to give over entirely.' He kissed her beneath the ear. 'I want to see you come apart. I want to know, tonight, that we are together when the plea-sure takes us.'

What did a woman say to that? To a lover who was adamantly focused on her needs, her pleasure before all else? Before his own? The truth would disappoint him. 'Darius…' She smoothed back his errant swoop of dark hair. 'I don't know if I can.'

'Yet you can for lesser pleasures,' he reminded her, not scolding her.

'That's different.' She played with his cravat, unty-ing the knot and slipping out the tiepin. 'You are in-credibly overdressed for the occasion, Mr Rutherford.' She gave him a slow smile. It seemed an age since she'd called him Mr Rutherford in truth. 'Allow me to do the honours.'

'I've a better idea.' Darius rose from the bed and beyond her into the pool of light cast by the lamp. 'Watch me.'

Chapter Sixteen

Oh, that was not fair. He was pulling out all the stops tonight. She leaned back against the pillows and watched, aware that his eyes never left hers, that the renewal of her just-sated arousal had as much to do with his gaze as it did with the voyeuristic delight of watching him disrobe, something that was orchestrated just for her. It occurred to her that a wedding night must be very much like this—an attentive groom, worshipping his bride, an ardent lover offering his body on pleasure's altar.

'Are you watching, Artemisia?' Darius's voice was a low, commanding drawl. He unfastened the cufflinks of his shirt and set them aside, a small, intimate gesture that was as sexy in its minutiae as the grander effort of slipping off his waistcoat and his shirt, leaving his chest on full display for her. She let her eyes linger over every muscled plane of him, seeing him this time as not as an objective artist, or from the viewpoint of a woman enraged, but as a woman who wanted him, who hungered for him.

'Yes, I am watching, I can hardly look away.' She gave a soft, throaty laugh. 'You are exquisite, Darius.' She could spend the night looking at every piece of him: the musculature of his shoulders and collarbones, the sculpted vee of him at the hips and pelvis disappearing beneath his waistband.

His hands rested at the waistband of those trousers, guardians of the last bastion of decency. 'Take them off, Darius,' she whispered, watching a slow smile take his face.

'As you command, my lady.' Darius let the trousers slide past lean hips and long thighs, drawing her eyes down his legs, over the curve of buttock and back. She needn't rush the perusal. This was hardly a repeat of seeing him naked and surprised from his bath. There was time. This was a man uncloaking for his lover, his power on full display, with a blatancy one could not fully appreciate making love clothed on a beach. This was raw masculine beauty revealed for her.

'Does this meet with your approval?' He was playing the servant warrior with her now, the knight at his lady's behest, ready to do as she bid, and her body was primed with desire. She could feel heat stirring between her legs, wetness gathering at her core. He might be asking the questions, but he was not waiting for her to give orders. Good. She was tired of giving orders, tired of being strong. Tonight, she wanted to be dominated, wanted someone else to take the lead.

Darius came to the bed and moved over her, his arms bracketing her head as they took his weight. Like this, pressed length to naked length, she was potently aware of the size of him, the power of him, all of him, not just the hard phallus jutting against her thigh, and she revelled in his strength. This was a man who knew how to take care of himself and, in the knowing, also knew how to take care of others.

He moved inside her, a reminder that this man wanted her, physically, emotionally. Her mewls and moans were not enough for him. He wanted her body, her mind, her soul. Her body she gave willingly. It was merely a vessel. The rest, less so. Yet she felt their tethers start to break free of their moorings as her hips lifted to him. Their bodies took up the rhythm of pleasure together; he set the pace, slow at first, a reminder that they needn't rush this. For the moment, they were in control. Correction. *He* was in control.

She gave a piquant shudder. He slid deep inside her and retreated like a lingering tide on the shores of her soul. She could look up into his face, his wide-open eyes, and see his naked pleasure on display, a reminder he was holding nothing back and a reminder that he was asking the same from her. Darius was leading by tempting, delicious example and she yearned to follow.

She let out a gasp as he came up hard against her womb and the pace changed to something fiercer, deeper, sharper. It was driving them now, their control slipping. She clung to Darius, legs and arms wrapped tight around him, holding him to her, the very posture of her body urging him onwards to the awaiting brink, every nerve of her, every muscle, wanting to crash with him.

There will be a cost, came a warning murmur.

She could not give him everything. What would be

left? What happened to her pride, her control, if she let it go? What happened when he broke her heart?

Her body didn't care. Her breath came fast, roused beyond logic. The decision was made. Just once, just tonight, she would fly with him and sort out the aftermath later.

Darius came into her hard, his body gathered and tight with desire, his eyes black flames as she met his gaze, let him see the desire matched in her own. 'Yes, Artemisia, yes, God, yes, let go.' The words were an incoherent litany of encouragement as she arched into Darius and leapt off pleasure's cliff with him, for him.

She had come for him and the knowledge of it, there at the last, had added a powerful intensity to his release. The very feel of Artemisia clenching, hot and wet about him, just before he withdrew to shudder his own completion, had undone him, drained him to the point of exhaustion. Darius thought he might never move again and that was fine with him. He was where he wanted to be, in Artemisia's arms, gently adrift in ecstasy's sea, pleasure pulsing over him long after the thundering physicality of release had abated.

Time and speech lost all configuration. They laid together, naked and warm and silent, attuned to one another's bodies, their quieting breath, the stilling of thumping hearts. Darius was aware, too, of the return of reason, the organisation of his thoughts, all of which centred around one essential idea: this was serious.

They were two weeks into February, into the exploration he'd persuaded her to undertake, to see what they might be. He did not need another two weeks to know he didn't want this to end. This was not an affair. This was...*for ever*. That was a strong, stunning concept to give space to in his mind. But once there, it was lodged. It would bear pondering, considering.

Artemisia snuggled against him, her hair tickling his chest and his arm clenched about her. He breathed her in, all sweet desire and winter spice. 'Artemisia, was it worth it? Letting go?' It was a lover's question, whispered in the aftermath of intimacy.

She lifted her head a fraction to look him in the eye. 'Yes, absolutely.' Her gaze was soft and frank, but he did not miss the unspoken reservation in her voice.

'But?' he coaxed gently and then sighed as her head settled back against his chest. He didn't need her answer. 'You think you'll regret this.' Despite his assurances, despite all the care he could demonstrably lavish on her, even in bed the doubt lingered between them. He ran his hand down the slim length of her arm in a light caress, his words an invitation to disclosure. 'Tell me, Artemisia? Who hurt you?' The primal man in him would hunt him down and exact retribution. She was too full of life to restrict her passions, yet she felt compelled to do just that.

'No one you know.' She gave a short laugh, as if she'd read his very thoughts. 'It was a long time ago and the fault was my own. But I learned. These things happen, Darius. No one is without scars.' All true, but he wanted to know hers, every one of them.

'Tell me about it.' She was trying to brush it aside. He would not allow it. They'd come so far tonight, he didn't want to stop here. 'Don't leave me out, Artemisia.' He was tempted to remind her he hadn't left her out. He'd shared his darkest regrets, his childhood. But he didn't want her disclosure because she felt an obligation. He wanted it because she trusted him with it. She sighed and settled. Darius waited and was rewarded.

'I was eighteen. My father had a protégé, Hunter McCullough, an Irish painter with immense potential. He spent a lot of time at the house and with me. We trained together and he flattered me, brought me little gifts. It was exciting to be the recipient of his attentions, although I knew he was a womaniser. The other artists at my father's studio talked. He told me I was his North Star, his one constant. Part of me wanted to believe him but part of me was cautious as well. My father was famous. People vied for his favour. My father had warned us to be wary of being used as means of getting to him.' Darius felt her shrug against him. Shrugging off memories or trying to evince a nonchalant insouciance?

'I was young and wild, burning with curiosity. It's hard not to be when there's constant talk in the workshop about the goings-on between men and women, and teasing, and models in various stages of undress. Hunter had stolen a few kisses from me on various occasions. I was more than willing to accommodate him on those grounds. What could a few kisses hurt? In truth, I enjoyed them. I had not intended anything more than kisses. I didn't understand how a man might misconstrue them as an invitation to more. My knowledge was theoretical, not practical at the time.' Another shrug. This time Darius felt himself brace. The story was changing tone, becoming darker.

Remembrances of other words she'd used once with

him came to mind. *Violated...against her will...unwilling...without permission.*

'One night, I was painting late. Everyone else had gone to an exhibition. He showed up at the studio, drunk and manic. His moods were mercurial. He was short on funds, *again*. A critic had slighted his latest painting. The world was against him, he said, but not me. He could always count on me, his one constant. Even drunk, he was an expert flatterer. It started as kisses, then we were on the posing couch and he was grabbing at my skirts.

'I told him no, I tried to push him off, but he didn't listen. He kept saying, what did it matter, we would marry and be the greatest artistic couple in London, we'd show them—them being the critics and creditors that dogged him—what he was really made of, greatness waiting to happen. No one would dare say anything against the son-in-law of Sir Lesley Stansfield.' She paused and drew a ragged breath. 'Then he took me...until he collapsed unconscious on me.'

Anger surged through Darius, anger at Hunter Mc-Cullough, anger at his sex. 'The bastard. That's rape.'

'That's what I said. He said I enjoyed it, that I'd wanted it, that I'd led him on with kisses, that I'd asked too late for him to stop. It wasn't fair. I even thought for a while he might be right. There was no way to put it to the test. I wasn't going to publicly accuse him. Women don't get to decide those things.'

'Did you tell your father?' Darius asked. He would call out any man who ever treated a daughter of his that way. He couldn't imagine any father doing less.

'Yes, and I told him not to believe a word of romance

from McCullough when he came begging for my hand. My father believed me and sent McCullough packing back to Ireland. Threatened to ruin him if he breathed a word against us. Since then, I've been more careful with men, seeing them as they are.' She sighed against him. 'Don't be mad, Darius. You can do nothing about it. It was a long time ago,' she repeated. 'I've made sure since then that my body is mine to give, not for anyone else to take.'

'I can be appalled, though,' Darius growled.

'Not tonight,' she whispered against his mouth. She swung over him, straddling him. 'I seem to recall you like this.'

He did like it. He liked it best when her back arched and her breasts thrust forward in the cups of her hands as she rode him, her hair falling about her as she claimed her release in the night not once more, but twice before they fell into pleasure's deep sleep.

They slept late, well past breakfast. They might have even slept later if there hadn't been an insistent knock at the door. It was the sound of raised voices, that of his beleaguered servant and the unmistakable clipped tones of an aristocrat, that roused Darius. He sat up, bleary eyed, and pushed a hand through his hair, his thoughts slow to assemble as Artemisia stirred beside him with a drowsy murmur. 'What's going on?'

Before Darius could climb out of bed, the door opened and his servant slipped inside, shutting the door firmly behind him and bolting it. 'Good morning, milord, Miss Stansfield, my pardon.' He was suitably flushed and cognisant of the awkward situation.

'What is it?' Darius was gruff. His servants knew better than to bother him when he was abed unless it was an emergency. A bolt of worry shot through him—was it an emergency? While he'd been indulging himself in Seasalter had something happened? 'It's not my father? My mother?'

'No, my apologies,' his servant stammered and then regained a sense of decorum. 'It's nothing of the sort. Sir Aldred Gray has arrived from the Academy and is demanding an audience.'

Artemisia stiffened beside him. He put a hand on her arm in reassurance. 'I will handle this. Stay in the room. Gray doesn't need to know you're here.' To the servant he offered instruction, his brain functioning at full speed now. 'Take Gray downstairs, see that he's fed. I'll meet with him once I'm dressed for the day.' Three-quarters of an hour should be plenty of time to cool the gentleman's heels and remind him who he was dealing with.

The servant left and Darius shared a glance with Artemisia. 'Not exactly the way I was planning on waking up this morning.'

'No, certainly not,' she said shortly, but her eyes said something more. They needn't worry about what happened when they went to London. London had come to them. But procrastination had cost them. They weren't ready.

Chapter Seventeen

Darius was ready to face the honourable Sir Aldred Gray an hour later. The honourable part was up for debate. The man had no reason to be here unless he doubted Darius was doing his job, a thought that rankled. Or, if he was curious as to what Darius was getting up to. Darius remembered with acute clarity that it had been Aldred who suggested he seduce Artemisia. That rankled even more, considering what had transpired these last two weeks with Artemisia. He was too aware that an outsider would see it as a lurid affair when in reality it was so much more and the decision had not been taken lightly.

'Gray, I am surprised to see you.' Darius entered the Crown's private parlour on the stroke of eleven and helped himself to hot coffee from the carafe on the sideboard, a convenient excuse for not offering his hand to shake. The shaking of hands implied a bonhomie Darius currently did not feel. Intruders weren't entitled to manners. 'My report is not due to the Academy for another two weeks.'

'I thought I'd come and have a look at your progress first-hand,' Gray said amiably. 'I admit to some surprise of my own when you decided to stay the entire six weeks.' He gave a knowing chuckle. 'Perhaps Seasalter has hidden charms?'

'I did not wish to make a hasty generalisation one way or the other on Miss Stansfield's work,' Darius replied evenly. 'As you pointed out in your letter, I have my reputation to consider. Whatever my opinion, I must be able to back it.' Darius took a chair. 'What can I do for you so that you may not be inconvenienced by an overlong stay?'

'Ho, ho, you don't want to share the bounties of Seasalter. I did wonder what juicy bit you had upstairs with you this morning.' Gray chuckled.

Darius wanted this man back on the road as soon as possible before he could pick up a whiff of gossip about himself and Artemisia, or before Artemisia felt like giving Gray a piece of her mind. Despite the promises he'd extracted from her, Darius half expected her to come charging down the stairs demanding an explanation. It would be the worst thing she could do and it would confirm the lascivious thoughts running through Gray's head.

'I was hoping to get a confirmation that Miss Stansfield's work was found wanting. I believe that was the job, wasn't it?' Gray waved his hand airily. 'It doesn't matter if the report isn't done. Just something to take back to the assembly so we can plan our strategy accordingly. It all must be handled delicately and that takes time.'

Darius crossed a leg over one knee. 'I promised the

assembly objectivity. That's what I'll give them. The board should prepare themselves for an excellent report. Her work on her latest collection is outstanding. It has quite impressed me.'

Gray shifted in his seat, growing uncomfortable. 'You know that is not what we want to hear.'

'Is the Academy not interested in the truth?' Darius pressed.

'I hardly think truth is the opinion of one man.' Gray levelled a strong gaze at him. 'I believe the letter makes that clear.'

'You mean the blackmail threat,' Darius said bluntly. 'If I don't do as the Academy wishes, it will seek to ruin me. Yes, the letter made that very clear, right at the bottom in closing. A less discerning mind might have missed it. This isn't about the quality of her work, but the quality of her gender.' That he so calmly voiced the accusation out loud was a sign of how much the last months had changed him. That he inwardly believed it was another.

'That can be no surprise. You're a smart man and you were there for our discussion.'

'But I didn't agree to it. I promised you objectivity. The Academy is a group of men who are intimidated by a woman who can out-paint them.' This was about repression wielded as a tool of the cowardly. But today was the first time he realised how intensely he wanted no part of it, could have no part of it, and still hold himself accountable to his code of honour. The world started to tilt on its axis once more. It was beginning to dawn on him in full what such a fight would entail.

Gray leaned back in his chair and studied him with

a sharp eye. 'I see she has bewitched you. I am sure
you are not the first man to fall for her bold charms.
I feared this might happen. Be careful that you've not
been impressed with her art as much as you've been
impressed with *her.*' It was not unlike the argument of
old, the argument of the unenlightened that suggested
there could be no reliable witnesses to witchcraft since
the only witnesses were the witch herself and the one
bewitched. How convenient. How unfair. How naive
that he'd once thought the modern world had come further than that.

Darius tensed, his thoughts and emotions raw with
new discovery and passion. 'You should be careful that
I do not call you out for slander, Gray. That is a woman's
reputation as well as my own that you are questioning.'

Gray shrugged. 'Take my advice, St Helier, look to
your own reputation first. It's worth protecting. Hers
is not.' He stood and looked about, waiting for an invitation, oblivious to the insult he'd dealt. 'Perhaps we
might pay her a visit? I wouldn't want to go without
seeing her. I'll stay the night here. Be a good chap and
arrange a dinner tonight.'

Darius rose. 'I wish I could, but she's gone on a
sketching tour. Not sure when she'll be back. I'll be
using the time to write my report. I'm not even sure
I'll see her before returning to London.' He was not
in the habit of lying and doing so now was risky. He
hoped Artemisia didn't prove him false with a sudden
appearance.

'Perhaps a look at her work, then?' Gray persisted.

'I could not arrange that.' Darius was quick to quash
the idea. It was a violation of Artemisia's privacy, she

would never consent to showing her work before it was ready. More than that, it was a trap for him. It assumed he had a certain intimate access to Artemisia, that he was no longer at best a neutral annoyance to her or at worst, an enemy. 'It's good to see a familiar face, but I fear you've made the trip for nothing.' A trip he must have started well before dawn to have made Seasalter before noon. Had Gray deliberately wanted to catch him abed?

Gray gave him a critical appraisal. 'Not nothing. I hope you know what you're doing, St Helier. If you choose to wage war on the Academy, you will lose.'

'I hardly think one person's opinion is a war.' Darius held the parlour door open. 'Funny you think so.' Maybe the Academy was more afraid than they let on. 'Best not to decide anything until the report is turned in, though,' he cautioned. 'I wouldn't like to think of you bringing back information to London only to have my report contradict it.' Sowing uncertainty would buy him time. The last thing he wanted was gossipy Aldred Gray spouting his speculations to anyone who would listen. But Gray had given him an idea.

Darius ushered Gray out to the man's carriage and saw him inside before it registered with Gray that he'd driven all this way for a half-hour meeting and was now on his way home. After seeing Gray off, Darius returned to the private parlour to unravel the events of the morning. If the assembly was expecting a war, he'd give them one. If the Academy saw his report as a cannon primed to blow a hole through their fortress, perhaps he should use it as such.

Darius sipped his coffee, ideas forming. He would

write to Basil Vellanoweth, the Duke of Boscastle, and his son, Inigo. Both were patrons of the arts. Inigo was a master at arranging 'things', whatever a fellow might need. He'd write to Lady Basingstoke as well, see if she might lend her person when she came to town for the Season. He would have to catch her between races. She would split her time between Newmarket and Ascot. Of course, his efforts would mean naught without Artemisia's cooperation.

He should speak to her immediately. His plans and her notorious impatience demanded it. She would be pacing upstairs. He could not bring himself to go up yet. He lingered over another cup of coffee, savouring the fire in the hearth, the patter of rain on the windows. The winter greyness of Seasalter seemed nostalgic in the wake of Gray's visit. He was going to miss this battered inn with its excellent wine that far outstripped the mediocre food and marshy beaches.

Darius blew out a breath, finally letting his mind acknowledge what Gray's visit had also meant. He didn't have two weeks left with Artemisia, not the way he'd planned. He needed to be back in London as soon as possible. The idyll in Seasalter was over. He pushed out of his chair and headed upstairs. He could not stop this from ending. All he could control was *how* it ended. His hand lingered on the door handle. Once he stepped inside the room everything would change. He only hoped Artemisia would see reason.

Artemisia stepped back from the window the moment the door handle rattled. Darius was back. Finally. She'd seen Gray drive away, seen Darius return inside.

She'd waited. And waited. She crossed her arms and faced the door. 'About time. I thought you might have left and gone with him.' It might have been better if he had, at least then things would have ended in a way she understood. Darius would have saved himself. She expected that. It was what men did.

Darius shut the door behind him. 'I needed time to think.' The quietness of his tone was telling. The more serious he was, the quieter he got. This must be serious indeed. Even braced for it, even knowing it had to be this way, his next words were still a blow. 'I need to leave for London as soon as possible.'

He was going to leave. She put on a brave face, trying to ignore the hurt that rocketed her through her and the surprise. Why surprise? This should *not* surprise her. She'd known from the start that he would go. She *wanted* him to go. She'd practically told him as much when he'd shared the letter. Darius couldn't ignore the threat the Academy had put to him for ever, although they'd done a fairly good imitation of it these past weeks. Seeing Aldred Gray in the flesh had no doubt made that threat very real.

She glanced at the bed, still rumpled from last night. It had been nice while it lasted. She only regretted the final two weeks had been stolen from them. 'So this is how it ends. Suddenly, swiftly.' This was like an executioner's blade, certain, sure, final and just as inevitable. They'd known from the start, from that night at Gann's party, this was only temporary. It had given them permission to set aside certain decisions and positions. Now those burdens and realities had to be resumed.

'Will you go today?' she asked with a calmness that

belied her inner turmoil. She was hating herself. She'd
made promises to herself she would not be hurt when
this happened, but somewhere, somehow, those promises had become broken things.

'No, not for a couple of days. We need to make plans.
I have an idea, but I need your consent.' He paused, his
gaze resting on her face, confused and then clearing.
Suddenly he was in motion, crossing the room, round-
ing the bed, taking her hands. 'Artemisia, this is not
the end of *us*. Did you think I was leaving *you*? You
did, didn't you?' He led her to the edge of the bed and
made her sit while he dragged over the room's single
chair. He sat before her, her hands in his. 'The Academy has tried to wrong us both. I say we fight back
and declare war.'

Artemisia gave him an incredulous stare, emotions
rioting. This wasn't just about desire any more. The
one rule that had given her licence for tasting forbidden fruit dangled before her, daring her to break it. If
she took his offer to join forces, that's what she'd be
doing. They would be twined together in more significant ways. The old thought returned: they would ruin
one another unless she put a stop to this now. 'We can't
win. The two of us against the Academy and years of
tradition? Darius, we'd be made a laughing stock.'

She knew what happened to rule-breakers. They
were labelled as eccentric, their credibility questioned
at every turn because they didn't follow the crowd, allowed to fade into the shadows if they were lucky. Not
everyone was that lucky.

He sat forward on the edge of the chair. 'It wouldn't
just be the two of us, Artemisia. I have friends who

would help, friends that others would follow. I will engage their services, and you should write to your friends. Lady Basingstoke, for instance.'

'What could she do? She's a horse enthusiast, not an art patron,' Artemisia argued. Her list of useful contacts would disappoint Darius if he meant to rally the troops.

'She's the subject of your prize-winning portrait. She could come to the exhibition. If she came, perhaps she could talk her in-laws and her rather large family into lending their consequence.'

'What exhibition?' Darius's enthusiasm was contagious. She found herself getting caught up in the theoretical possibilities he proposed.

'Your exhibition. The Academy won't have you— fine. We'll show them we don't need them. We'll stage your work at a smaller but elegant venue on the Strand. We'll open a few days before the Academy's spring art show, give people time to spread word of mouth about it and, with luck, we'll upstage the Academy.' Darius grinned. 'They're afraid of us, Artemisia. I saw it in Gray's face today. Threats are all they have. So, we call their bluff.'

Artemisia disengaged her hands and rose from the bed to pace. She needed space in which to digest this fantastical scheme. He was talking sheer craziness. 'What if we lose? You're asking a lot of people to put themselves out for us.'

'Then we lose. We were going to lose already by doing nothing,' Darius reasoned. 'But we won't lose, Artemisia. My friends are powerful and your art is good.' He paused. 'The reason you are being censored, denied a voice, is not just.'

His praise brought a soft smile to her face, and her heart warmed despite the objections of her mind. Even in the face of adversity, Darius believed in the power of right. It was not naivety that drove his belief, but his belief in himself. He could make things right by the sheer dint of his will. 'As lovely as it sounds, Darius, I can't ask you to risk all that for me.'

She ached to go to him, but she didn't dare touch him or she would lose her own sense of rightness. This was her fight, alone. He made it too easy to believe otherwise, a sure sign of the feelings he raised in her. Dangerous feelings. Dangerous beliefs. Such beliefs had betrayed her before. 'I stand by what I told you in the beginning. Turn in your report the way they want it and let me go.' It was best for his reputation and best for her own soundness. This way, she could not be disappointed in him or in herself.

He speared her with a look, his brow furrowed. 'That sounds very much like giving up to me. I didn't think you were a coward.'

'I'm not giving up. A good general knows when to retreat the field, when to save lives instead of pressing on foolishly, and that's what this is, Darius. You are pressing on foolishly for the sake of principle.' She shook her head, stalling further protest. 'I'm not giving up. I'm saving you. You can't save me, but you can save yourself. Even if we were to win, it would only be one battle in a larger war.'

Always. There would never be a clear finish line to cross. That line would keep moving as long as men were afraid. She had to make him understand. 'It wouldn't only be about art, Darius. When they can't win there, they will make it personal.' His friends couldn't protect her from her own follies.

'Heaven forbid they find Hunter McCullough somewhere.' Or her other two lovers. They'd been rather practical men in the end and had left when she didn't give them what they wanted, which hadn't been her. They'd made it clear they'd do anything to advance their careers. Through them, the Academy would paint her with a whore's brush.

'They wouldn't dare breathe such scandal about a viscount's wife.'

The words left her breathless. Stunned. He couldn't mean it. That would engender a whole other fight. They would have a two-fronted battle on their hands. 'Is that a proposal?' If so, it was the icing on a mad cake.

'It's part of the plan. You're right. If we remain as we are now, people will speculate we are lovers and they won't be wrong. But marriage would change that. Marriage would give you the protection of my name, my house,' Darius argued. 'Marriage to me will give you everything you've ever wanted.'

'Not on my terms, but yours. It undermines everything I've worked for. It proves the Academy right, that a woman can achieve nothing on her own. People will say it was marriage that made my acceptance, my art, possible, that I am tolerated because I am Viscountess St Helier.' Could he see that?

Darius nodded in contemplation. 'What if marriage was aside from all that? What if it was simply because I love you and it just happened to further the plan?' He was crushing her resistance, spinning a fairy tale. Fairy tales were fictions. She needed to remember that.

'No one would ever believe it. No one would separate the reasons. If I wasn't a whore, I'd be an opportunist. Aside from that, your family would never countenance the match and society would follow.'

Darius rose and went to her, an edge of anger in his movements. 'I'd prefer you not talk about yourself in those terms,' he growled. 'I mean this proposal, Artemisia. Even if Aldred Gray hadn't shown up today, I would want this. Marry me. I don't want us to end. Whatever happens with your art, I want us.' He was intoxicating and persuasive up close. She could smell the clean linen and spice of him, see the intensity of want in his dark eyes, feel it in his touch. And her body believed it. It was thrumming with the possibility of what he offered.

'Darius, it's impossible. I will ruin you. You would hate me in time, a shorter time than you think. It's not really love that drives you, Darius, it's responsibility, it's your innate desire to take care of those around you.' She tried to reason with him, with herself. It would be too easy to believe him, to take everything he offered, to lay down the fight or at least share it. To accept would be to change herself. She wasn't sure she wanted to change. She wanted to remain intact, yet Darius had already changed her, softened her, made her believe in things long dead, that her independence wasn't contingent on living alone, that she was worth loving just as she was.

'Say yes to the exhibition, Artemisia. Let me prove to you what is possible.' He had her in his arms now, she could feel the strength of him flowing about her, her resistance overcome by his resolve. 'Give me a week's head start, then pack up your paintings and come to London. I will give you a triumphal entry and together we will give the Academy hell.'

Artemisia sighed and looked up into his face. 'I like the sound of that.' Why not? She couldn't fight both Darius and the Academy simultaneously. She would take it one thing at a time, starting with the Academy first.

'You'll see, Artemisia,' Darius whispered at her ear. She could feel him smile against her skin. 'We can change the world.' Maybe they could, she thought as he bore her back to the bed. But it hardly mattered. In the end she would still have to leave him. Best to recognise it now so it would hurt less when it came. Women like her weren't meant for men like him, not in the long run. She had to remind herself that from here on out, everything was a prelude to farewell.

Chapter Eighteen

London welcomed her back with better weather than it had farewelled her with in December. March was still brisk and it would see its share of rain, but for today the sun pierced the grey clouds and the wind had chased away the worst of the soot so that, by the time the coach reached the outskirts of town, there was a facsimile of spring in the air. One could argue London in spring was London at its best.

'Will you be happy to be home?' Artemisia asked Addy, who'd been peering out the coach window for the last twenty minutes in order to catch the first glimpse of town. Addy had not been happy to leave Seasalter. More to the point, Addy had been reluctant to leave Bennett Galbraith and his obsequious attentions.

'I am, I just hope Mr Galbraith doesn't forget about me,' Addy said wistfully.

'How could anyone forget you, Addy dear? If Mr Galbraith does, it is his loss,' Artemisia assured her. Privately, she thought there was every chance he might forget about her sister and she would be satisfied with that. Mr Galbraith was a rake of the first level. Artemisia wanted him as far from her sister as could be managed.

It should have been quite telling to Addy that he made no arrangements to come up to London during the Season, a clear signal that he lacked the funds for town even for a short while and that he hadn't the connections. He was beneath the notice of a daughter of a knight of the realm. But Addy didn't see that. She saw only the excuses he offered: he didn't like town, it was too crowded, too noisy. His supposedly wholesome self preferred the country. He'd even tried to persuade Addy to stay, but Artemisia had quickly squelched that. Addy could not stay alone without her sister for a chaperon. She'd been exceedingly firm on that point.

'Mr Galbraith won't forget you,' she repeated. 'Perhaps he's worried that you will forget him,' she postulated with a teasing smile. 'Maybe right now he's imagining you being swept off your feet by all the London beaux, men who love town as you do,' she reminded Addy. She could not see Addy appreciating life in the country permanently.

'Ha, ha, very funny.' Addy gave a short laugh. 'I'm not the sort to attract bevies of beaux. Men don't fall at my feet like they do yours. I'm too…' She hunted for a word and failed to find it. 'I don't know what, but too something.'

Too young, too beautiful, too innocent, Artemisia supplied silently. Her sister was going to stay that way if she had any say in the matter. 'When the time is right, you'll meet someone,' Artemisia assured her gently.

'The way you met Darius?' Addy enquired slyly. 'You must be excited to see him.'

Excited wasn't quite the word for it. She was somewhere between excited and anxious. It was her turn to have doubts. It had been almost two weeks since Darius had kissed her goodbye at the Crown amid a rumple of bedsheets and lovemaking in the predawn darkness. He was going to pave the way for her and she was to follow. She'd packed up her paintings, closed the farmhouse and done just that.

Had things gone as he'd planned? Had he succeeded? Or had he met with obstacles? Had he had time to think about the reality of their situation? If so, had he realised how much he risked and how little she was worth it? Had he decided to distance himself from her? She'd told him once she wouldn't blame him if that was his choice, that she understood. In theory, she still did. But that had been before...before lovemaking on beaches and in beds, before wild beliefs that he could order the world to their liking, that he would marry her. He wouldn't marry her, they both knew that. But it was a nice thought.

'Are you going to tell Father you and Darius are in love?' Addy asked. The buildings were taller now and better built. They'd passed the outskirts.

'We are not in love,' Artemisia corrected. 'My relationship with Darius is my business and while we're in London the relationship *is* strictly business.' It might never be more than business again. That was what was truly eating at her as they drew closer to the Stansfield town house on Gower Street just off Bedford Square. Had that morning at the Crown been their last morning? Was everything that was to occur in London just a slow fade to forgetfulness, an easing erasure of what had once been?

'Not in love?' Addy protested. 'The two of you spent weeks closeted away together.'

'Sketching, painting,' Artemisia snapped a little more sternly than she'd meant to. 'I had an enormous amount of work to accomplish.' Work that had been carefully packed in a waterproof trunk. Her future was riding on that work. Perhaps the Academy would like it, perhaps they would be swayed by Darius's report and all other preparations would become unnecessary. It would be the best possible way for this to end. It was another fairy tale she'd spun for herself.

'I saw how he looked at you and you like him, Arta. Don't try to tell me otherwise. You don't tolerate fools.'

'I do like him, but that's not love, Addy. I hold him in esteem. He is intelligent and kind in a way many men are not. There is a selflessness to him.' One that he had to be protected against or he'd be the maker of his own downfall. 'He is the son of the Earl of Bourne,' Artemisia reminded her. 'Whether or not we are in love is irrelevant. He isn't just an art critic. He has obligations we cannot begin to imagine.'

It really was over, then. Perhaps she'd needed to hear herself speak the words out loud in order to be convinced. She could stop worrying. There was nothing to worry about. Worrying assumed there was room for possibility—that something could or could not be. She'd not been aware of how much possibility she'd allowed to exist until now. Apparently, she'd allowed for more than she'd thought. She thought she'd been very careful not letting her heart get carried away. She had not been carful enough, it seemed.

'You're the daughter of a knight. You talk as though we're peasants, Artemisia.' Addy toed her with her boot, half-teasing, half-scolding.

'You're right,' Artemisia said in conciliatory tones. There was no need to step all over Addy's finer feelings. Besides, she needed Addy to remember their standing when it came to Bennett Galbraith. They were definitely too high in the instep for him, even if they weren't high enough for the grand Rutherfords of Bourne. While her carriage was rolling up in front of a town house on Gower in Bloomsbury, Darius was quartered in the West End. He was at the centre of Mayfair while Sir Lesley Stansfield lived among intellectuals, scientists, writers, businessmen and professional artists, the occasional émigré. Bloomsbury was always interesting, but it wasn't the aristocracy.

The steps were set and the girls were handed down into the bright sunlight. Artemisia blinked and looked up at the town house's façade with its long windows, white shutters against red brick. This was home, as were the studios in the converted mews. She was not ashamed of it.

Inside, Anstruther waited for them in the hall, welcoming them back and giving directions for trunks. 'There will be tea in the rose room in an hour. I am to tell you your father wishes to speak with you, Miss Stansfield.' So her father was home. Her stomach tightened. Did he know something? Had Darius been here without her permission to unveil their plan?

'I'd rather take tea in my studio, Anstruther. Please

tell Father I'd be happy to speak with him there. Have the footmen bring my art trunks immediately.' She wanted to be unpacked before she met with her father, wanted to have her work on display. Perhaps he meant to dissuade her from confronting the Academy. It would be harder to do with proof of her excellence staring back at him.

Sir Lesley Stansfield stared at the canvases lining the edge of Artemisia's studio. His gaze was slow and lingering; there was no rush. Artemisia sat on the small sofa she'd appropriated for her private working quarters and sipped tea, waiting in silence. When he came to the last one, the pintail duck, he said simply, 'Daughter, you've been busy. Your retreat was not spent in vain. This is an impressive collection of work.'

Artemisia smiled at the praise. She knew the work was good, but to hear her father say it meant everything to her. Darius wasn't the only one who strove to please their parents. She wondered if it was something a child ever grew out of. 'I'm glad you approve.' She fixed him a cup of tea as he took a seat across from her.

Her father lifted a dark brow. 'I said it was good, I didn't say I approved.' He took the cup and saucer and added another cube of sugar. He and Darius had a sweet tooth in common. 'It's beautiful work, Artemisia. There's a sense of a real collection about it: the consistent theme, the unified palette, the subject matter. It's thoughtful, well constructed and well executed. It carries a narrative with it, as I'm sure you intended, not just in each individual painting, but across the series.'

He sipped his tea and sighed. 'But it's a risk. I am sure you know that, too.'

Artemisia lifted a shoulder. 'The Academy asked to see something new, something they felt I hadn't showed them in twelve years of work. They might have meant that, or not.' She tried to keep the sarcasm from her tone. Her father would not appreciate having the Academy maligned. 'What I've done is new. It's daring, it's different and yet, if one looks closely, it pays homage to the important parts of the English tradition. Constable paints scenes from nature as well.' She practised the arguments she would make in a few days at the Royal Academy's March meeting. At last she asked the pertinent question. 'Will you be there for the meeting?' He had nominated her, at her request, but he'd not been there in December. She'd wondered if that would have made a difference.

Her father shook his head. 'I think it's better if I am not.' She felt disappointed; she would have welcomed his attendance, her father's support.

'Better for whom?' Artemisia queried coolly, shooting him a hard stare over the rim of her teacup.

'For both of us, Artemisia,' her father snapped. 'You pride yourself on your self-sufficiency. You would never forgive yourself or the Academy for accepting you on grounds not your own. I can't imagine you would want to invoke nepotism,' he scolded. 'Even so, there are other considerations. I must have a career left when this is over. You will need me to have that career. You can take shelter under that canopy and repair your losses if need be. But that can't happen if I go down with your ship.'

Artemisia bristled. 'You think I will fail.' Did he think that because he also knew it was a foregone conclusion, that the Academy was stacked against her even if she had produced the *Mona Lisa*? Or because he didn't believe in her talent in general despite his kind praise? She wasn't brave enough to ask, not just for the sake of her own self-worth. She didn't *want* to see her father's own weakness, his innate selfishness. She'd seen it before in Italy when he'd put his grief ahead of raising his daughters. She knew the weakness was there. She tried not to remind herself of it. He was the only parent she had left.

'You think I threaten your self-sufficiency,' Artemisia accused. 'I'm not sure I find that very flattering.' Nor did she like the reminder of how alike they were. Wasn't this akin to the same reasons she built mental walls against Darius's incursions? She had to have something left when he was gone. Above all else, she had to protect herself. Like father, like daughter.

He met her gaze with tired grey eyes. 'I've worked hard for my career, for my fame, for my chance to give my daughters a life worthy of them. I will not allow that security to be threatened in my waning years.' Even his voice held a weariness she'd not heard before. 'How do I explain this to you, who has so many masterpieces left to paint? You have all the passion for painting, for living that I once had, but now lack. Not by choice, but by virtue of time.' He sighed. 'How many masterpieces do you think I have left? I will be lucky if I have one.'

'Father, you have years left to paint,' Artemisia protested. She'd never known a life when her father hadn't painted. Even when her mother was alive, he'd buried himself behind an easel, painting, always painting. He was only fifty-five.

'Yes, my dear girl, I have years left to paint. But to paint *well*? Ah, there's the question. Mary Moser, your own mentor, stopped exhibiting at fifty. I've been lucky to paint this long. How much longer will my eyesight hold? How much longer will my hand be steady enough to produce excellence? The masterpieces I have left won't be paintings but students, the people who will carry my legacy forward.'

'All the more reason to champion me *and* Addy. She's become very good,' Artemisia argued. She was being bold, but this was her chance. How did her father not see the obvious? 'Let me be your legacy. There have been several parent–child partnerships through the Academy's history.'

He held up a hand to stop her recitation. 'I know all of that, Artemisia.' He dropped his head in his hands. 'I wish it could be different…' He let his sentence trail off. He didn't need to finish it. Artemisia set her cup down and rose, turning away from him and looking out the window so he wouldn't see the injury he'd dealt her. Any legacy attached to her was fraught with speculation, with a shadow of question about her competence, her longevity. *She* would never be good enough. No wonder her father didn't want to tie his kite to hers.

Mary Moser had stopped exhibiting in her fifties because she'd married, not because her skills had failed. Angelica Kauffman, the other female founder, had kept painting after marriage, but only because she'd left England and gone to Rome. Despite their careers and their immense competence, they weren't even allowed to attend the assembly meetings. Legacies needed sons. Sir Lesley Stansfield's son had died with her mother. A daughter would never be enough.

Artemisia gripped the windowsill until her knuckles were white with pain as the unspoken reality swept her. Her father had lost more than a wife all those years ago. He'd lost the hopes on which he'd built a lifetime: a beloved partner, a child, an heir for his legacy. No wonder his grief had endured, had defined months of their lives in Italy. 'You must have hated us, Addy and me.' Did he still hate them? And yet he'd taught them to paint.

'I don't hate you. I've never hated my beautiful daughters. I love you and Addy. But I am an old man, Artemisia. I cannot risk anything more. I need to have something left…' he lifted his head '…for all of us, in case my girls need me. If Addy wants to marry well, I will want to bring all I can to bear for her.' He could not do that with scandal attached to his name. She noticed he said nothing of her marrying well. Perhaps he despaired of her there, too.

It was difficult to be angry with him on those grounds. She knew the kinds of needs he meant— significant life needs, like the protection he'd given her when she'd gone to him over Hunter McCullough. He'd not hesitated to use his influence then. He would not hesitate to use that influence or resources to help Addy make a good match, or perhaps later to secure futures for any potential grandchildren. Those things were worth saving himself for. She understood that if he had to choose, her choices had put her outside that circle.

'Artemisia, be careful. You are an associate of the

Royal Academy already. You've won prizes, you've gained recognition. No one disputes your talents, only the title bestowed upon them. Be careful you aren't throwing away what you have achieved with both hands.' For his sake, for Addy's sake, for her own sake. If she was too scandalous, he and Addy would have to distance themselves from her.

She could understand it, even empathise with it, but even so, she could not accept it as her own decision. She was on her own. Just as she'd always been. *You have Darius*, the little voice of hope whispered optimistically in her mind. Did she? Or would she learn at the crucial moment he'd decided to save his own skin instead?

Chapter Nineteen

The crucial moment had arrived. Darius watched it unfold from his seat in the assembly. Artemisia had been allowed to hang her works beforehand, assembly members had been allowed to browse the offerings before the meeting was convened. Artemisia was called upon to give a talk about her work and the inspiration for her collection. She'd been articulate and intelligent, discussing the theme of the work, the inspiration for it and her design choices. He'd been fiercely proud of her as she'd moved among the men viewing her work, stopping here and there to redirect thoughts and potential criticisms. He'd been even prouder as she'd delivered her presentation.

She'd made concessions for the occasion in the hopes of gaining favour, much as she'd done the last time. Her wayward curls had been tamed into an elegant, conservative twist at the nape of her neck and secured with a tastefully plain gold comb. She wore a mulberry dress of merino wool suited for afternoon wear, appropriately cut with a high neck and long sleeves trimmed in a sharp, clean, white lace.

Despite her efforts to look conservative, she'd managed to make tradition look sexier than ever. His hand itched to pull the comb from her hair, to let all that curling, tumbling luxury spill untamed over her shoulders. He wanted to undo the laces of her dress and slide the propriety from her body. Was she wearing silk beneath the wool? He itched to discover that, too.

Two weeks without Artemisia had been two weeks too many. He'd not seen her since her return to town. They'd agreed it would be too risky. They did not want any association to be noted that might suggest to the Academy there was a potential conflict of interest. Seeing her today, so composed, so assured, was a revelation and a reminder of why he cared for her, why he was committed to her cause. He'd never met anyone like her. She had changed his world in remarkable ways from picking up a paintbrush again to his understanding of things he would have once simply not seen. Now he wanted to change hers. And he couldn't.

Artemisia finished speaking and sat down to polite applause. It was all so courteously done that one might not have even noticed what was really happening. Certainly, three months ago he'd not have noticed. But today, he saw it and his heart sank. Her hard work, her brilliance, her arguments, even her concessions, wouldn't be enough. They were going to refuse her. Everyone knew. He knew. Artemisia knew, yet everyone was playing their parts to perfection. Anger stirred in him at the farce unfolding.

'St Helier, perhaps we might hear from you on the paintings?' President West called on him. 'You spent time watching the development process.'

Darius rose, not daring a glance Artemisia's direction. What was going through her mind? Did she think he would denounce her? Did she hold out an ounce of hope that his testimony would tip the scales? Or was she so collected because she already knew the outcome? 'I submitted my report this morning. It is available to anyone who wishes to read it. In short, I will share the highlights here. First, I find Miss Stansfield's work to be singularly unique in its style and use of colours. Secondly, I find her skill to be outstanding in blending her own personal style with the traditions of the English school. I am of the opinion that she brings much insight and talent on which the English school can build. I fully support her elevation to a Royal Academician.'

Darius sat down to a room full of silence. Aldred Gray lifted an almost imperceptible eyebrow in his direction. President West nodded his head as if his opinion was well received. 'Thank you for your insights and your time.' Shortly after that, President West dismissed guests and candidates so that the Academy could discuss and vote in privacy.

Artemisia left Somerset House without a single glance in his direction. He wished he could be with her to await the news. Darius left for his club to hold his own lonely vigil and to run through plans for the inevitable. This was not the end. They would fight, yet he hoped it wouldn't come to that, that the Academy would accept her brilliance.

* * *

Aldred Gray found him shortly before six o'clock. Gray took the chair opposite and ordered a brandy. 'I thought you'd be here. Word has been sent to Miss Stansfield. She's probably reading it right now.' Gray sat back and took his glass from a waiter's tray. He swirled it about and put his nose to it before tasting. The damn man was going to make him beg for news. Either that or he was watching for a reaction to see just how invested Darius was in Artemisia's situation.

Darius chose not to give Gray the satisfaction. He took a slow swallow of his own drink. 'How will Miss Stansfield feel about the news?'

'We've chosen not to elevate her status. She is welcome to remain as an associate, however.' Gray made it sound as though maintaining her status quo—something she'd already earned—was a grand favour. 'We do thank you for your honesty, St Helier. We have all done our best for her; her father, with the original nomination, you with your time invested, your incredibly detailed report, the Academy with its probation. We've done everything possible, perhaps even more, to give her a fair hearing.' He clapped a friendly hand on Darius's knee. 'You can rest assured this decision was not taken lightly.'

'I was never worried about that,' Darius replied drily. There'd never been a question of the decision being taken glibly. The Academy had taken it with the utmost seriousness of a general planning a campaign. They'd executed it with attention to every detail to ensure their success and their image.

Gray missed the wryness. 'You played your part and

the Academy is grateful to you once more.' He ordered another round of drinks and launched into a dissertation of the newly approved candidates and the upcoming spring show.

Darius listened with half an ear. Gray was thankfully very good at entertaining himself, requiring little from him to keep the conversation going. So that was how it was going to be. The Academy was willing to view his opinion as a necessary demonstration of fairness towards Artemisia, part of the play of justice they'd constructed. They would allow him to retain his position within the fold if he distanced himself from her now.

They'd wasted no time in offering the olive branch to him. They must be highly concerned about his reaction to their decision, concerned enough to fear some well-based repercussions and his consequence. They'd be right. They had to have rapprochement with him. An earl's son could not be so easily dismissed as an artist's daughter. He finished his drink and set the glass down. He rose abruptly. Gray might or might not have been in mid-sentence. Darius didn't particularly care.

'You must excuse me, I am expected somewhere this evening.' He paused and then mentioned offhandedly, 'A copy of my report will appear in *The Times* tomorrow, adjacent to the list of newly approved RAs, in abbreviated format, of course. Perhaps you'll be kind enough to relay that news to President West? Have a good evening, Gray.'

That felt good. Darius couldn't help but smile as he collected his coat, hat and walking stick at the cloakroom. It was freeing. There was no more waiting to see how things would go. Decisions had been made.

The next step was to go to Artemisia. That was a reason for celebration, too. They needn't pretend to avoid one another now.

She needn't pretend sophisticated indifference or cool acceptance of the Academy's decision here in her private studio. She was alone here and could give herself over to rage and disappointment. The note had come an hour ago with the return of her collection, carefully packed with the Academy's thanks, best wishes and the reminder that she would always be welcome as a royal associate. She'd read the note stoically under Anstruther's watchful gaze, given directions to have the paintings taken to the studio and then she had retreated.

Artemisia stared at the paintings lined against the wall. They were starkly beautiful. Perhaps too stark, message and all. Had she done this to herself? She had been very deliberate about the message of protest behind her work. Darius had warned her and she'd forged on any way. Her gaze landed on the pintail duck. How could it be she'd completed that only a few weeks ago? Seasalter seemed like another lifetime. She wanted to be there now, tucked up before the fire in the farmhouse parlour, Darius beside her, a warmed glass of the Crown's fine red in her hand.

She shook her head against her self-pity. She'd allow herself this one night of disappointment, but no more. It would solve nothing. She shouldn't even allow herself this much pity. She'd known her bid would end this way. She'd had weeks, months, to mourn this loss. And yet the unfairness of it all hurt so damn badly.

But there was no time for drowning, for wallowing.

Her battle was over. She needed to turn her attention to Darius and how she could best protect him from his own nobility. He'd stirred her heart today when he'd spoken on her behalf, as foolhardy as it was. He'd been so commanding, so confident, she'd almost believed he might sway them. For a few moments, he'd given her back a hope she'd disposed of.

It had taken all of her willpower to walk out of Somerset without a glance for him. She'd wanted to run to him, throw her arms about him and kiss him. No one had ever done as much for her as he had in those words, publicly endorsing her against all odds, a decision that would cost him unless she could convince him otherwise. That convincing would mean giving her up, setting aside his plans to champion her outside the Academy.

A knock at her studio jolted her out of her ruminations. The room had fallen dark as she'd daydreamed. She turned up the lamp and opened the door. 'Darius!'

He nearly knocked the lamp from her hand as he swept her into his arms, kissing her hard. He smelled of the spice of his own soap and clean linen. 'You were magnificent today, my darling!' He took the lamp from her and set it aside. He was dressed for the evening in a dark cloth coat, single-breasted with tails over pale, tight-fitting breeches, and an embroidered waistcoat in a rich sapphire blue. He was dressed for going out, clearly.

'I wasn't magnificent enough,' she said. Had he heard the news? She suddenly felt guilty she'd not sent word. Had he been waiting to hear all this time? 'I thought you would have been told.'

Darius waved a dismissive hand. 'I know, I heard. Gray came to the club to enlighten me. Their decision does not make you less magnificent.' She was in his arms again. 'Since when have you ever defined yourself based on their standards?' His ebullience faded, replaced by seriousness. 'I was proud of you today. You were everything you should have been.'

Tears stung at his words. 'Don't, Darius,' she warned. She hadn't cried yet, but his words would break the last of her resolve. What he'd done for her today, and what he continued to do, would undo her. 'Come sit, we must talk.' Perhaps talking would allay her tears. She tugged at his wrist, but he remained fixed in place. 'What is it?'

'This is the studio?' He glanced around, his gaze falling on her sofa.

'It's my private studio,' she answered carefully, following his train of thought. 'I don't paint with my father's students any more. I moved in here several years ago after the incident with Hunter McCullough. It was obviously not a good idea for me to continue to paint with the group.' It would have been an invitation to more trouble. Darius seemed to relax as he followed her to the sofa.

'Gray was insufferable.' He took up the conversation. 'He told me I could rest easy in knowing that I'd done everything possible to ensure you a fair hearing. The Academy was thankful for my objectivity. I had played my part well for them.'

Artemisia heard the edge on his last words. 'I assume that was their method of announcing their forgiveness of your errant ways,' she said coolly. Was he looking to her for absolution? 'You should take the offer, of course.' It seemed she wouldn't have to save him after all, the Academy had done that for her. For him, this couldn't have gone better. He'd emerged with his honour intact, he hadn't been compelled to sacrifice his principles for a lie, or his position for the truth.

'I most certainly should *not*.' Darius frowned at her. 'They have done you a gross injustice.' His gaze considered her, warmth and hope pooling in her belly. 'This is not over. I told Gray my report would appear in *The Times* tomorrow.'

Artemisia gasped, 'No, you didn't. You will alienate the Academy completely by publicly setting yourself against them.' More to the point, by aligning himself so directly with her. 'I thought we'd decided I was a lost cause.'

Darius reached for her hands. She wasn't fast enough to pull them away. It was hard to argue when he was touching her. Everything seemed more compelling. 'I don't know that we can win for you, but what about the others who come after you? There will be other women with talent who want what you want. This fight is about you, but it's also about them.'

'But it doesn't have to be your fight. I always thought I'd be in this alone and it's fine. You needn't sacrifice yourself.' He'd better take that offer while she could still make it. It was getting more difficult to let him go, to want to fight alone. He'd changed that for her and she wasn't sure yet if she had thanked him for it.

'I know it doesn't. But I want it to be. I was denied a chance at something I loved. I think it's my fight, too. They'll be careful not to alienate me too much.' He leaned in and kissed her cheek. 'I need you to do something for me, darling; change into a ballgown. My carriage is waiting out front to take us to the Elliots'.'

'Dancing is the last thing I feel like doing tonight,' Artemisia said.

'I'm sure it is, which is why it's the thing you *must* do tonight.' Darius rose and offered her his hand. 'Tonight, you dance and laugh as if the Academy's decision does not pain you in the least. They wanted to put out your fire, Artemisia. You need to show them they've done the opposite: they've fanned it. You don't need them to be a successful artist.' He gave her an experimental twirl that made her laugh, brightening her spirits. 'Put on your dancing shoes, Artemisia. We have declared war on the Academy.'

Chapter Twenty

They danced that night, a glorious, sweeping waltz that left Artemisia breathless. Darius was an exquisite dancer, navigating them through the crowded Elliot ballroom with athletic grace and confidence, his hand firm at her back, his mouth teasing her into smiles of her own with its infectious grin. For a few precious moments she could get lost in him, his eyes, his touch; she could forget the disappointments of the day, she could believe in the fantasies he wrought.

They danced the next night, too, and the one after that. She felt invincible in Darius's arms as they sailed across London's dance floors. She was buoyed by his confidence and the vindicated satisfaction of seeing his well-articulated editorial regarding the recent RA selections by the Academy appear in *The Times*. Darius stole kisses in moonlit gardens, and her studio in the mews became their refuge. There might be no more lovemaking by night, but they had the afternoons, long, lazy afternoons spent in the studio. After such interludes, she was happy to put on her fashionable ballgowns and dance the nights away with him.

Darius had proved inventive in that regard. Well aware that even two dances a night with her would draw speculation, Darius limited their dances to a single waltz and then cannily arranged to have them dance in the same sets so they might at least partner one another for a short time. She was starting to have fun in London, starting to see the charm her sister saw in town. It was different when one had an attentive and influential escort. Darius was all that and more: escort, lover, believer, champion. Although, as one week faded into the next, she was aware of a certain anxiety settling over her.

Everything had been too perfect. There'd been no response from the Academy *yet* to Darius's editorial. Were they simply going to ignore it? For Darius's sake, she hoped so. Grown adults should be able to tolerate and accommodate a difference in opinions on occasion. As for herself, her situation remained unsettled. What was she to do now? She said as much to Darius on a grey afternoon towards the end of March.

'What do you want to do?' Darius asked, drowsy from cosy lovemaking before the studio's fireplace. His hand idly combed tangles from her hair as she snuggled in the crook of his arm.

'I want to be an RA, but that's not going to happen.' Artemisia raised up on an arm to look at him.

'No, that's not going to happen. But what do you need that for?' Darius argued.

'RAs can teach at the Royal Academy. They can mould the minds and styles of future artists, their opinions have weight in shaping the direction of the English school,' Artemisia itemised.

'Can you not do those things without the initials?' Darius asked. 'Can you not teach? Can you not exhibit your work or publish treatises on art? Can you not wield influence from outside the academy?'

'I can, but I would lack status. Who wants to be taught by a rejected candidate? It would be an exercise in futility.'

His hand went back to stroking her hair in a thoughtful motion. 'Those who have also been rejected.'

'An academy of misfits?' Artemisia questioned. 'I can't see the benefit in catering to mediocrity.'

Darius laughed. 'Now who is the snob, Artemisia? I am not talking about misfits. I'm talking about people like you, others who have been passed over because they didn't fit the mould, but whose talent deserves recognition.'

Artemisia shifted in his arms, considering. 'Other women.' A little spark of excitement flickered. 'An academy for women? For girls?' She liked the idea. 'There are so few women even as associates in the academy because there's no place for them to study. Art schools don't take female students.' She'd been lucky in that regard. She had a father to teach her. Mary Moser and Angela Kaufmann had also been protégées of their fathers. But what about the girls who didn't have artistic parents? How would she ever breach the bastion of the male-dominated academy without an army?

Darius had talked of an army before, an army of well-placed advocates like Lady Basingstoke. But what would they advocate for? Just her? That seemed a wasted effort. She needed foot soldiers, so to speak. She might be able to recruit a few female artists who were already trained, but there was no depth, no longevity in that. She would need to raise her army from the ground up. 'The Academy wouldn't like it.'

'No, I don't think they would,' Darius said slowly. 'They might take away your associate status. I would think very carefully about that if you set yourself up in direct opposition.'

She laughed softly. 'Says the man who was just moments ago suggesting I strike out for my own and eschew the protections of the Academy.' The flicker of excitement was dimmer now.

'I fully believe it's a possibility given that they aren't going to elevate you. But everything has a cost—perhaps the trade-off is worth it.' His words were thoughtful and slow. 'It's important to know what that price is upfront. We make better decisions that way and have fewer surprises.' She wondered how autobiographical that comment was. At some point, he had decided his painting came at too great a cost to himself and to others. Perhaps, at some point, she needed to decide the opposite: that the cost of *not* painting, of not challenging the institution, was a price too high for herself and others to pay. 'All evil needs to prosper is for a good man—or woman—to do nothing, is that it?' She softly paraphrased Burke.

'Yes. What shall we do, Artemisia?' It was the one thing they'd not discussed since the night the Academy had declined her nomination. 'I think the world is waiting on you. The Academy certainly is, as am I.

I have plans in motion, but they mean nothing without your consent.'

'The Academy?' She sat up, her mind too alert now for drowsy after-play.

'Why do you think they've not responded to my editorial? They're waiting to see if you're going to make a fuss or if you will happily accept the limitations of your gender and remain a compliant associate. They won't start the war, Artemisia. They're happy to have your talent under the aegis. They have nothing to gain by fighting you. But right now, you're not fighting. You're making it easy on them. They're hoping you are done, that you have accepted your place.'

She reached for her shift and popped her head through as if to underscore her words. 'The honeymoon's over, isn't it? We can't just dance the night away and pretend all will work itself out.'

'No.' Darius sat up, too, and reached for a shirt, his voice quiet. 'I have a lease available on a nice property on the Strand just around the corner from Somerset House. It would serve as an excellent venue for an exhibition. We can run the show the month of May and open it three days before the Academy's spring show, make ourselves the first show of the Season.' He paused, his eyes hot on her as he let her digest the idea. While she'd been burying her head in the sand, ignoring next steps, he'd been busy. 'Shall I sign the lease, Artemisia?'

There would be no denying or misconstruing their attentions. The Academy would not overlook this slap in the face. 'Who would sponsor the show?' Artemisia ventured.

'The Duke of Boscastle. I've already contacted him. He is willing to lend his name.' Darius fastened his cuffs. Putting on his armour, she thought. Each piece of clothing arming him to face society.

'The Academy may exile you, Darius, if they know you're behind this.' They would see his signature on the lease and they would know he'd orchestrated the show no matter who the sponsor was.

'They may. You are not the only one taking risks.' He rose and came to help her with her laces. 'Nor should you be. Why should I ask you to risk everything and not risk anything myself? That seems unfair.' And fairness mattered to Darius very much. Fairness was a type of responsibility to him, she was coming to realise.

She was silent, pondering her options as his fingers left her, her laces tied. She did not want him ruined for her and over something that might not bear fruit. 'I think you risk too much. You have little to gain and much to lose while I have little to lose and much to gain,' she pointed out.

'Losing recognition as an associate is no small thing. You risk plenty.' Darius smiled softly. 'But neither is doing nothing. If you don't do this, Artemisia, you will have to settle for the crumbs off their table.' There would be no forward momentum. Ever. She would be taken with limited seriousness by some, perhaps with even less by others. She shuddered at the thought. She'd worked too hard to be considered a hobbyist, a dauber, someone who'd achieved the status of associate simply as a courtesy to her father. She was starting to better understand her father's refusal to argue for her. She needed to stand on her own feet, on her own merits.

He'd given her the power and the permission to break free on her own. But she had to do the actual breaking. No one else could do it for her. This would be the ultimate test of her independence, her own self-sufficiency. It both frightened and thrilled her.

She held his gaze and whet her lips, making the decision. 'Sign the lease, Darius.' There was just enough time to put a show together. Four weeks if they planned to open at the end of April, a week before the Academy show. She ran the timeline in her mind: barely enough time to advertise, to get the pictures hung, a caterer arranged, to send out invitations, to arrange reviews and their publication.

A smile wreathed Darius's face and he swept her into a celebratory hug. 'Good girl. I am proud of you. We will make this a show the London Season will remember.'

He kissed her hard on the mouth and she let herself forget for one more day that, even if they succeeded, it didn't change the other reality—that nothing, not even taking on the Academy, launching herself as a valid, independent artist, could change them. At the end of this, she would still be an artist's daughter and he would still be an earl's son. There would be no place for them together in society. She would still have to give him up. Or content herself to a life as his mistress, a life of restrictions not much different than a life of bowing to the Academy's limitations. It didn't seem fair.

The Academy didn't play fair. Darius thwacked the rolled-up newspaper against his leg in frustration, the noise a little too loud in the late-afternoon silence of

White's. The few men in attendance looked up from their seats and went back to their reading. After reading the society column in not one, but three newspapers, it was no wonder his father had wanted to meet for drinks and to discuss certain developments. The Academy had taken their distemper beyond the parameters of the art and made it personal.

They'd also not been as neutral or as accepting as Darius had thought. True, they'd been waiting for Artemisia to show her beautiful flaming colours. If she hadn't, they might have left their evidence unreported, their case unmade. But Artemisia had not gone silently, and the Academy had been ready. Sources now 'noticed' the trend that had been established over the past several weeks that Lord St Helier had bestowed considerable attentions on Miss Artemisia Stansfield in a manner that was of a questionable nature. Their aspersions that she ought to know better damaged her reputation, insinuating that she was using her 'charms' to reach above her station. Those aspersions left him in a difficult position; either he was naively flaunting her or he was deliberately parading his lover in front of society, a lover who was not worthy of his attentions publicly.

'Darius, how are you?' His father approached the nook he occupied.

Darius rose and shook hands. His father looked well except for dark circles beneath his eyes. 'A new coat, I see,' Darius commented as they sat. 'You're keeping your tailor busy.'

They ordered drinks and made small talk about the new bill his father was sponsoring in Parliament about the repatriation of artefacts from foreign countries, his mother's latest charity ventures, the newest acquisitions to the Bourne collection. The drinks arrived and, once assured of no further interruptions, his father got straight to the point.

'It seems you are making some artistic acquisitions of your own these days, Darius. I read your editorial in the paper a few weeks back. I had drinks with Boscastle the other day after Parliament. He's excited about the exhibition. Your efforts are very bold, though, especially when they are accompanied by a rather personal interest. It's clear your efforts on Miss Stansfield's behalf are not entirely from an artistic perspective.' His father's greying brows furrowed. 'Is she your mistress? Is that why you're doing this?'

'No, she is not my mistress. I know better than to flaunt a mistress in society's face or to abuse my status and reputation in order to foist her talents upon the art world. Such assertions malign both her and me,' Darius said in low, firm tones. He was a grown man. His father usually did not interfere in his life or question his choices. It was somewhat embarrassing to have those choices called into question now.

His father took a swallow of brandy and gave them each a moment to compose themselves. 'It's just that your mother had such hopes for this Season. It's time to start looking to your nursery and your mother feels this year's crop of debutantes is spectacular. We wouldn't want you to miss out because of a misunderstanding. I am concerned that the gossips, fuelled by those in the Academy looking for some revenge, will put an indecent twist on your winter in Seasalter,' his father ventured. 'If the gossips learned of it, they would turn it into something sordid. No one would actually believe you spent six weeks there gathering information for your report, not when it involves a woman like that.'

Darius bristled. 'A woman like what? Do you *know* Artemisia Stansfield?'

'I know women like her. All men do,' his father said severely. 'She's a veritable siren. She's not only lovely, but she's confident and intelligent and she does not need to keep her chastity, so she employs herself to the greatest extent possible. She's able to give men a fantasy they cannot get with a debutante. It's intoxicating and you wouldn't be the first man to be caught up in such a spell.'

'You do her a disservice,' Darius growled. 'I mean to marry her.'

Chapter Twenty-One

His father did not react immediately. He took a slow drink and appeared to give the pronouncement some thought before he met Darius's gaze with a flinty stare. 'You most certainly do not want to marry her. You only think you do.' His father was quick to dismiss the idea. Old ghosts began to rise. This had happened before when he'd wanted to tour Europe, to paint.

'If you and Mother met her, you would think differently. She comports herself well. She understands society.' Artemisia had navigated balls with ease and élan, unflustered by titles. Her father's status meant she was no country bumpkin come to town. She knew how to go about.

'Your mother? Meet her? She should not even be in the room with a woman like Artemisia Stansfield.' The Earl of Bourne nearly choked on his drink, a rare lapse in his father's usually impeccable decorum. 'Miss Stansfield is not what the earldom needs and she is not what you've been raised to seek out in a wife.' He leaned forward and dropped his voice. 'Let me remind you of what you've conveniently forgotten. She is an artist's daughter. She has no lineage, no bloodline, no pedigree, no land, no fortune. She has only a father who has acquired some small amount of fame and a title. Start thinking with your brain, Darius.' His father sat back. 'This surprises me. You've always done what is right.' He had, much to his regret.

'You mean required. They are not necessarily the same thing.'

'They are for earls,' his father was quick to correct.

He'd given up his paints to please his father. He'd been a boy then, impressionable. He was a man now and he'd be damned if he gave up the woman he loved because someone else told him to. There it was—*loved*. He loved Artemisia Stansfield. He would move society's mountains for her, including his own father's resistance. 'I've already asked her,' Darius offered boldly.

His father arched another brow. 'Have you? What did she say?'

'She said no.' But he would ask her again when she saw the possibilities, not the fantasies, when the success of the show was behind them, when he'd proven himself to her.

'Good girl. At least one of you has their head on straight.'

Darius fixed his father with a hard stare. 'Father, I love her.' He tried the declaration out. It felt good, just as it had felt good to have made a decision to confront the Academy.

'Fine. You can love her all you want. I have nothing against that. Just don't marry her. Men like you and I, we don't marry for love. We marry for the earldom. Honestly, Darius, I thought by now you knew that.'

'But you and Mother…' Darius said.

'Your mother and I knew our duty. And so do you. I have every faith in you, Darius.' His father smiled reassuringly, a glimmer of kindness in his eyes that Darius thought misplaced.

'You are asking me to give up the woman I love.' Just as his father had asked him to give up the thing he loved most when he was sixteen, the thing that drove his passion.

His father gave a small, sad smile. 'Do you think you are the only man to do so? This is what men of responsibility do. It is how we keep our power. This is why we don't mingle with women outside our sphere, so that we are not tempted by the impossible.' The last was meant as a subtle scold, but Darius did not miss the shadow in his father's dark eyes. What mystery lurked there?

'I am not asking anything of you that I have not done myself. I promise you, in time, all will come out right. Your mother will help you find a worthy bride this Season. Your wife will run your house, bear your children, your heirs, and you will come to care for her. Treat her with respect and she will treat you with respect and all else will follow. Marriage is one of many arrangements you will make in your life. To consider it to be any more than that leads us down the road of unnecessary disappointment.'

Darius stared at his father, his personal understanding of the small world of his family shattering and reforming with alacrity. He understood all this in theory, of course. Any man inheriting a title did. He'd just never applied those theories to his parents, or to himself. Until now, there'd been no need to. Realisations rocketed through his mind. His parents had not been a love match. His father had loved another. He would never admit as much. His father was too much a man of honour to suggest his wife was not the sole object of his esteem. That honour, that sense of responsibility to the house of Bourne, had suggested the right course of action was to set aside his personal preferences. Despite whatever pain it had caused him, he was asking his son to do the same.

'I appreciate your insight,' Darius said sincerely. He disagreed with it and found it uncomfortable, but he would not treat his father's pain with callous disregard nor his wisdom. It did, however, make the situation more difficult. He admired his father—even at nearly thirty-five his father's approval was important to him. His father had been the stick by which he'd measured himself, a man of no vices, a man who saw to the welfare of his family and his people. And yet, wasn't being a slave to tradition a type of vice? When did tradition demand too much of a man?

He would not give up Artemisia. It would be like ripping out his soul a second time, and it would be worse. He did not think he could patch it over this time. With her, he'd got a piece of himself back and more. She'd opened up the world to him. Through her, he'd started to see the world differently. He'd broken out of his unwitting blindness. His world would never be the same. He didn't want it to be. He didn't want to go back. The war he waged against the Academy had come home.

* * *

The problem with wars was that they escalated. Artemisia leaned back against the squabs as her carriage made slow progress towards the showroom on the Strand. She closed her eyes, trying to ignore the headlines from the latest gossip column, but the words danced even behind her eyelids.

Timeline of a scandal

This article had dared to outline, based on the speculation of second-hand sources, what had transpired between her and Darius in Seasalter, painting a lurid picture of a lusty affair in which she'd successfully seduced him.

Darius wouldn't like it. He would not like that she'd been defamed. He would not like that his strength of character had been maligned, portraying him as an innocent victim—as if a man his age could be an 'innocent' and maintain any amount of credibility.

It was not the first account. Ever since the early advertisements regarding her exhibition had come out the war against her had escalated. In the evenings she and Darius would dance, and in the morning the papers would lash out.

Artist stealing a march on Season's debutantes!
Earl's heir flaunts mistress!

Never any names, of course, that's what kept it from being libel, but anyone in town could guess who the articles referred to. She and Darius had become a 'point of interest' in lieu of any other gossip as the population in town grew daily in anticipation of the Season.

What had once been a private professional skirmish between her and the Academy had become public. It spilled over, involving others. People were choosing sides. She saw it at the early balls. The traditional conservatives followed the Academy and the old guard. The more liberal crowd, headed by the show's sponsor, the Duke of Boscastle and his ally in all things, the Duke of Newlyn, supported Darius and, by extension, her. Last night, she'd received her first outright snub. A woman had actually excused herself from the ball, citing Artemisia's attendance as the specific reason she was leaving early.

Darius had responded by whisking her out to the dance floor for an unprecedented second dance, a waltz in which he'd held her scandalously close. She'd thought at the time there was something more at work in his decision last night than the woman's slight, but there had been no opportunity to discuss it. Time together was precious little these days as they prepared for the show.

The carriage pulled up to the kerb and Artemisia got out, hiding the newspaper beneath the seat. Out of sight, out of mind. She'd promised to meet Darius this afternoon and work on hanging pictures. With the show just a week away, there was much to do. She was grateful for the busyness. The show was a welcome distraction from the scandal. The exhibition was her reminder that, while the Academy and society were choosing to make this scandal about more than her art, her art was the reason for all the preparation, all the effort and all the sacrifice, although she doubted anyone newly come to town even realised it. That was how thorough the gossip column campaign had been in moving everything away from Darius's articulate editorial about her overlooked candidacy to an attack on her morals.

Darius met her at the door with a kiss on the cheek. 'Another bad column?' he guessed.

'How did you know?' So much for hiding it. It might be under the seat of the carriage, but it was apparently written all over her face.

'Your jaw is tight and you've got sparks in your eyes.' Darius laughed it off. 'I've seen you angry before, remember. All you're missing is a bucket of cold water.' He helped her out of her outerwear. 'Was it awful?'

'This person has written a timeline of what they presume was our pre-existing affair in Seasalter.' She untied her bonnet. 'The bothersome piece is that it's not necessarily a lie. The report is somewhat accurate.'

Darius swore under his breath. 'I should call Aldred Gray out for this. I am sure it was he who put the idea in the reporter's head. He suspected you were upstairs in my bed that morning. But he has no proof. That's the damnable part of this.'

'No duelling,' Artemisia said in all seriousness. She did worry someone might push Darius's honour too far. 'What better way to besmirch a woman's cause than to destroy her reputation? Men have been doing it for centuries. No one is even thinking about my art any more.'

'We'll change that. Come and see.' Darius took her hand and led her through the house. The place he'd leased for the exhibition was an old half-timbered Tudor-style building that had been a shop, a set of offices and a wealthy man's house over the centuries. They climbed the stairs to the upper floor where the space widened out into an enormous area. She could imagine it filled at one time with clerks' desks, but now it was empty and open with windows letting in light and overlooking the Thames. The room was severe, no decorative architectural distractions except the thick black timbers overhead.

'It's perfect,' Artemisia turned about slowly, taking in the space. The plainness of the walls would be an ideal complement to the austerity of her paintings. Even the black Tudor-style ceiling beams favoured the palette of her collection. She smiled. 'You are perfect, Darius. Thank you.' She recognised this place for what it was: a gift, a token of how deeply his affections for her ran. She did not think for a moment he'd selected this place because it was the first one he'd found. This place had been chosen with great deliberateness for its location as well as for its other qualities. That deliberateness and what it suggested touched her, scared her.

'Darius,' she asked quietly, 'do you think anyone will come?' She couldn't bear to fail so utterly in front of him, not after the lengths he'd gone to. He'd put his reputation on the line for her with his personal friends and his professional acquaintances.

'They will come. Boscastle's sponsorship guarantees it, you needn't worry,' Darius assured her. But would they come back? What would the show prove? That she could draw attention or that her art was appreciated?

She walked to the windows and stared down at the Thames sparkling beneath them. Seasalter lay at the other end of the river. How she wished she could sail away, to Seasalter or even beyond, perhaps to Italy.

'Will they come for the art, though, or to gape at the seductress?' That would be even worse than opening the exhibition to an empty hall.

They'd not spoken of it, but she was well aware in all the gossip columns that she was the villain, not Darius. He was merely misguided, under her spell, but there was always room for him to return to the fold. All he had to do was denounce her, admit his folly and all would be forgiven. It should have angered her, another sign of how unfair the world was. Men simply couldn't make mistakes. Instead, it gave her hope that, when all this was over, he would have a place when she left.

'I've a surprise for you, it came this afternoon.' Darius pulled her away from the windows and towards a large paper-wrapped package leaning against the wall. 'Lady Basingstoke brought it. You just missed her by half an hour.'

Genuine delight rushed through her as she undid the paper. 'Lady Basingstoke sent the portrait!' Artemisia tore away the last of the wrapping, revealing Lady Basingstoke beside her champion thoroughbred. She stared at the painting she'd done two years ago, tears stinging at all it meant. The painting had won its category that year at the Academy's spring show. It usually hung in pride of place at Castonbury Abbey up north, but Lady Basingstoke had brought it to London. For her. This was an endorsement, a reminder to all that Lady Basingstoke and her husband stood with her.

'Lady Basingstoke is a powerful ally. She defied the conventions of the racing world when Warborne won Epsom. She will want to champion another woman wanting to break down barriers in her own field.' Darius came to stand with her and study the painting. 'Perhaps now you will believe me when I tell you people will come for the right reasons. We do not fight alone, Artemisia.'

Boscastle, Newlyn, Basingstoke. No, they certainly did not. The list of allies was impressive. 'Will your father come?' Artemisia asked carefully. The Earl of Bourne would be a natural ally, a supporter of his son and a regular feature in the art world, yet there'd been no mention of his participation.

'I want to do this on my own,' Darius answered firmly.

Some of the joy she felt over Lady Basingstoke's endorsement faded. 'Your father disagrees with your pursuit.'

Darius nodded. 'We had a frank discussion at White's yesterday.'

'Ah, that explains the waltz last night. I thought there was a bit more to it than Lady Cartford's snub.' She also thought, although she kept it to herself, that the 'frank discussion' was about more than the art show, but about her.

'He'll come around,' Darius said confidently. She didn't argue the point. It didn't matter. The Earl of Bourne didn't need to come around. She would be gone and the point moot. She had cost Darius enough. She would not cost him his family.

Darius took her in his arms and danced her into a silent waltz. 'It doesn't matter, as long as the two of us stand together, we can accomplish great things.' She wanted to believe that. She truly did, but she knew how the world really worked.

Chapter Twenty-Two

When Addy breathlessly informed her the Earl was here, Artemisia's first assumption was that Basingstoke was calling and Addy had mistaken the title. Basingstoke hadn't inherited yet. She knew no other. 'Send him back here to the studio and have Anstruther make a tea tray,' Artemisia smiled at the prospect of her guest. Lady Basingstoke's husband was good company. It would take her mind off the exhibition's opening tomorrow and early reviews.

Darius had held a private showing yesterday for art critics and key newspapers. She was anxious to see what they had to say and being idle was torture on her nerves. If it had been up to her, she would have spent the day fussing over the paintings, arranging and rearranging what had already been decided, checking and rechecking catering details. But Darius had firmly forbade her from the exhibition hall until the show opened.

'Back here?' Addy questioned. 'I thought you might prefer to greet him in the drawing room or in the rose parlour.'

'I want to show Basingstoke some works.' Artemisia unbuttoned her smock and set it aside. The best thing about a visit with Phaedra or her husband was that one needn't stand on ceremony.

Addy shook her head, her voice an aghast whisper. 'It's not Basingstoke. It's the Earl of Bourne.'

Darius's father. The man who put responsibility above all else, even his son's painting.

'The rose parlour, then, most definitely.' Artemisia gave her wrinkled skirts a worried smoothing, not that it would help. She'd been painting on a rather personal project this morning and hadn't taken much time with her appearance, thinking she'd be alone. She caught sight of her hair in the little mirror she kept above the brush-washing station. It was a frizzled mess of a braid. 'Do I have time to change?' She debated the idea of making Bourne wait another twenty minutes and decided against it.

'Let me do something with your hair.' Addy reached for the pins in her own and pulled them out. She made a few expert twists of Artemisia's plait and pinned it at the nape of her neck in the semblance of a bun. 'It's better than nothing.' Addy smiled nervously. 'This is good, isn't it? Darius's father is here, the show opens tomorrow. He's probably visiting because Darius wants the two of you to meet.'

Artemisia offered her sister a soft smile. 'Perhaps.' She didn't want to dash Addy's hopes, but she didn't think Bourne was calling to become friends. If Bourne had come all the way to Bloomsbury to look down his nose at the Stansfields, he would be disappointed. The Stansfields might not have the Mayfair address of the

Rutherfords, but their cook could lay out a tea tray like no other.

She exchanged a conspiratorial smile with Addy as her sister gave her hand an encouraging squeeze. 'Bourne will love you. How could he not? You both have a passion for art, that's something to start with, and you both care for Darius, albeit in different ways,' Addy offered with her characteristic optimism before she set off to order tea.

How could he not?

Oh, there was plenty not to love about her. Artemisia was all too aware, as she made her way to the rose parlour, of the flaws she possessed in the eyes of a man who had ambitions for his son.

What does it matter if he likes you or not? You're not marrying Darius anyway, her conscience reminded her. *Give Bourne your assurances and send him on his way.*

'Lord Bourne, how nice of you to call. Is there something I can help with you? A portrait, perhaps?' Artemisia pasted on a polite smile and entered the parlour as if she received earls in her work clothes every day. She wouldn't apologise for it. Lord Bourne's call was unsolicited.

Darius's father turned from the window which overlooked the flower garden, in possession of his own polite smile, a smile that lacked Darius's warmth. 'Miss Stansfield, it's good of you to receive me.' There was no accompanying apology or excuse for the spontaneous nature of the call. Nor was there any warmth in his words or expression, just neutral, well-mannered politeness. He was a handsome man, nearly as tall as Darius, and well dressed in afternoon clothes: a jacket of blue superfine and a tasteful cream waistcoat embroidered with pheasants. His hair was dark like Darius's and only just beginning to show signs of greying at the temples.

Artemisia gestured that they should be seated and the tea tray arrived on cue, giving her something to do as she rallied her defences. Bourne had meant to take her by surprise. She didn't need a lot of imagination to guess why, nor a lot of time. Bourne got straight to the point once he had his teacup in hand.

'I've come about my son, Miss Stansfield. The two of you have become linked in unfortunate ways recently because of the exhibition.' He carefully sipped his tea, his dark eyes, so like his son's, were alert as he waited for Artemisia's response.

The man was a masterful tactician. Darius must have inherited some of his skill there from him as well. Artemisia did not miss the insinuation that the only reason Darius's name was linked with hers was the art show. There was no other reason—not an illicit romance, nothing that implied the existence of relationship. Bourne would want it that way.

Artemisia replied with silence, saying nothing but calmly sipping her own tea and waiting for Bourne to continue. This time, Bourne opted for a more reconciliatory approach. 'It is unfortunate that the gossips don't allow men and women to be business partners or even friends without turning it into something sordid, but that's the reality. I am sure you will be glad to have the show behind you so you can go on with your life without fearing to open the newspapers every morning.'

'Thank you for the concern, my lord, but I don't fear it.' Artemisia smiled over the lip of her cup. 'Any publicity is good publicity, after all. As you said, society will make its own gossip no matter what the truth is.' It was mostly bravado. She *did* fear opening the newspapers and seeing that someone else had taken another stab at Darius, at her.

Bourne smiled coolly. 'Of course, it's different for you, isn't it? For a lady, her reputation is everything. This kind of scrutiny in the papers would have sunk a debutante.'

Artemisia let the implication that she was no lady pass unremarked. 'It's a good thing, then, that I'm not a debutante and I do not go under so easily.' She selected a little frosted cake from the platter and popped it into her mouth as yet another reminder that she was no debutante. She'd eat what she wanted, just as she'd do as she pleased, not just with tea trays, but with life. Bourne could say his piece, but he could not intimidate her.

'I'm glad we understand one another.' Bourne set aside his tea. 'You know your place, that's an admirable quality. Sometimes it is easy to forget that place when one is working closely with another. May I assume, then, that you will have nothing further to do with my son once the exhibition is concluded?'

It was not a question, it was a warning. 'Your son is an adult. I think he can make up his own mind about who he spends his time with.' Artemisia continued to drink her tea. Darius would be furious if he knew his father had come to interfere. It was because of that fury that Artemisia wouldn't tell him. She did not want to be the cause of family discord. No good could come of pitting Darius against his parents. Such a situation had already broken him once. She did not want Darius feeling he had to choose between her and his family, his heritage, especially when he didn't really have choice. She'd already refused his proposal once. This visit from Bourne only reinforced that she'd been right to be sceptical.

Bourne's mouth compressed as he considered her next move. His eyes narrowed—whatever debate he'd been holding with himself had been decided. 'Miss Stansfield, you are known for being outspoken. Allow me to be blunt with you. The Countess and I have hopes of our son making a match this Season with Worth's granddaughter, among other potential girls. I would not want him to be distracted now that spring is upon us.'

There was so much insult in that comment Artemisia wasn't sure which piece to be offended by first—being labelled a mere distraction, a frivolous whim Darius had undertaken, or that such frivolity was acceptable as long as it was in the winter when no one would notice. 'I appreciate your concern, Lord Bourne.' Artemisia rose, signalling the interview was at an end. Never mind that it was rude to do so, never mind that Bourne outranked her. She wasn't going to win his favour no matter what she did.

'The concern is not for you, Miss Stansfield, it is for my son,' Bourne corrected, rising. 'I am sincerely hoping the scandal has blown over in a few weeks' time.' Even that was insulting—she was worth no more than a few weeks' notice.

'I am sure it will if I am truly the frivolity you claim I am.' Artemisia gave a cold smile. 'If you will excuse me, I have work to see to. My butler can see you out when you're ready.' Then she left the rose parlour, her head held high, and returned to the sanctity of her studio and buried herself in that work.

Artemisia put on her smock and laid out her brushes like a surgeon laying out his tools: the fan brush for feathering, the filbert for blending, the rigger for the delicate lines of eyebrow. She smiled to herself, as she considered the painting *A Lord at His Bath*. She would need the rigger today. She was nearly done with this project she'd worked on in her spare time: Darius at his bath, the way she'd seen him that first night.

What would Bourne say to that? Perhaps he'd like to flash the picture around to all those potential debutantes he'd spoke of. At one time, the idea would have made her laugh. Not today, though. Today, the idea was a reminder of what was to come. She and Darius would part ways. Soon. What other choice did she have? He would go on to marry one of those decent girls like the Earl of Worth's granddaughter and she would just go on, a notorious artist who'd defied the Academy.

This painting would spend its life at the back of a closet. She would never show it to anyone, not even Darius. It was too bad, she felt she'd done excellent work on it, enough perhaps to even earn a ribbon at the spring show if the Academy wouldn't hold her 'poor behaviour' against her. They would, though. As long as she was an associate she could enter her work, but they could not afford to recognise it without resurrecting the question of why she'd not been named an academician. It was one of the many things she'd lost when she'd chosen this path. It was a silly thing to regret. A ribbon was just silky fabric. Only it was more than that.

It represented validation from experts, from peers, that her efforts were good.

Why did she want validation from men who didn't respect her enough to admit her to their ranks? It was a false validation at best, she reminded herself. Is that what she wanted? To settle for a lie? For limits? Those were the very things she was fighting against. She deserved—*other women deserved*—to be recognised on an equal footing with their talented male counterparts. But the fight was hard and the costs were mounting. Artemisia picked up a brush and determinedly began to paint. There was no room for doubt—she'd passed the point of no return a long time ago.

Darius found her still working several hours later. Spring twilight was settling outside her windows when he appeared at the studio, carrying a picnic basket. 'I've brought dinner. Your sister said you'd been in here for hours.'

She wondered what else Addy might have mentioned to him. Hopefully she hadn't blurted anything out about Lord Bourne's visit. But Darius seemed in too pleasant of a mood for that to have been the case.

He set the basket down before the hearth. 'I'll start a fire while you wash up.' It wasn't a question. It was his way of deciding she'd worked long enough for the day. 'What are you working on? I thought you might take a break after the winter collection.'

'Nothing. It's private. I'd rather you didn't see it.' Artemisia pulled a drop cloth carefully over it and set about cleaning her brushes, the smell of turpentine mixing with the scents of dinner and fire. She pulled off her smock at last and joined him at the low table set before her second-hand sofa. She studied the dinner offerings. 'Champagne? What's this for?'

Darius grinned and reached into the picnic basket. 'For this. The first reviews are in, right on time.'

He handed her a stack of newspapers and let her scan them as he popped the cork. She sat down and gave them her full, nervous attention. *The Times*, the *Herald*, the *Post*, and two other smaller papers, had all liked the paintings. Words like 'fresh', 'evocative', and 'thought-provoking' popped from the pages, interspersed with phrases like, 'a new direction', and 'a blend of naturalism and realism'.

Darius handed her a glass of cold champagne. 'Here's to success,' he toasted. 'You've done it, Artemisia.' They drank and he paused. 'What is it?'

'Don't you think it's too soon to celebrate? What if no one comes tomorrow?' She folded up the reviews. 'Reviews are one thing, but what if good art simply isn't enough to bring out the people?'

'People will come, not just tomorrow, but all month, and I think you'll sell every painting.' Darius fixed her a plate of cold meat and bread. 'Is that all this is? Opening day megrims? Or is there something more?' He fixed his own plate and settled across from her.

'The costs are mounting and today I was acutely aware of everything this fight has taken. I'm not sure what I'll be left with when this is over.' She took another swallow of her champagne, the coldness of it easing her throat.

'You might be looking at it all wrong, Artemisia.' Darius gave her a smile that warmed her. 'This show is not the end, it's not even an end in itself. It's the beginning of your rise. Not just your rise, but the beginning of opening the art world to women, truly opening it, so that one day it will no longer be remarkable when a woman does something. We won't have to say "the first woman" to do something, because it will be expected, it will be a matter of course. What you have left is the future.'

Artemisia smiled and Darius laughed. 'You've made a convert out of me, my darling. I didn't understand what the fight really was three months ago, but you showed me things I'd never thought about.'

She nibbled at her ham and cheese. 'Speaking of conversions, what about you, Darius? You don't have to do anything. You're male. The world is already yours. You don't need to fight. What do you get from all of this?'

'I've got a piece of myself back—the courage to draw again, to paint again.' His eyes glistened, desire lighting them, a reminder that preparations for the show had kept them busy recently and apart. 'Most of all, I get you, Artemisia, a woman who is afraid of nothing. I've never met anyone like you.'

She shook her head. 'These days I'm afraid of everything. Of who I am, of what I'll become, of what it will cost me and others. I'm afraid of losing you.' The words were inadequate. She wasn't as brave as he was with expressing his feelings, nor was she as confident in them. She didn't quite trust them herself.

'You won't lose me, Artemisia.' His voice was low, a husky, determined growl that sent a thrill racing through her even though it would only lead to temptations best avoided. Why torture herself like this with one more night?

Darius came around the low table and sat beside her on the sofa, his eyes hot on her. 'Do you want to know what I am most afraid of?' It was hard to imagine Darius afraid of anything. If anyone was fearless it was him. 'I'm afraid of going back to what I was: half a man, barely feeling, blind to injustices, wrapped up in myself, not maliciously, but still wrapped up in myself none the less. I'm especially afraid of never feeling with another person the way I feel when I make love with you, when I lie with you, when I talk with you.'

'Oh, my dear.' She cupped his jaw with her hand. He might have to face that fear. She sincerely doubted Worth's granddaughter, whoever she was, would ever reach the depths of him. Darius was a complex, private man. That he'd let her see so much of him, that he'd bared secrets to her, had spoken volumes about his depth of feeling for her. He'd trusted her and, in the end, she'd trusted him. But trust couldn't change anything. It could only remind them of what could not be and what would eventually be lost. But not tonight. Tonight, he was hers, and she was his. There was something she could still give him.

'Darius,' she breathed against his skin, her lips brushing his jaw. 'Would you sketch me? Tonight?' She rose from the sofa, her fingers at her hair, pulling it loose from its pins. She let it fall while his eyes burned. 'There's paper and pencil in the desk over there. Go get it,' she instructed in a throaty whisper. Her hands worked the buttons of her dress as he looked up from gathering supplies.

'Artemisia, what are you doing?'

'Taking off my clothes. Have you ever done a nude before, Darius?'

'No.' He swallowed hard as he returned to her, his body showing signs of being more than ready to engage in her decadent game.

'Good.' Artemisia licked her lips. 'I'll be your first.'

Darius gave his head a wicked shake. 'No, you'll be my only.' He took her by the hand and led her to the sofa with a wicked whisper, 'Allow me to arrange you, my dear.'

Chapter Twenty-Three

Arrangements had gone off perfectly. Darius discreetly scanned the exhibition space while giving a good impression of paying attention to Worth's granddaughter—May, April, June? He didn't recall her name except that it was a month in spring. She was a lovely girl with more than her share of spirit, but Darius had other things and other people on his mind. Servers were circulating with afternoon champagne and cold hors d'oeuvres. An elegantly draped table of teacakes and other sweet delicacies was kept full along with an enormous silver punch bowl. It was no small feat given that the open space of the hall was crowded.

Crowded. That was his favourite word today. He wanted to crow in celebration. A footman had brought word just fifteen minutes ago that carriages lined the street, still disgorging passengers looking to attend. Everyone who was anyone was here. In one corner, the Dukes of Boscastle and Newlyn held court with their wives, entertaining a large number of their friends. In another spot, near the portrait of Warbourne, Lady

Basingstoke and her husband talked with fellow horse lovers. The scene was repeated throughout the room, clusters of Darius's friends and supporters holding 'mini-parties'. Art critics moved through the crowd, studying the paintings. Darius had spent time with each of them upon their arrival, walking them through the collection and offering a narrative for the paintings. So far, all had been suitably impressed. Artemisia could expect another round of glowing reviews.

Darius smiled at something Miss Worth said. Not because it deserved a smile, but because he was happy and pleased. He was content. When Artemisia arrived she would see the visual proof of her success. She should be here soon. He'd persuaded her to arrive an hour and a half after the opening. He thought there was some confidence and élan in the idea of arriving like a guest to one's own party. It would signal that she had not been nervous at all over society's reception of her work outside the Academy's show.

That contentment wasn't only because of the show's opening success. He thought he might have been content without it, although it would have made things more difficult. He was content because he was with Artemisia, because he'd found his path and his voice once more. There would be struggles. He would need to deal with his parents. But those struggles no longer seemed insurmountable as they once did. Together, he and Artemisia would make a life together, one full of creating opportunities for others.

There was a burst of activity at the entrance and Darius's smile widened. The celebrity of the hour was here, accompanied by her sister and her father. He'd left her early this morning, asleep on their blankets in the studio, a note beside her pillow. She'd been tousled and naked—*very* naked. There was a vulnerability to Artemisia when she slept. He would like to draw *that* some day… Artemisia with her armour off.

None of that vulnerability was evident at the moment. Today she'd dressed carefully, perhaps to complement her paintings. Her gown was a subtly pretty but unassuming rose lawn, embroidered with delicate white flowers at the hem. She wore a simple gold chain at her neck and her dark hair was done up in a riotous pile of curls. Like her paintings, her clothing was understated elegance, a point one could not overlook when she stood beside her flamboyant father dressed in a coat of bright peacock blue and a figured waistcoat of jade green. Sir Lesley Stansfield was a showman. Artemisia wanted to be something more. *His*, Darius thought. She was his.

Despite itching to go to her, to take her by the arm and parade her around, to announce to everyone in every way that she was his, Darius did not go to her at once. He remained content to let her make her own entrance, to greet her guests and drink in her success. He wanted to do nothing to jeopardise that. Perhaps the worst thing he could do would be to claim her openly. It would affirm the things speculated in the newspapers about their relationship, the wicked suppositions Sir Aldred Gray had posited. He forced himself to listen to Miss Worth, who certainly deserved better from him than she'd got, and he counted the minutes until he could approach Artemisia.

* * *

She would wait for Darius to approach her. That was the plan. But that plan hadn't included him smiling at a pretty, fresh-faced girl. Artemisia had spotted him immediately upon entering the room. Despite the crowd, he'd stood out: tall, and handsome in a jacket of dark blue superfine, his hair carefully combed, his jaw freshly shaved. Last night he'd been all stubble and tangles. She felt herself flush a little from more than the heat of the room. Last night had been a slow, decadent burn. Her skin still remembered the caress of the paintbrush on her skin as Darius had feathered it across her breasts and down her belly. He certainly wouldn't be doing *that* with Miss Whoever She Was. It was all for show, she reminded herself. Darius could not come racing over to her without doing them both a disservice.

Artemisia kept her eyes firmly away from Darius as she circulated throughout the room, greeting people, nodding here, stopping to talk with others there. The Duke of Boscastle invited her and her family over to join him for a toast, much to her father's delight. 'Dukes flock to your standard. The show will be sold out before the week's end,' her father said in low tones. 'You've done well, my dear.'

Had she done well? Her father's words niggled at her as she drank her champagne and accepted congratulations. What had she done? She'd painted the pictures. She'd tweaked the Academy's nose by arguing with them. Had she invited these guests? Were any of them her contemporaries? Had she arranged the venue? The catering? Had she held the private show for early reviews and then seen them published the day before opening in key newspapers? Could she even have achieved this much if she'd tried? The answer to both questions was alarmingly *no*.

She did not have an entrée to the Duke of Boscastle. She was not on personal terms with other leading art critics. Her contemporaries were not here today. They were all over at the Academy, hanging last-minute pictures for the show in three days. This was all Darius's doing. Everywhere she looked, it was all Darius: his friends, his connections, his ideas. He had done this for her.

On the one hand, her heart wanted to swell with the effort her champion had put forward on her behalf. She understood all too well the risks he'd taken, the work he'd exerted for this. Today was his success, just as her success was his success. But light must have darkness and there was darkness aplenty behind this wonderful occasion. These people had come for him, because he'd asked. They'd not come for her exclusively.

Artemisia excused herself from the group, her party spirit suddenly dampened. She wandered to a window, taking in the view of the Thames as the realisation swamped her. It only seemed to prove her point: this was not her victory against the Academy. This wasn't her victory for women. This wasn't even a personal victory for her as an artist. She'd not drawn this crowd. Darius had. Nothing had changed. She was still, most unfortunately, right. Men ruled the world. Men decided who had access, who had acceptance. A woman alone did not. A woman alone was nothing but a novelty that was tolerated until she became annoying. *Tolerated.* That's what the Academy had done until she'd over-reached herself in their opinion. Then she'd been dismissed.

Someone approached from behind. Darius, perhaps? Who else would have the audacity or permission? Surely her posture suggested she wished a moment of privacy. 'To your success, my dear Miss Stansfield.' A hand offered her a glass of champagne.

She turned, taking the glass with frosty tones that made her disappointment over the interruption plain. 'Sir Gray, I am surprised to see you here, or perhaps not that surprised. Has the Academy sent you to spy?'

'It's a public exhibition, Miss Stansfield. Everyone who buys a ticket is welcome.' He held up his entrance stub. 'You've had a very good turnout. St Helier has rallied his troops for you.' He winked, his words picking at her wounded feelings. Hadn't she been thinking the same thing? How many others would conclude similarly? 'You've upstaged us, opening three days in advance.' He gave a bland shrug. 'Perhaps you were worried no one would come if you opened on the same day.'

'Perhaps I opened today so that I would not detract from your show. I was getting the excitement out of the way,' Artemisia countered sharply. She would not show any doubt to this man who had so shamelessly led the attack against her.

'*Touché*, Miss Stansfield.' He held up his glass in a brief salute and drank. 'Tell me, what do you think happens after this? Let's assume all the best. Let's assume you sell every piece of artwork, that the negative press calms down, that someone not in St Helier's pocket takes up a liking for your artwork. What does that get you? What happens the next time you hold an exhibition?' He took another swallow of champagne before offering his hypotheses. 'Do all the same folks turn out because St Helier asked them, bribed them, offered them favours, whatever he does? How much art do you think his friends can buy? How many art critics can he keep on influencing, especially once his own standing suffers a blow?'

'How dare you suggest he bribed anyone for a review,' Artemisia all but growled.

'It's an uncomfortable realisation. I see you hadn't thought of it.' No, she hadn't. Darius had, however, carefully selected those he approached, ensuring a good early set of reviews. Perhaps the line between bribery and cautious audience analysis was a thin one.

'I don't need to think of it. I am quite confident my work speaks for itself, just as I am quite confident in the integrity of the critics you malign by the attack on their own credibility,' Artemisia threw back, but it was too late. The little bomb he'd dropped over her ramparts was already exploding. Would she ever be able to believe anything anyone wrote again? Was this what it had felt like for Darius growing up? Wondering how true his talent really was and unable to know because of his position? Would there always be a hidden agenda? The doubts were starting to mount up.

'I didn't come over here to spar with you, actually, Miss Stansfield. I came to make sure you saw the future. Consider this an embassy of good will. You care for St Helier. The Academy admires his eye for art and his value to us as a critic, as well as his very direct connection to the house of Bourne. The Earl keeps many artists employed with his purchases. The Academy is willing to make amends with him, welcome him back into the fold.' Gray exchanged champagne glasses on a passing tray. 'Let him go, Miss Stansfield. He can have his status, his reputation back before it's really truly gone.'

'Assuming I mean to keep him, that there is a relationship between us that transcends our business arrangement, why should I?' Artemisia kept her words even, her gaze steady. It was becoming too much, really. First Darius's father and now Sir Gray, both of them begging her not to ruin Darius. Between them, her self-esteem would be in tatters.

Gray chuckled. 'I'll give you three reasons.' He ticked them off on his fingers. 'Because you can't win. Every time you produce a piece of work or an exhibition people will resurrect the scandal and drag your name through the mud. They'll drag his, too, if you stay connected. Second, you will always wonder if your success is really yours or if it's because of him, assuming there is any success after this. Third, there is the humanity of it. You do care for him and you simply don't want to ruin him.

'You are not meant to be a countess, Miss Stansfield. When I say ruin him, I mean ruin his family name, as well as this "career", if I may use that word, he's carved out for himself. How long do you think love would last under those conditions? When you've taken everything from him?'

He nodded across the room to where Darius was once again with another smiling debutante and her parents, standing in front of the pintail duck. 'Let him go lead the life he was meant to lead.'

She tossed back the last of her champagne, too fast, the fizz clogging in her throat. 'Do you think it's that simple? If I walk away, what's to say he won't follow me?' Darius had spotted them and was walking her way at last.

'You overestimate your appeal, Miss Stansfield.' Gray followed her gaze, marking Darius's progress. 'St Helier has always been a man who has done what was required of him. You might admire him for that, but he will leave you for it.' He gave her a nod. 'Good day, Miss Stansfield. Thank you for your time and consideration.' He melted into the crowd before Darius could reach them. Coward, Artemisia thought. The man would not dare to say such things to Darius in person. Then again, he didn't need to. It wasn't Darius he needed to sow doubt with. It was her, because she already had doubts, doubts that ran parallel to the ones he'd voiced. He merely affirmed them.

Hadn't she already had such realisations? Hadn't she already argued with herself that she should leave him? That nothing good could come of being with him? Yet there had been good. She'd allowed hope to flicker, however briefly. It had flared last night. Last night anything had been possible, even today when she'd walked into the exhibition that hope had still burned. But Gray was right. It was selfish to keep Darius.

'Champagne?' Darius grabbed two glass from a passing tray.

'No, thank you. I've had enough champagne for one day.' She needed her wits clear. Decisions would have to be made and soon. The sooner the better. She'd let this linger far too long as it was. She should have ended this in Seasalter.

'You did it, Artemisia, you've dazzled them,' Darius toasted and drank anyway. 'This is your day. I've already had offers for five of the paintings. Boscastle's friend, the Duke of Hayle, wants two for his hunting box.' She smiled but the words did not excite her as they might have earlier. Of course Boscastle's friend wanted a painting. Isn't that what Gray had suggested would be the case?

'You are not pleased.' His smiled faded and he drew her into an alcove. 'What's wrong, Artemisia? Did Gray say something to upset you? I should have come over sooner when I saw him with you. The man's a cad on the best of days.'

'Nothing I haven't heard before. I can handle the likes of Sir Aldred Gray.' Artemisia shook her head in dismissal. 'It's just that this show is all you, all your effort.' She would be honest with him, he deserved that and more. 'This is not my doing. This doesn't prove anything has changed.'

'How can you say that when it's your paintings that are getting all the attention?' Darius replied.

'But I didn't bring the people in. You did that.' She had to make him see this was an artificial victory.

'Does it have to be you or me? Can't it be *us*? Can't we be a team, Artemisia? A seamless team where it's not clear where one begins and the other ends?'

That was when she knew without a doubt she had to let him go. He would not make the decision to leave her. She would cost him everything. The Academy would not forgive him again, nor would his family if he became a seamless extension of herself. She reached for the curtain and drew it across the alcove. 'Kiss me, Darius.'

It would be a goodbye kiss. As long as she stayed, Darius would be pulled in two directions, forced always to give up something he loved. She would not put him in that position again. It had to be her. She had to be the one to leave and she would, tonight. While he was celebrating at the exhibition, she would pack her things and go.

She would take one last piece of him with her and then she would take her leave. It would break her heart to do it, but she had years and years ahead of her to mend it and miles to put between them. The miles would help. Where she was going, he was unlikely to follow her. That would be to the good. He'd been far too persuasive up until now. Perhaps it was for the best. She still had her own dreams, her own ambitions, and they could be realised in other places, just not here.

Chapter Twenty-Four

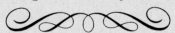

She wasn't here. Darius sank on to the sofa in Artemisia's studio, trying to tamp down on the panic that threatened to run away with him. But it was hard and he was losing the battle. Artemisia was gone in a very absolute way. The room felt different. The blankets and sheets had been picked up and folded away from their tangled camp by the fire. The hearth was cold and swept. Most telling, though, was that her brushes were gone, the turpentine was gone. Her blank canvases were gone. Her smock was gone. Artemisia went nowhere without her paints and she didn't intend on coming back.

It was the last that had him dumbfounded and panic erupting. Why wouldn't she come back? The thought seemed so extreme that he couldn't truly bring himself to accept it. He should have come last night. He'd been busy with sales. He'd sold four more after he'd told her about Boscastle. There'd been a bidding war for the pintail duck. It had gone to an avid fisherman whom Darius didn't know particularly well. He'd thought Artemisia would like that, a sale that wasn't directly connected to one of his acquaintances.

There'd been money to handle and to watch over, quite a lot of it, even though the paintings would remain on display until the show concluded at the end of May. He'd had some misguided romantic notion of bringing the money to Artemisia and pressing it into her hand as some kind of proof of the self-sufficiency she valued above all else. She had earned this, no one else. His champagne and cold shrimp hadn't earned it, just her paintings.

He was too late and that knowledge recast the way he understood yesterday afternoon. Where he'd seen resounding success, she'd seen reliance on another, she'd seen another validation that men got what they wanted. She'd not seen or had not accepted her part in that victory. She'd not accepted that they were a team. Had it been that which had set her sour? Did she not want to be a team? Had he misunderstood that in some way? That cut him deeply, not only because it would mean he'd misread her, but because he'd misread what their relationship was based on. He'd thought they were a partnership, taking on the institution of the Academy together. But she'd only been in it for herself.

That couldn't be right. That wasn't the Artemisia he knew. She liked her self-sufficiency but she wasn't selfish. Darius rose and began to move about the room, looking for something, some sign that she hadn't simply left him, that she would return. At the back of the studio an old easel stood draped in a holland cloth. He'd seen it already and paid it no mind. This time he caught the outline of a form beneath it.

Darius pulled off the sheet and stared at the painting beneath. It was him, that first night at the Crown, dripping from his bath. It was quite an experience seeing oneself represented naked on canvas. He wasn't entirely sure he was comfortable with it, but it wasn't the nudity that bothered him, it was the other things that she'd captured: the way his body was turned slightly away from the viewer, the way the exposed curve of buttock and thigh denied the revelation of more intimate parts. There was a shadow across his face, cast there by the firelight in the background, making his expression inscrutable and haughty, all the better to hide himself, not just his body but his thoughts, his soul.

The art critic in him saw the excellence in the work, each brush stroke reinforcing the narrative; even in his bath a lord dared not let down his guard. Responsibility and the need to put on a brave, impenetrable front remained always—even when naked, a lord was never truly naked, he couldn't afford to be. Hence the need for not depicting his full extent. She'd seen all of him that night. If she'd wanted to tease him, or make an erotic painting of him, she'd have painted a different view. No, this one was meant for something more. If one saw his privates, he might appear to be too human, less lordly. Men were judged by such things. A man's phallus size was his own private business and it was scrupulously guarded, not that he needed to be ashamed of his.

It was the message of the painting that mattered and his heart broke. She was letting him go, letting him choose responsibility, letting him choose to fulfil the expectations that life had placed in his path, letting him be the future Earl of Bourne—*A Lord at His Bath*.

How dare she? Anger filled the cracks in his heart, a stopgap against the emerging pain. It would not last, but he would take the reprieve for now. How dare she decide for him what was best? How dare she decide to sacrifice *them*. It was not for her alone to decide.

The door to the studio opened and he looked up, hope flaring. Perhaps she'd come back? It was only Addy. 'Is she not here, then?' Addy was pale, as surprised as he that Artemisia was gone.

He shook his head. 'She's taken her paints.' Addy would know what that meant. 'Did she not say anything to you? Did she talk about leaving?' How long had she known she would go? How long had she hidden that decision from him? When they were making love at the Crown that last morning before he'd come to London? Sooner? Later? Had she decided last night? Or at the last moment at the show?

Kiss me, Darius. It had been a kiss for the ages, exciting and erotic in its intensity, knowing that discovery lay just beyond a thin curtain of fabric. He'd never thought it would be the last kiss. He pushed the thought away. He couldn't think like that. It would not be the last time he kissed her any more than the night before last would be the final time he'd made love to her. They were just beginning. It was too soon for last times.

'No, she said nothing.' Addy's own betrayal showed plainly on her face. The sisters were close. It made him wonder what had happened that had caused Artemisia to hide her decision from even Addy. He wished he could think of something to say to take away Addy's pain. Addy sagged on to the sofa.

'I don't understand it. Why would she leave? The

show was a success, her reviews were good and she had you.' She shot an accusing glance at him. 'Did the two of you fight? I thought everything was going well between you, despite the papers' gossip. Your father came by earlier this week and I thought it was a good sign, that perhaps you'd proposed. It would be like Artemisia to say nothing until everything was final, but why else would Lord Bourne call but to interview his future daughter-in-law?'

Darius was only half listening. His thoughts were still rooted back on the first sentence. 'My father was here?'

'Yes, didn't you know? I thought you had sent him. Artemisia never did say how the interview went.'

'I did *not* send him and, no, it was not a visit of matrimonial intent.' At least not in the way Addy was thinking of it. He wasn't surprised Artemisia hadn't shared the outcome of the visit. His father had called to warn her away, perhaps even threaten her, although he couldn't imagine threats carrying any weight with Artemisia. She cared little for what someone claimed they might do to her. Unless the threats weren't against her, but someone she cared for—like him, like her family.

Darius began to pace, a fuller picture coming to him. His father's visit. Aldred Gray's visit at the show. His own mention of his father's discussion. He'd not been overly specific with her, but she'd guess the gist of that conversation. Combine the content of those visits with the doubts he knew she harboured in her own mind and she'd begin to see obstacles and sacrifice. She would not see solutions because she didn't want him to suffer for her. She didn't want to wreck his family. She didn't want to steal his life. She didn't understand his life was nothing without her. It was tired and empty. She'd done it because she loved him. If there was a silver lining, that was it.

She loved him. Too much to let him suffer.

That was unacceptable.

'Where do you think she went?' Darius covered up the easel. It was like drawing a curtain over a part of his life, a part that was over now. 'Did she go to Seasalter?' But even as he said it, his gut knew she hadn't gone there. There'd be too much pain, too many memories. It couldn't be her refuge any more. Grief twisted in his gut. He'd ruined that for her. 'If not Seasalter, then where?'

Addy shook her head. 'I don't know. Somewhere she can paint and not be found. Shall I close things up?'

'No, go on. I'll just be a few minutes.' Darius wanted a moment to gather himself. It would probably take more than a moment. His world felt empty, shattered despite the success of the show. He might never be 'gathered' again. An abyss yawned before him, a life without Artemisia. He leaned his head against the wall, desperate to stop the darkness from swamping him. He did not know right now what that life looked like, or how he'd get through it. Maybe he didn't need to know. Maybe he just took things one day at a time, one decision at a time. Maybe that was how he got through it. It was how he'd got through those first days at Oxford, the first days after setting aside his painting.

He made an impotent fist. His father had taken that from him, using his mother as a weapon, using the title, using a lord's inherent sense of responsibility against him. His father had tried those same tactics again. Rage stirred in his darkness. His father had been here, had convinced Artemisia to give him up, just as he'd tried to convince Darius to give her up. But what had worked with a sixteen-year-old boy could not be allowed to work on a man with power of his own.

Arguing with your father won't bring her back, it might even cause the very thing she left to prevent, his conscience argued.

So be it. Darius raised his head. He couldn't bring her back, but that didn't mean what his father had done should go unanswered. He had nothing left to lose. The woman he loved had left him. There was for him but darkness and despair. It was time to confront the Earl.

'You went behind my back. You chased her away, the woman I loved, the woman I planned to marry.' Darius faced his father from the marble fireplace of the Bourne town house drawing room. Morning sun slanted through the tall windows, catching the wisps of hot tea steaming from the porcelain service set on the low table where it sat untouched. One look at his face upon arrival and his mother had insisted a cup of tea could put anything aright. If his father's weapon of choice was responsibility, his mother's was tea. Tea was for peace, but there could be no peace, not this time. This time, his father had gone too far.

'You look like hell, Darius.' His father crossed an elegant leg over one knee, looking immaculate, clean-shaven and undisturbed by his son's unannounced visit. Perhaps he'd anticipated this and Darius's arrival wasn't so 'unannounced' after all.

'I *feel* like hell,' Darius retorted. 'I feel as if my life has been pulled out from under me, stolen from me. Most of all I feel betrayed by my own father, a man I admire, which makes it a double betrayal.'

'You need sleep.' His father shook his head. 'You are distraught and since you cannot take out your disappointment on Miss Stansfield for her desertion, you are striking out at the nearest target.'

How like his father to make this his fault, as if by managing his own emotions better this would cease to be a problem. 'Darius, this may come as a surprise to you, but she had no intention of accepting your proposal. I asked her and that is what she told me. Now, I can see that the news hurts,' he began.

Darius interrupted. He would not believe that, never mind that Artemisia had made similar noises to him. He'd always expected to talk her out of them. He'd planned on using the success of the show to prove so much to her. Now, he would not get that chance. 'What was she supposed to say? You ambushed her in her own home and put an impossible question to her.'

His father gave a long-suffering sigh. 'I did it for your own good. You failed to see reason, so I went to the one person who would.'

'My own good? Like giving up my painting? Was that for my own good, or yours?' Darius kept his voice level, acutely aware that his mother sat pale-faced and silent on the sofa, looking nervously between her husband and her son.

His father's voice raised fractionally. '*That* was for Bourne. Nothing we do is just for you or I.' It was the first show of emotion his father had demonstrated. 'You are my son, my heir, the future of the earldom. Your mother—'

'No.' His mother's voice was stern in the silence. 'Do not make this about me, not this time. I will not be leveraged against my own son.' Darius had not heard his mother speak to his father so directly in years. 'Our disappointments do not need to be repeated by him.'

His father glared at them both, his eyes landing finally on Darius. 'You will let Artemisia Stansfield go because it is demanded of you. It is the right thing to do.' His father gave a wry, cold smile. 'Besides, why argue over it? What's done is done. She is gone and you can't bring her back. Why seek conflict that cannot be resolved?' He made a peaceful gesture with his hands.

'No.' Darius hated the idea that his father might win by default. The pieces that had shattered inside him last night and jabbed at his broken heart until dawn quieted. Letting her go was not the right thing. Letting his father exert his power like this was not the right thing. For the first time since Artemisia had left, he saw a way forward.

He faced his father, calm settling over him. He was sure of his direction now even if the path to it was still undefined. 'I will find her and bring her back and I will marry her, your opinion be damned.' He'd rather do this with his parents' support, but if not, he would do it alone.

His father's eyes narrowed. He rose. 'I see you cannot be reasoned with at the moment. I have other appointments to keep. We will discuss this later when you are more reasonable.'

There was a long silence after his father left the

room. Darius exhaled into it, feeling a weight leave his shoulders. He'd declared himself. There was nothing left to do but the next thing. He had to move forward now. Any faltering on his part would equal victory for his father. 'I am going after her,' he announced to his mother.

She nodded. 'Do you know where she is?'

'Possibly. I think she may be headed to Italy.' The idea had come to him last night as he'd paced his rooms, thinking where she would go, where could she paint? He'd let his mind sift through all the conversations, all the walks on the beach, all the campfires and rainy afternoons in the farmhouse until he knew without doubt where she'd gone. He'd bet every pound note in his pocket she'd gone back to the beach where she'd learned to paint. She'd been happy there and in Italy she might have more freedom than she did here.

'If I leave now I can race to Dover and catch the first ship, maybe even catch her. She might still be there if the shipping schedules aren't amenable.' He was only a day behind her, he would eventually catch up to her in Calais, or Paris, or somewhere on the overland road to Italy.

'Unless she takes a boat the entire way,' his mother offered cautiously. 'I don't mean to undermine the idea, Darius. It is a noble gesture. Perhaps the kind of romantic overture a girl dreams of, but it might not get you the results you're looking for.' His mother reached for the teapot and poured out two cups. 'Come and sit, we need a better plan if we want to get better results.'

We. Such a small word and yet so powerful. Darius sat beside his mother and took the teacup. 'Thank you,

Mother.' A little bit of hope flickered among the ashes of his rage and disappointment. He had an ally.

'Have you thought of what happens if you catch up to her? You'll profess your love, she'll resist because she loves you, too. You will have the same arguments I suspect you've already had all over again because nothing has changed. Ask yourself, what will be different this time?' Nothing. His mother was right. He could not go to Artemisia empty-handed. He needed to go to her with obstacles overcome.

His mother nodded towards the pocket of his coat. 'Do you still carry that journal with you? This might be a good time to use it.' She rose, tall and regal, less brittle than she'd been, and made her way to the escritoire in the corner. There was a certain life to her this morning that Darius found heartening. 'I am going to write a letter to my future daughter-in-law while you plan how you're going to win her back.'

'What about Father?' Darius asked, drawing out his journal. He didn't want to leave things this way with his father.

'He will have to find his own way, Darius. Just as you have found yours.' She smiled softly. 'Time does heal a great many things. Give him that, Darius, and I think things will come aright eventually.' But it wouldn't be tomorrow, or next week. It might be years. He could not make his father change his mind. 'Focus on what you can effect.' His mother smiled from her desk.

Yes, a plan. He could effect that. He began to write, his own mind focused now on something other than his grief. What obstacles had to be overcome? What solutions were needed? Artemisia would want to win not just a battle, she'd made that clear enough. She would want to win the war. For that there were things she'd need, and allies, and he could get them for her. She just needed to be a little less stubborn and accept them, as a wedding gift.

There was some satisfaction in seeing that list take shape, but it was not a guarantee of success. They would take time. They would not be accomplished overnight. What needed doing was monumental and he would have to act quickly. He did not want Artemisia to think he'd let her go. He would see this through. For him, for her, for *them*.

Viscount St Helier had become a whirlwind of activity. Even society noted it. By day, he was present at every art exhibition great or small, talking with artists, with patrons, with critics, anyone of note in the art world. By night, he attended every ball, talked to men of import and danced with their daughters. Only the most astute among society had noticed the spark that drove him was darker, more desperate, than a simple search for a bride. He was a man with a goal, a man driven to lengths for a purpose.

In late July, he spent a week in Seasalter, making undisclosed arrangements with Owen Gann regarding the use of an abandoned property near the Stansfield farmhouse. Then he had packed his trunks and disappeared from society as the Season ended. There were rumours he was taking a short tour of the Continent before winter. Some speculated it was to acquire art from private collections. Perhaps he was on an errand of his father's, after all—there'd been a noted encounter between the two of them at White's prior to his departure.

Rumour wasn't entirely wrong. There *had* been a heated encounter. Not about art, though. He was going to the Continent to do some collecting, but again, not technically about art. He was going to collect Artemisia just as soon as he could find her. When he did, he was going to lay his heart and her dreams at her feet and hope it was enough. If it was not, then and only then would he give in to the despair he'd worked feverishly to hold at bay.

Chapter Twenty-Five

Bagnoli, just outside Naples, Italy
—late August

Someone was watching her work. The hairs on the back of her neck were prickling from something other than sweat and sand. She was not unused to the sensation. She'd become something of a local sensation in the time she'd been here. It was not unusual for the village children to come down to the beach and watch her paint, or play nearby in the sand as she worked.

But these eyes felt different. Intense, as if they were studying her and not the painting itself. Intense, as if they were a pair of burning black eyes that could sear a hole in her heart. She'd not let herself think of that specific pair of eyes for a long time now. They were part of her past. Darius Rutherford was not coming for her. There was no purpose. Even if he did come, she would only have had to send him packing. This was her life now.

Whoever was here was coming closer. Today, she

was alone on the beach and not expecting any company. Apparently, company had found her anyway. She did not like uninvited company. Artemisia reached for her walking stick, a thick, club-like, handleless cane of hawthorn she kept handy in case she needed to be stern with the stray dogs so common to the areas around Naples.

'Whoever you are, I suggest you keep your distance. I am armed.'

'And dangerous. Woe to any man who crosses you.' The warm laugh froze her for its familiarity and for its ability to conjure intimacy after months of trying to forget it.

She turned slowly, using every second to steel herself against the sight that would meet her eyes. Darius was here. Why? For what reason? What could coming here now accomplish? There were questions and anger. Why now when she'd put her life back together?

She had a small villa on the hillside that caught the breeze off the sea. She painted on the balcony sometimes. She went into Naples and exhibited her work with other artists on occasion. No one cared about her past here. There were people who remembered her father and were happy to extend their acquaintance to his grown daughter. But more than that, they knew nothing of her, only her art. All of that was suddenly at risk the moment she raised her eyes.

She gave herself the luxury of staring at him for a long moment before she spoke, plenty of time to take in the changes of a summer. He was a study of dark and light: his black hair, his eyes, his skin tanned from the Italian sun, his body dressed in what would pass for dishabille in England, no jacket, no waistcoat, no cravat, only a white linen shirt open at the neck showing off the tanned vee of his chest, and buckskins and bare feet. It was an intoxicatingly sexy look. 'Darius, what are you doing here?'

'I've come to see you.' He came closer, each step reminding her of the power of his presence. His confidence was still the same, only magnified. There was an ease to his step. 'How are you, Artemisia? I've missed you.' To his credit, he didn't try to kiss her, didn't try to presume upon their past.

'I've been here all along.' There was a bit of a bite to her tone. Again the question came—why now?

He gave her a breath-taking smile. 'I couldn't come empty-handed or it would have been for naught. We would have had the same old arguments.' He paused, his eyes making her hot. 'It's nearly dinner time. Would you join me at the local trattoria and let me tell you what I've been up to?' He winked. 'I hear they have a good red.'

'We'll be the talk of the village tomorrow.' But she was already packing up her things.

'I don't mind.' Darius set about helping her, folding up the easel and storing her papers in a case. He paused, considering. 'Do you? Is there someone you'd prefer didn't know I was here? You needn't worry. I have no claim to you. I expect nothing.'

But he wanted a claim, she saw that clearly in his eyes. 'No, there is no one, there's *been* no one.' She'd had offers, of course, but it had been too soon. It might always be too soon.

He smiled, relief easing his shoulders. 'I have not

been with anyone since you left.' His dark eyes were solemn. 'You nearly broke me when I discovered you'd gone.' His voice was quiet, barely audible above the gentle susurration of waves on the shore. 'There were days when I thought about giving up, when I didn't want to get out of bed, empty as it was.' His voice was raw with emotion. She reached out a hand to him automatically. He took it and didn't let it go.

'But you did because people were counting on you,' Artemisia surmised softly. How was it possible that they hadn't touched for four months and yet it was so natural to do so? How was it possible she'd thought she might be over him? Recovered? She was not.

'Yes. People were counting on me.' He looked out over the sea. 'Are you terribly hungry?' He smiled when she shook her head. 'Come walk? I've come to like Italian sunsets and we were always good at beaches.'

'We're a long way from Seasalter.' Artemisia gave a nervous laugh. They were being so careful with one another, both of them unsure of their reception.

'All of your paintings sold from the show,' Darius said. She nodded. It seemed the right place to start, at the very place where they'd last seen each other. Then he began to unfold his plans. 'It was a lot of money. I used it in your name to open an art school for girls in Seasalter.'

'You opened a school? For girls?' Artemisia could barely choke out the words. His announcement had her reeling. It was overwhelming, really. That he'd spent the intervening months doing this for her, for others.

'Actually, *you've* opened it. I've just started it. I don't want to mastermind your dream, I just want to be part of it with you, alongside you. It was your dream, after all. You are its architect.' His eyes were thoughtful. 'I think that's where change has to start; with education. One woman raising attention to an issue and causing a scandal lasts only so long, then it's put away again, the issue ignored until next time. That doesn't change anything. But mobilising a community, like the art community, does bring change.

'When female artists walk among that community in proportion to its population, with their heads held high, with training and with intelligence and pride to speak their minds and share their opinions, that's when change will come. It won't happen next year. It might take a generation or two, but some day, no one will think twice about a woman's nomination as an Royal Academician.'

Artemisia swiped at tears. Someone understood at last and that it was this man touched her beyond words. 'Tell me about it. Where is it, this school that will change England?'

Darius smiled. 'Owen Gann helped me locate a building near the farmhouse, an old fishery that is now vacant.' Artemisia nodded again. She knew the property. 'Addy is even now recruiting students. The school will need you, though. Those girls will need you. You are their inspiration.' He raised her knuckles to his lips. 'They aren't the only ones. I need you, you are my inspiration, too. I never would have thought about a school for girls, or even known there was need for one if it hadn't been for you. We are not finished, Artemisia.'

No, they weren't. The tingling of her hand where his lips passed was further proof of that. But how could it end differently? 'And earls' heirs who want to paint? Is there room for them in that new world, too?' she asked softly.

'Yes, I think there might be.' He smiled, but they weren't out of the woods yet.

'And your family? Where do they feature? Because they must, Darius. I left as much for my art as I left for you. You've already given up too much for them. I could not be the source of another rift.' A hundred art schools couldn't change that. 'You're still heir to an earldom.' His parents, the people he loved, still had expectations.

'Yes. That hasn't changed. My parents have come to understand that while I will always respect the interests of Bourne, I will make my own choices when it comes to my wife. In fact, my mother has written you a letter.' He patted his coat pocket. 'My father will come around. I won't promise it will be easy, but I *do* promise it will be done. Not in a moment, not in a week, but I think over the years, it will be accomplished.' He gave her a wicked smile. 'I think grandchildren will go a long way in easing that path. But before there are grandchildren, there should be a wedding.' He knelt down in the sand. 'Marry me. Say yes, Artemisia. There are no more obstacles standing in our way and I want desperately to get off the sand before a wave comes.'

'This was why you waited to come.' It was all falling into place. The school, the students, putting it in Seasalter. He'd given her her refuge back. He'd proven himself, not just that he loved her but that he respected her objections to their match and he'd systematically set out to overcome them just as he'd set out to win her heart, one trusting piece at a time. 'Yes, Darius Rutherford, I will marry you.' She laughed, pulling him up and kissing him hard on the mouth as a wave fell over their feet.

'Just in time, too.' Darius laughed against her mouth. 'I was afraid you'd make me wait until the tide came in.'

'I think four months is long enough.' Their kisses became softer, longer, as the sun fell to the horizon.

'I never want to be without you that long again.' Darius's mouth moved to her neck. 'Will you marry me tomorrow, Artemisia? I passed a church in the village.'

'Tomorrow? Here? You don't want to wait and do it in England?' she murmured. She would be beyond making plans soon. Best settle it now while she had possession of her thoughts.

'Here. Tomorrow. In the place where you were happiest.' Darius pulled back. 'Is it too soon? Do you want time to plan? Women set such store by their wedding day.'

'It's not too soon for for ever to start.' She wrapped her arms about him. 'Tomorrow night, I'll paint my husband.'

'Before or after we make love?' Darius swung her out of the way of an oncoming wave.

'During.' She laughed.

Epilogue

Seasalter, Kent—December

Artemisia Stansfield-Rutherford, Viscountess St Helier, strode thoughtfully through her studio in the Seasalter farmhouse. It was hardly 'her' studio any more, she mused, studying the eight bent heads concentrated on their paintings of home. The glass-walled room had become a classroom this past month ever since the Stansfield School of Art for Girls had opened in November, its first term running November through March.

Artemisia stopped beside each girl to study her work, offering a quiet suggestion or a compliment as needed. The pupils ranged in age from ten to fifteen. Today, they were painting their homes from memory and would make gifts of their work to their families when they left in a few days for the holiday break. She stopped beside an easel, studying the girl's painting. 'Use a rigger here, Emily, it will help you with your fine detail.' Emily was one of Darius's many coups. She was the daughter of a painter who was a royal associate with the Academy and who saw the logic of training a girl with talent to maximise that talent.

Artemisia smiled as she looked across the room at the girls busy and intent on doing their best. Some of them came from artistic families, others came of their own raw skills. Some came on a scholarship, others came because they could pay. Each one, regardless of who their parents were, filled her with warm satisfaction. Eight was a start and it was enough for now. Eight was what the farmhouse could hold until the fishery was ready.

Her great-aunt would have loved seeing all the girls gathered together, filling the bedrooms upstairs, sitting in the chairs around the dining room table with she and Darius at the foot and at the head every night, governing manners and conversations with Addy holding court in the middle. Mrs Harris was certainly thriving. She adored cooking for eleven and Elianora still came up and baked twice a week.

Near the door, one girl stirred, her nose wrinkling in an appreciative sniff, catching the scent of ginger biscuits. Artemisia looked at the watch pinned to her bodice, although she didn't need to. She, and every girl in the studio, knew what time it was. If it was Friday and there was the scent of ginger biscuits, it was half past three without doubt.

Artemisia dismissed class, following behind the girls on their way through the decked halls of the farm-house—courtesy of Addy and her insatiable holiday spirit and the Christmas party that would take place to-morrow—to the dining room where a platter of freshly baked and iced ginger biscuits in the shape of little men were piled high on a platter beside a pitcher of cold milk. Addy was already there, seated at the table, reviewing sketches from the morning session. Artemisia smiled at her sister over the girls' heads, both of them laughing at the girls devouring the platter. Girls should have healthy appetites, just like boys.

Addy had been a wonder this autumn. Artemisia was still not sure how her sister had managed to have the school ready upon their return, but she had. She'd even organised the opening ceremonies, complete with an impressive guest list including representatives from the Dukes of Hayle and Boscastle and an appearance from the Basingstokes, who'd offered a scholarship for a girl with a talent for animal portraiture. Artemisia was forced to conclude that Addy was growing up. She was twenty-one now, no longer her baby sister, and more than ready for more responsibility.

Artemisia snatched a biscuit from the platter before they were all gone and took a bite. Somewhere in all the noise of eating biscuits, the sound of the front door opening reached her. It would be Darius and Owen Gann. While she and Addy instructed, the men spent their days restoring the old fishery for a time in the near future when the needs of the school would outstrip the capacity of the farmhouse. Her hand went surreptitiously to her waist. That time would be soon, very soon.

'Still biting the heads off men, I see.' Darius stole a kiss from behind. He smelled like hard work and outdoors.

'Only the small ónes,' she replied with a laugh.

'Cowards, the whole lot of them.' Darius chuckled. They'd laughed a lot since they'd come home from their honeymoon in Italy. Even in the face of adversity. Despite the opening of the school, despite the happiness of their marriage, there were still rough edges around their success. There would always be those who resisted change, who chose to stall progress and the opening of minds by sowing dissent. They would never stamp it all out, but they could laugh and they could persevere, and therein would lay their victory.

'How is the fishery coming?' Artemisia drew her handsome husband out into the hallway for a bit of privacy, something that was hard to come by these days.

'We've got the classrooms framed downstairs. You could easily teach classes there next autumn and I might even have time then to take one.' He winked mischievously, wrapping his arms about her. 'Although I'd miss my private lessons.' They'd made a habit out of keeping Sunday for themselves, packing a picnic and drawing on the beach together. Darius's already commendable skill had improved greatly and she had hopes he would choose to place his work in their modest end-of-year exhibition.

'What about the dormitory rooms on the second floor?' Artemisia asked, turning in his arms to face him. She popped the rest of the biscuit into his mouth, making him talk around the crumbs.

'They're coming along. Are you getting tired of sharing your house with eight girls?' Darius laughed. It was admittedly an unorthodox start to married life.

'No, it's just that we might need one of those rooms back in a few months,' Artemisia offered coyly after he swallowed. She had news to share with him that might cause a choking hazard.

'Why? Is your father moving in?' Consternation flared across Darius's usually confident features, proving even an earl's heir could be intimidated by the prospect of one's father-in-law sharing his roof.

'No.' Artemisia gave a slow smile. 'But someone else might be, a little someone else about this big.' She made a cradling gesture with her arms and watched Darius's jaw drop.

'A baby? We're having a baby?'

The euphoria in his face nearly brought her to tears, so touching was the sight of his abject happiness. Had she ever made anyone so happy? The idea that she could was still new to her. Then the euphoria was gone, replaced by worry.

'Is it what you want, Artemisia? I thought we'd decided to wait.'

They *had* decided to wait, feeling that the school was a big enough venture without adding parenthood to the mix, but nature seemed to have other ideas on that account.

She offered him a broad smile. 'It's fine, Darius. More than fine.' She paused, fiddling with his neckcloth. 'I suppose now your parents will have a reason to visit.'

That was another rough area. His father's reaction to their marriage remained uncomfortable territory. On the surface, he gave nothing away as to his discontent, as was the Rutherford way. But beneath that surface, his displeasure was evident. While two dukes had sent emissaries to the school's opening, England's largest collector of art had not made an appearance, although his wife had.

There was hope in that, Artemisia thought. Lady Bourne had made herself a regular correspondent with her son and her new daughter-in-law. Artemisia knew little of mothers, having lost hers so early, but she knew a mother valued a son's happiness above all else. Lady Bourne was undoubtedly torn between her son and her husband, but she was finding her own power. She'd even made a small speech at the school's opening about the importance of encouraging women's talents in the same way men were professionally encouraged.

'When shall we tell the others?' Darius asked, kissing her throat and making it clear the hallway wouldn't be private enough soon.

'Tomorrow, at Addy's Christmas party.' Artemisia smiled. 'She declares it's become a tradition since it was so successful last year.' Last year's party had been marked with the surprising return of Elianora's fiancé, Owen Gann's younger brother.

'Well, big news will certainly become the tradition. First Elianora's announcement and this year, ours,' Darius murmured against her ear. 'I wonder what the big news will be next year?'

'That your father is coming for the holidays?' She laughed, but she was serious, too. She would like nothing better than to seal her husband's happiness and see that rift overcome.

Darius raised a dubious brow. 'One can always hope.'

'Right now, I hope you'll come upstairs with me,' Artemisia whispered, 'We have time before dinner to celebrate on our own.' She took his hand and led him upwards. There were many things she hoped would come to pass. She hoped Bourne would come, that Bourne would accept his son's marriage. She hoped the Academy would one day rescind their decision on her rank. But she would be happy without those things because she'd found something more, something better.

She shut the bedroom door behind them, her eyes fixed on her husband stripping out of his clothes. There was no more glorious creature than a man well-loved by a woman unless it was a woman well-loved by her man.

* * * * *

*If you enjoyed this book, why not check out
Bronwyn Scott's The Cornish Dukes miniseries*

The Secrets of Lord Lynford
The Passions of Lord Trevethow
The Temptations of Lord Tintagel
The Confessions of the Duke of Newlyn

*And look out for the next book in
The Rebellious Sisterhood miniseries,
coming soon!*